# CUT

By Kevin Outlaw

**Published by Hartley Publications**
**P.O. Box 100, Devizes, Wiltshire, SN10 4TE**

**FIRST EDITION: 2005**

**ISBN: 1 873313 098**

**Typeset and make-up by Wentrow Media.**
**Printed by Elite Colour Print.**

*With thanks to:*

*Mum and Dad,*
*my brother, Rus,*
*and Amy.*

*Harshest critics, biggest fans.*

CHAPTER 1

Ethan was awake. His damp sheets were knotted into a terrible noose, his pillows screwed up and thrown aside. The bedside lamp was overturned and hanging by its black cord off the edge of the table. Red figures on the digital alarm clock blinked on and off, counting seconds dutifully. Four-thirty in the morning.

A crack in the curtains revealed only darkness.

He had slept for less than an hour.

'Damn.'

He sat forwards, drawing his knees up to his chest and running trembling hands over his eyes. The sweat was pouring down his back, sketching awkward designs along the ridges of aching muscles. The hairs on his arms prickled in the unnatural chill of the bedroom; his head throbbed from the one-too-many beers he had swilled down the one-too-many painkillers with the previous evening.

Without thinking, he reached out and touched the far side of the bed. Cold. Empty. He was still alone.

'Damn.'

Without realising, he had made his hands into white fists, scrunching damp bed-linen in his palms. He forced himself to exhale, relaxed his fingers. The darkness creeping through the curtains continued creeping.

Time to get up.

As soon as he swung his feet out onto the floor miniature steel vices clamped around the muscles of his lower back. Recently bruised and slowly healing ribs made their presence felt in their usual malicious way. His swearing, while quiet, was exceptionally creative.

He kept his breathing shallow, minimising his discomfort. Stood.

When he picked up the lamp, and switched it on, hard orange light was thrown across the room, blazing his naked portrait against a full length mirror by the door. Roughly one third of his body was black, blue, or purple. It looked almost as bad as it felt.

The smile he tried on was awkward, so he settled instead for his more natural scowl. Missing out on at least one big race was nothing to be smiling about.

He turned and examined his back in the mirror. The bruises ran around the right side of his body, and then clawed their way up like twisted black fingers.

Easing into a robe made him feel better. Not being able to see the bruises and grazes and scabbing cuts was easier. If only it was possible to throw a robe over the thundering, bone-cracking memory.

Painkillers helped, but he had taken enough in the last twenty-four hours to fell a champion racehorse.

He couldn't . . . wouldn't . . . take any more.

His hands were clenched again, so tightly the muscles in his arms were trembling.

No more painkillers.

He moved into the kitchen, and switched on the coffee percolator. He prepared four rounds of buttered toast with Camembert
and drank enough black, unsweetened coffee to float his last dose
of painkillers out of his ears.

There were some benefits to be gained from not racing for a
few days. No weigh-ins. No scales.

The sun rose, flickering sporadically as its wide, yellow beams
caressed the empty street beyond the kitchen window. Birds - who
knows what kind? - chirped in the trees, serenading the dawn.
Ethan could envy such a simple existence.

At seven-forty-five, he ran a bath, lacing the water with numerous herbal potions recommended to him by his Governor, Charles
Lesterton. Lesterton had taken more than his share of spills
during his time as a jockey, and he knew every trick going for getting back in the saddle as soon as possible. He knew, as well as
Ethan did, being out of action meant no wage. Ethan was barely
covering the rent at the best of times.

The rent . . .

He slid carefully into the steaming water of the bath, and stared
at the cracks in the ceiling.

The rent . . .

Another bill he was storing up in the vain hope it might suddenly vanish in a puff of smoke. Another undeniable, unpaid,
unaffordable expense. More worry, more stress.

And for what?

The flat, his home, was one of five similar self-contained prop-
erties, thrown together within the black-brick skeleton of an old
public house.

The building itself was a monstrosity. It brooded next to the
main road of the village like something out of a Hammer horror
movie. Black ivy clawed up the crumbling walls and wrapped
around the windows. Gutters drooped and sloshed rain during
heavy downpours. Rogue tiles, green with moss, lifted in high

7

winds and threatened to decapitate innocent passers-by. A friend of Ethan's in the building trade told him once, the whole place stood only on a miracle.

Inside, every effort had been made to at least make the flats look homely, but it was impossible to disguise the cold and damp, and the sense of impending loneliness the walls themselves seemed to generate.

Ethan kept his flat spotlessly clean, but no amount of air freshener could stop the place smelling like an old cemetery, and on more than one occasion he had been tempted to dig out the sealed fireplace in the lounge to check there wasn't a body decomposing in there.

Ethan was the only tenant. The other flats remained empty and foreboding.

The impression was, and always had been, if he left, the premises would be levelled. He had no intentions of leaving. The flat was only a twenty minute walk from Lesterton's stables, about as good as living on the grounds as he could hope for.

His eyes flicked together. He could almost smell the damp creeping into the top corners of the room, could almost sense the dirty, worming fingers of green rot probing for a way in. He felt like he could just rot with everything else.

Maybe he would turn up at the stables around nine. Anything had to be better than staying in the flat. He might not be able to ride, but he could show his unflagging enthusiasm for his chosen profession. Crazy, stupid profession . . .

Crazy . . .

Stupid . . .

He woke suddenly, his nose full of herbal remedy bubbles, and stinging lukewarm water in his eyes.

He splashed around until one flailing hand lighted on a towel. Wiped his face. The waterproof clock, stuck to the beige tiles with black suction cups, was reading nine-fifteen. Sunlight reflected on the rims of the chrome taps like tiny, mocking smiles.

'Damn,' he said, which was becoming something of a mantra for the day.

Gritting his teeth, he dragged himself out of the bath. His mouth was dry and furry from the combination of beer and drugs and cheese. Gargling with mouth rinse helped.

His pale, unshaven features, wreathed in steam, blinked out at him from the bathroom mirror. He looked like death.

He dressed in workable trousers and a sweater, and hobbled to the front door, determined to at least show his face at the stables, perhaps help with the afternoon feed or some other job that wouldn't prove too taxing. Something of the day could still be salvaged.

The door to the flat swung open. The corridor beyond rolled leisurely, without carpet or wallpaper or any effort to look remotely decorated, towards a front door he alone had used in the last few months.

The door was open.

There were bags in the hallway.

One suitcase. Numerous other boxes. Pots, pans, blankets, lamp shades. Homely things.

In the gravel forecourt, a small Escort had been backed up close to the building. The boot was open.

Someone was leaning against the car. A woman. She was talking on a mobile phone. As Ethan watched, heart thundering and bouncing painfully around his ribcage like a rubber ball, she threw her head back and laughed, and her face . . . By God.

Her face.

Ethan quietly back-stepped into his flat and closed the door, leaning against it. His breath had quickened but seemed to be having trouble squeezing past a blockage in his throat. His hands were drawn fists, the fingernails cutting into white palms. The blood had drained from his face. He closed his eyes. Too late

9

though, too late. He had already seen her.

He rocked his head back, swallowed hard. Composed himself. He was fine, just fine. She was just a girl. He was okay. Better than okay. Really.

The front door slammed.

Christ. She was in the building.

He moved back through to the bathroom where it was still hot and steamy; looked at himself in the mirror.

He couldn't let her see him like that, broken up and smashed, shaking and tired and battered.

'Damn,' he said, hands wrapping around the rim of the basin. 'Damn, damn, damn.' He ran the cold water, splashing his face. If he kept doing it, sooner or later he would wake up. He would wake up because this wasn't the movies. This was real life, where old flames didn't turn up out of the blue and move into the apartment upstairs.

Real life, damn it. Real life.

This wasn't Never-Neverland.

He straightened up, looked himself directly in the eye. 'Okay,' he said quietly. 'You can do this.'

His reflection didn't appear convinced.

He closed the cold tap, it squealed horribly, betraying a plumbing system far older than he was. Condensation ran in confused patterns across the mirror, slicing his face into a hundred equally terrified pieces.

'Okay,' he said, with slightly more conviction. 'Okay.'

When he went back into the hallway, the bags that had been stacked by the door were gone. Most of the boxes too. The front door was closed.

He took a painful, careful step, locked his flat behind him, closing off his only escape route.

Now what? Leave? Head for the stables? Wait?

Go upstairs?

He faltered in the corridor. His nerves buzzed and shook, shivering fear and excitement through his body. She had come back, beyond all reason, all hope. She had come back. Should he play this cool? Did she want him to play this cool? It had been almost a year. He couldn't look too desperate, too needy. He had to look powerful. He was a man. Cool was best.

Surely, cool was best.

His nervous mouth curled into the simple grin of a love-struck teenager.

Maybe she knew he lived here.

Maybe she was waiting for him to go and say hello. Maybe she had picked this very apartment so she could be close to him again. Maybe she had finally realised she couldn't live without him.

Maybe she needed Ethan as much as he needed her.

Maybe, just maybe, the waiting had paid off. Perhaps the nights of being alone, the terrible dreams, had all been worthwhile. Because she was here. Here, now.

That was all that mattered.

He turned and looked at the stairs, steeling himself for the ascent. His ribs grumbled, but they had no choice in the matter. He was going up there and he was going to play out this fantastic black-and-white movie matinee. He was going to knock on her door and she was going to open the door and he was going to say something witty and endearing that would remind her exactly why she had fallen in love with him in the first place. He was going to walk into her flat as calmly as she had walked back into his life.

He was going to be happy again.

He looked up.

She was standing there, at the top of the stairs. Watching him. 'Hello,' she said.

His stomach folded into a neat package, and casually dropped through the floor. He visibly slumped, which was not the best first impression he could have made. His mouth worked foolishly,

11

desperately attempting to generate that witty and endearing comment he had planned.

'You're not her,' he said.

## CHAPTER 2

'I love you,' she said, and, though she wasn't speaking to him, Ethan could imagine how it must have felt to hear those words whispered by this girl - this girl who wasn't who he had thought she was - in the dark of night, with her lips close, her body closer. Her soft voice held, in its round, flowing vowels, the kernel of a promise that might never be fulfilled but which was tantalising enough to rejuvenate hope with her every word.

He sipped his coffee, waited patiently for her to finish her telephone conversation. Around them, the café bustled with the lunchtime rush of fried eggs and dripping bacon sandwiches. The smell of grease and pig fat, ketchup and eggs, permeated the air and made it all the harder for him to enjoy the cucumber sandwiches he had ordered.

The waitress knew him, and would occasionally swagger past with a refill for his coffee, and a suggestive wink. She did not look overly pleased he had arrived that afternoon with a female companion, especially such a beautiful one.

And by God, she was a beautiful one.

As she continued her mobile phone conversation, Ethan watched her over the rim of his cup. It was easy to see how he could have mistaken her for his ex-fiancée, she had many of the same characteristics. Her hair was about the same length, cut raggedly to the shoulder, the same auburn colour. She had the same pale complexion, the same delicate, thin lips. Her eyes were green, rather than brown, but they had that wide, innocent look about them, and they glimmered playfully as she teased the man on the other end of the phone. She even had the same way of playing with her earrings when she talked.

Besides, Ethan must have seen his ex a hundred times a day since she left him. In a stranger's walk, a girl's wave.

She was always there, a ghost walking in his shadow, occasionally flitting into his field of view when he least expected it.

He put the coffee cup back on its chipped saucer and within a few seconds the overly-familiar waitress, Liz, appeared with a steaming jug. 'Who's your friend?' she pried, with all the subtlety of a crowbar.

'My new neighbour, Karen,' he said.

'She talking to anyone special?' The leading question was terribly, almost painfully, transparent.

'Her fiancé,' he said, quietly enjoying the way Liz suddenly relaxed. Her prickling gaze was replaced with something a little - certainly not a lot - less icy. The beginnings of an unkind smile, or partially disguised sneer, played around the bright red smear of makeup that indicated where her lips were. It was not an attractive smile, by any means.

'That's nice,' she said, wiggling off back to the counter. Two other white-clad waitresses moved around like unrecognised circus performers, balancing plates and cutlery and other sundry utensils. Every plastic-covered table in the café was occupied, and there was a sense of barely contained panic among the staff as

14

they scampered backwards and forwards. Ethan watched other diners scoffing their way through cardiac arrest-inducing meals. Karen went on talking on her mobile.

It had just turned one, by Ethan's watch, and he had managed to procure his favourite table by the window. From here, it was possible to look out over Lesterton's rather substantial stables. No horses on the gallops at that time, but the lads could clearly be seen moving through the quadrangles, organising the midday feed. Ethan was vaguely aware he had promised himself he would assist with that part of the daily routine in order to secure a few brownie points.

He glanced at Karen.

Brownie points weren't everything.

'Yes, Honey, I'll see you soon.' She looked at Ethan and rolled those beautiful airport-novel eyes. Her long fingers strayed along the white collar of her flower-print blouse, then up to her diamond earrings. 'Yes. No. Yes, I told you, I'm having lunch with my new neighbour. Ethan. He's a jockey too -'

'Apprentice jockey,' Ethan whispered.

'Yes. No, he's nice. Isn't that a weird coincidence?'

He sat back, watching her perfect pink lips forming the seemingly tireless string of words. She spoke quickly, but every syllable was formed precisely. No noticeable accent, only the taint of expensive schooling.

'It's just lunch, Honey. It's okay. No. Don't be silly. He's a gentleman. You'll like him. Of course you're going to meet him.'

Ethan drummed his fingers on the table, picked up the pepper mill, put it back, folded a paper napkin into four. The sun streamed through the window, warm and comforting. He tapped his foot, balanced his spoon on the rim of the sugar bowl, examined the poorly covered-up cracks in the white-washed ceiling, studied the backs of his hands.

'Honey, I have to ring off now. Yes. Ethan's bored. I'm being

15

rude. Yes. Yes. Okay already. Yes. I'll only sleep with him the once.' She looked at Ethan and winked. He drank his coffee. 'See you later. Okay. I love you too.'

She clicked her phone closed and slipped it into her handbag. 'He sounded nice,' Ethan said, damningly. His father, a wonderfully demented Colonel who ran his family like the one-hundred-and-first battalion, had always told him, in that gruff and uncompromising way Ethan loved so dearly, 'Nice people are just people who haven't got enough balls to go after what they want in life'. Ethan had always believed there was a fine line between nice and decent. He didn't really consider himself to be either.

'He is nice,' Karen said, adding sweetener to her own coffee and stirring it vigorously. 'You may have met him. He's a jockey.'

'So I gather.'

'Jamie Redthorn. You know him?'

Ethan's eyes widened. 'The Jamie Redthorn?'

'I suppose so.'

'He's the reason I started racing. When I was twelve I watched him racing at Ascot. He was partnered with an uncertainty that had been racing a little in Ireland but had never really proved itself on the other side of the water. Horse called Silly Chicane. It was a huge race, a dozen serious contenders. Silly Chicane should have balked, but Jamie got up on the last furlong and destroyed everybody on the field.'

Karen raised an eyebrow.

'He looked so . . .' Ethan gestured uselessly. 'I knew then, when I saw him waving his whip in the air, I wanted to do that. I wanted to be like him.'

'I'll make sure I get you his autograph.'

Ethan flushed red. 'Sorry, I must sound pretty stupid. How did you two meet?'

A small movement played across her face, flickering and illusive. Momentary. 'Let's talk about something else,' she said.

16

'Fine, let's talk about you.'

'Oh really, how dull.'

'What made you want to move to a neighbourhood like this? Did you draw a short straw?'

'I moved for my work.' She looked beyond the window, at the rolling fields and banks of trees, beyond which the towering chimney stacks of industry belched dragon-breath at the sky. The landscape, dependent on the outlook of the beholder, ranged from beautiful to desolate. 'Mainly,' she added, somewhat superfluously.

'What do you do?'

'I'd rather talk about you,' she said.

'There's nothing to talk about. I am what you see. As much depth and complexity as a paddling pool.'

She leaned close, resting her chin on one delicately cupped hand. A silver bracelet on her wrist twinkled in the sunlight, spangling her face with isometric flares of white. Damn, she was pretty. Audrey Hepburn Breakfast At Tiffany's pretty. 'Paddling pools may look shallow,' she said, 'but there's always a few feet in them.'

A young couple on the next table looked over, clearly happy in the generically happy-couple kind of way, then leaned in and whispered to one another. They weren't local, and had probably recognised Ethan from some newspaper story somewhere. All the regulars knew his face, and the faces of the more famous jocks at Lesterton's stables, and they were way past the gawping stage. These two people were only seconds away from coming over to say hello in an excited rush.

'Do you want to get out of here?' Ethan asked.

'Got anywhere in mind?'

He stood, doing his best to disguise the shiver of pain that fluttered across his features as groaning muscles realigned along his back. 'Not really,' he said. 'But the smell of bacon is driving me

17

crazy.'

Karen rose, dabbing at her face needlessly with a paper napkin. 'Wherever we go, you know you're not going to get out of answering my questions.' Her eyes were wide and beautiful and shimmering.

'New rule,' he said, taking her hand. 'We alternate questions. No lying. No passing. No phone a friend.'

'What are we playing for?'

He grinned, dropped enough money on the table to cover almost twice what they had eaten, and led her out into the street.

A quiet Tuesday afternoon allowed them to roam freely around the village without interruption. No pedestrians, no how-do-you-dos, no lovely-days, just the perfectly flat calm of a day without hurry. Karen and Ethan moved through that calm like ripples, distorting the beauty of silence with a sudden laugh or silly remark as they walked down towards the perimeter of Lesterton's grounds. There, by the crumbling dry stone wall, and the towering Oak Ethan had climbed in his youth on a drunken dare, watching white clouds peel away from the sky and fluster across the bright face of the sun, they stopped. Ethan stretched out in the long grass; Karen sat against a flat stone on which the moss grew in hungry flourishes.

For a while they didn't speak. Somehow, that seemed perfectly natural. Ethan closed his eyes and listened to her breathing. A cool breeze bristled the dry grass like there were invisible children running there, and for the moment, blissful minutes, Ethan forgot about his injuries. For the first time since the accident, he didn't need to fight the urge to crunch painkillers.

'It's my turn,' Karen said, eventually.

'For?'

'A question.'

'Shoot.'

'Who is she?'

Ethan raised himself on one elbow. 'Who?'

'New rule. No playing dumb.'

'You learn fast.'

'You're evading the question.'

'What is the question?'

'Who is the girl you mistook me for this morning?'

'Nobody.'

Her lips rolled back from teeth more deadly than any sharks in a disarmingly bright smile. 'No lying. No passing.' He stuck his tongue out. She crossed her arms and tilted her head to one side so hair partially fell across her mouth. 'I've never seen somebody so disappointed to see me before.'

'I didn't realise it showed.'

'You aren't as mysterious as you think you are.'

'Don't take it personally.' He snatched at handfuls of grass thoughtlessly, ripping it out of the ground in clumps. 'I wasn't disappointed, I was just expecting someone else.'

'Who?'

'I thought you were an old . . . acquaintance.'

'Girlfriend?'

'Only one question at a time. My turn.'

'This is the same question, you've only given me a partial answer.'

'You're making these rules up as you go along.'

'It's a woman's prerogative.'

He sank back into the grass. It seemed safer there. 'Fiancée,' he said, reluctantly.

'Really? What happened?'

He stretched out his right hand, index finger raised. 'Now, that is clearly a new question. My turn.'

'Strict, aren't you?'

'I believe in fair play.'

'Fine. Go ahead.'

'Why don't you live with Jamie?'

It had sounded like such an innocent question in his head, but even as he spoke the words he could hear the unintended slight Karen would surely believe it was meant to be. An uncomfortable silence was the only response.

'Sorry,' he said. 'I retract that question.'

'Don't,' she said quietly, almost inaudibly. 'I agreed to the rules of the game. I have to answer.'

'Really, that's not necessary.'

'I'm not sure he loves me.'

Ethan sat up. 'I don't think you should go on,' he said.

'He says he loves me, treats me . . . kindly. He's never cheated on me, as far as I know, but. . .'

'You don't believe him.'

'It's just words to him. When you tell somebody you love them, they shouldn't just say it back.' She glanced off towards the shimmering heat-haze horizon, where the twist of the road disappeared from sight. 'There should be more than that, shouldn't there?'

He laced his fingers together, bowed his head in contemplation. One wrong word could destroy everything. 'What else can someone say?'

'Why should they say anything? Love isn't about words. Love isn't about silly words.'

'Then why are you with him?'

She shrugged, and all the hopelessness in the world settled across her shoulders. It was a defeated gesture and yet, somehow, full of pride. Ethan watched her wrestle the words she needed into a knotted sentence. 'I love him and I think, one day, I can make him love me in the same way.'

'And until then you'll continue living in apartments by yourself?'

'You think I'm silly and melodramatic.'

'Not at all.'

'I need that distance, that space. If I'm with him he'll never try harder, he'll never need to love me in the way I love him.'

'So you're giving him an ultimatum?'

'You're getting a lot of free questions out of me. I think it's my turn.'

Ethan gestured that she should proceed. The leaves of the Oak tree flapped against each other, winking and nudging in the wind. Faint voices carried across the expanse of shimmering green fields, from the direction of the yard. Lesterton had no races today, and that meant he would be plodding around the grounds like a bear with a sore head, looking for some stable hands to intimidate. Ethan considered himself to be blessed he was in Karen's company rather than the trainer's.

'What happened with you and your ex?' she asked.

His gaze drew back to level with hers. She was watching him with an almost frightening intensity. He squirmed, picked at his fingernails. 'We grew apart.'

'New rule. No clichés. And you have to give me her name.'

'Melissa. And that wasn't a cliché.'

'Be honest. Nobody just grows apart, there's always a catalyst.'

'Relationships aren't a science. Sometimes things happen and you can't stop them, no matter how you might want to. Sometimes you don't even know what those things are until they take your legs out from under you.'

'What does that mean?'

'It means we grew apart.'

'You said you play fair. Do you want an easier question?'

'Please.'

'Are you seeing anyone right now?'

He sighed heavily. There were girls, three of them. None of them were girlfriends. None of them were serious. They used him and he used them. He doubted any of them really knew why.

'Ethan?'

21

He blinked. The sun dipped behind a cloud, enjoying a playful hide-and-seek moment. A shiver ran along his spine. 'I don't think so,' he said.

'Why not?'

'I can't answer that.'

'Why?'

'Because you said no clichés.'

'Try me.'

'Would you believe I haven't met the right person yet?'

'I'm more inclined to believe you met the right person and you've never got over it.'

'Melissa?' Ethan snorted an unpleasant laugh through his nose that was even more bitter than he had expected. 'No. Melissa was wrong in every conceivable kind of way. I don't need her any more than she needs me.' His words lacked any kind of real conviction.

'Aren't you looking for her replacement?'

He looked hard at Karen, at the suede skirt, split to the thigh; at the thick curls of her hair; at her wet, pink lips. She was similar to Melissa in so many ways.

'No,' he said, unconvincingly. 'Why would I be looking to replace her? I don't want someone else like her. I want someone better.'

Karen swept back cascades of hair in a matter-of-fact kind of way. Nothing overtly sexual in the motion, but still Ethan could not help but avert his gaze for fear the beginnings of some unfortunate desire might be seen in his eyes. 'You didn't grow apart, did you?' she asked, as though she was inserting a scalpel under his skin. 'She left you.'

'You see a lot of things,' he said.

'I'm very observant. Why are you so ashamed about it?'

'I'm a man, I'm supposed to be the heartbreaker.'

'I didn't take you for that type.'

22

'Everybody's that type.'

The sun re-emerged from behind the banks of smoky cloud. 'I hope not,' Karen whispered.

'You're disappointed.'

'I don't know you well enough to be disappointed.'

They sat in silence for a while. Ethan continued pulling clumps of grass out of the earth, and tried to think of something funny to say. Karen wrapped an earring around her finger. The day wore on relentlessly.

'I'm sorry,' he said. He didn't know why, but he meant it. 'Maybe we should stick to a safer line of questioning.'

'Like what? Favourite colour?'

He saw the spark of amusement flare in her eyes again, and latched on to it hopefully. 'I can guess yours.'

'Go ahead.'

'Pink.'

'What makes you say that?'

'Your lipstick.'

'I wear lots of different coloured lipsticks.'

'But pink is your favourite.'

'Maybe.' Her gaze ran over his trousers, his sweater, his jacket. All black. 'Your favourite colour is black.'

'Wrong. It's pink.'

She raised a perfectly pencilled eyebrow suggestively. 'Are you flirting with me?'

He cleared his throat, turned away. 'Sorry,' he said. 'Didn't mean to make you feel uncomfortable.'

'You're the one that looks uncomfortable.'

She stood, running the creases out of her skirt with delicately manicured fingers. He watched her feet - her knee-high boots - as she approached. 'Do I make you feel awkward?'

His throat worked soundlessly.

She walked around so she was standing behind him. Crouched.

'Are you scared of me?' she asked.

'I don't even know you,' he said.

Her hands rested on his shoulders, her lips moved down close to his ear. Her breath was hot and seductive. 'That can be rectified,' she said.

CHAPTER 3

Trevor Dalton was peculiarly ugly.

He was ugly, not through any outstandingly ugly feature - no big nose or crooked mouth - but rather through a combination of rather ordinary features. His face was almost entirely without character. His nose was neither too big nor too small; it was not too wide, too flat, too pointed, too narrow, or too bent. His nose was simply a nose, entirely practical and without feature. Likewise, his eyes seemed almost devoid of life, of colour even, being hard grey orbs set in the hollows of his face.

There was no quirk to his mouth, no interesting tick on his lip, no unusual movement that might catch somebody's eye.

In truth, Dalton's face was made up of such completely ordinary components the resulting combination was a surreal and unnatural sculpture. It was almost as though he was trying too hard to look normal, like he was a body-snatching alien unaccustomed to the novelty of human flesh and all its vagaries. Even his efficient stride seemed mechanical, practised to perfection.

He dressed in black at all times, when he wasn't on the back of a horse, and he conducted himself in the stiff-backed, tight-collared way expected of the English gentry. He drank tea on the lawn in the afternoon, played croquet, and remained quite sober even while drinking.

To anybody he met, he was a sinister shadow of a man, a creature that could be anyone or anything at any time. Those people who saw him walking down the street might even be compelled to cross over, or duck into a store, not out of fear, but out of some crawling sensation under the skin that couldn't be scratched away.

When Dalton spoke, it was with the crisp, hard British vowels and consonants of a seriously expensive education. Even when he was being genuinely friendly, he sounded like he was being patronising, and there was always enough pomp in his grandiose stories to fill any room with an air of superiority. Not that his superiority was entirely without grounds, he was, after all, an expert.

He was an expert at making love - or, at least, having sex, because he was never in love - and his options, when it came to a bed in which to spend the night, were extensive, despite his physical unattractiveness. He was an expert socialite, knowing exactly where to be, and when to be there, in order to maximise his potential standing in society. But above all else, he was, and always had been, an expert horseman.

He was the definition of British High Society. He was also the definition of a complete bastard.

*

Dalton's visitor arrived a little after two o'clock in the afternoon.

At the time, Dalton was sat around the back of his rather expensive, rather desirable, country house, basking by his pool

26

with a cocktail in one hand and a drooping cigarette in the other. He was wearing a black silk shirt, unbuttoned to the waist, and black Chinos with a Gucci belt; an ensemble strangely contrary to the warm weather.

Sat in his Day-Glo deck chair, he looked something like a lost penguin.

His eyes, disguised behind designer sunglasses, were fixed on some point in the Heavens, beyond the extent of human vision and imagination.

Had he been asked, at that time, what he was thinking about, it is likely he would have said 'nothing'. This was probably about as far from the truth as it was possible to get.

Dalton, at no point in his life, had ever thought about nothing. There was no way of making money out of thinking about nothing, and money was largely the driving force in Dalton's day-to-day activities.

As he stared into the sky, at something that possibly wasn't there, he was making plans. Beneath his calm exterior, he was paddling like crazy.

'Don't get up,' his visitor said, sitting opposite.

The sun glittered on the bobbing water of the pool, and the suitably tanned bodies of the women swimming in it.

'Wasn't planning to,' Dalton said. He remained staring at the blue tracts of sky that showed through whispers of discarded clouds. His bland, strangely ugly, unimportant face revealed nothing of his thoughts.

The girls in the pool splashed and giggled and generally paid Dalton and his visitor no attention. Several hours from now they could be asked who the guest had been, and they would not even be able to recall if there had been one.

The visitor ran a handkerchief around the back of his neck. Said nothing.

'It's my day off,' Dalton said. 'This isn't going to be about business, is it?' He sipped his cocktail through a straw, drew on his cigarette until the last embers crackled to death against the filter. Waited patiently for a response.

'Newbury,' the visitor said.

'I repeat, this is my day off. Look over there.' Dalton waved towards the general direction of the pool, without rising. 'See those women?'

The visitor glanced at the pool. There were six girls in total. All beautiful. All toned and tanned and designed by God Himself to slam every last brain cell a man had into dust with just the slightest look.

As he watched, he was reminded of Ulysses. These were the modern-day Sirens. An interesting distraction, but a distraction. A deadly one.

'What about them?' he asked.

'Those women are the only things I am interested in today.' This was a lie, albeit a very convincing one. 'This is my first day off in six months.'

'It must be nice to be able to take the time to pamper yourself.'

The girls splashed and played.

'Everybody should take the time to pamper themselves once in a while, or . . .' Dalton shrugged. 'What's the point?'

'The people I work for don't agree with time off,' the visitor said. He made no secret of the hungry, curious way in which he watched the women swim. 'I'm not sure many people do. There's always an angle. Every party is an opportunity to get further, to meet that right person who will keep the money coming in. Every handshake, every greeting, is potential cash flow.' He stopped, looked in his handkerchief as though he had wiped something interesting off the back of his neck. 'Even now, you're thinking about Newbury, and what I've got to say.'

'Do you think you know me?'

'We're the same.'

'I wouldn't be so sure.'

'We'll see.'

'You have a business proposition, I assume?'

'Perhaps.' The visitor sucked his teeth thoughtfully. 'Who are all these women?'

Dalton fished a packet of cigarettes out of his trouser pocket and waved it towards the visitor vaguely. The visitor shook his head. 'I roll my own,' he said.

Dalton lit himself a cigarette, and puffed his way through half of it. 'I don't know,' he said.

'You don't know what?'

'The women.'

'You don't know them?'

'Maybe that one.' Dalton pointed out the most attractive girl. She was lying by the edge of the water, her mocha-latte skin glowing lustily.

'Maybe that one, what?'

'Maybe that one I slept with. She looks like my type. I probably said she could come round and use the pool.'

'And the others?'

'Her friends, probably.'

'Doesn't it bother you having all these people you don't know around the place?'

'Are you kidding? Look at them, they're beautiful.'

'Transient, though.'

'Who cares? I like to surround myself with beautiful, useless things. They're like trophies. Lacking in conversation but nice to look at.'

The visitor folded his handkerchief neatly and put it in his shirt pocket. He looked incredibly uncomfortable in a beige Ralph Lauren single-breasted jacket, and tie. He looked, very much, like he had dressed for a business meeting. 'It was trophies I wanted to talk about,' he said. 'But I don't like the idea of talking in front of

29

these girls.'

'Girls make you nervous?'

'When I don't know who they are.'

'Trust me, they couldn't give a damn about what you have to say. They're too busy having fun.' Dalton flicked ash. 'Maybe they've got the right idea.'

'Even so, I'd rather not talk in front of them.'

Dalton drew steadily on his cigarette, washing down the smoke with the last of his cocktail. 'Why? What is it you want to say?'

'I wanted to talk about Newbury, two days from now. You're riding, aren't you?'

'I am.'

'You're riding for Lesterton, right?'

'Who told you that?'

'It's true, isn't it?'

'Actually, no. It's not.'

'I thought . . .' The visitor paused. Two of the girls had started kissing; it was exceptionally entertaining. 'I heard you were riding for Lesterton sometimes.'

'Sometimes. Emphasis on the some.'

'So who's riding for him at Newbury?'

'O'Hara.'

The visitor scratched his jaw. 'O'Hara. . .'

'There's a certain degree of loyalty among Lesterton's people that can sometimes be . . . frustrating.'

'Do you think there's a distinction between loyalty and honesty?'

'I think there can be.'

'And O'Hara? What's he like?'

'Difficult. But I've put some pressure on him recently. Think it may be starting to show.'

'Enough pressure to make him pop?'

'Perhaps. He's a difficult man to rile, but I've taken a few of his rides recently. He's a little concerned I may be taking a few more if things don't change.'

The visitor studied his hands. 'And you intend to keep this pressure on?'

'You ask a lot of questions.'

'Character flaw.'

'We all have those.'

Dalton stubbed his cigarette out. It died, with a stubborn hiss, on the arm of the deck chair. A minute sneaked away quietly, while it thought nobody was watching.

'What are you riding?' the visitor asked.

'Nothing with a chance of winning.'

'You're certain of that?'

'Positive. There's only one horse in this race as far as I'm concerned. My guess would be, you've come to the same conclusion, or else you wouldn't be here.'

'Perhaps.' The visitor pulled a laminated card from his shirt pocket, handed it to Dalton. 'That's my personal number. If you want to talk some more, ring me.'

'What would we have to talk about?'

'Something that may be of mutual benefit.'

'I don't think I'm interested.'

'And that's why I'm not telling you any more for the time being.'

'I'm fickle. Stick around and you might be able to change my mind.'

'But I can't take that risk. You decide you're interested, we'll talk again.'

The visitor stood, watched the two girls kissing in the pool. 'You have a nice view here,' he said.

Dalton slipped the business card into his pocket, shook another cigarette from his pack. 'What's this all about?' he asked, searching for his lighter.

The visitor smiled. 'Winning.'

CHAPTER 4

Dinner consisted of microwaved chicken curry and a bottle of red wine, the extent of Ethan's culinary expertise. The study of food preparation had never been high on his agenda. Still, Karen seemed more than happy to join him in his small, but tidy, ground floor apartment. For her company, he had traded his assistance, limited as that might have been in his current state, unpacking the various boxes in which her life had arrived that morning.

Her flat, directly above his own, on the first floor of the early nineteenth century, three-storey premises, was actually larger, but smaller windows and illogical corners and doors meant an air of dinginess pervaded even on the sunniest days. His own little residence, with the wide bay windows looking out onto the yards of Lesterton's grounds in the valley below, was definitely the more desirable of the two.

'I'm sorry about the food,' Ethan said, waving a fork at the plate of bright red rice and chicken.

Karen looked at him carefully, the light from the single candle in the centre of the table reflecting in her eyes in glittering flashes. The kitchen brooded in contemplative darkness. 'You apologise too often,' she said, quite seriously.

'Sorry.'

She sipped wine, dabbed her lips on a napkin. He watched her, drinking in every movement, every tiny nuance of her facial expressions.

His left hand drew into a fist on the table. He spooned rice into his mouth, and carried on watching her.

'Of course,' he said, 'I wouldn't normally eat this kind of thing.'

'Not healthy enough?' she asked.

'You can't trust these ready-made meals. Full of additives, colourings, bad stuff. But considering the circumstances, I think I can get away with it.'

'Then why the cucumber sandwiches at the café?'

'That was different. That was outside.'

'Is this a pride thing?'

'Maybe. I can't let people around here know I'm injured. I won't let them see me in pain.'

'Why?'

'I don't want anything in the papers.'

'Does it matter?'

'People have to trust me with their horses. I had an accident on the gallops. That doesn't look good.'

'Everybody has accidents.'

'There's a lot of money at stake in these races. People are investing in my ability, trusting me with their most valued assets. I can't show weakness. I won't.'

She tilted her head slightly. Her eyes drew narrower. He could almost feel his skin prickle as she watched him. 'You seem kind of big for a jockey. I think you probably carry more weight than Jamie.'

'It's a constant battle.'

'So what's different about tonight?'

He shrugged, and even that simple action sent a reminding spark of pain crackling along his back. 'I'll have to work a little harder once I'm fit, but I figure while I'm incapacitated I might as well make the most of it.'

'It must be hard.'

'Being trodden on by a horse? It isn't easy. I've seen horses break their own legs in an attempt to avoid landing on a fallen jockey in the past. Guess I just got lucky.'

'How did it happen?'

'I fell off. It happens sometimes.' He pushed rice around on his plate, forming Pilau mountains on a lake of curry sauce. 'I was exercising one of the more frisky colts. He bolted, my mind was elsewhere. I slipped. I'm lucky it wasn't much worse.'

'Where?'

'Where what?'

'Your mind. Where was it?'

A taste of wine, a thoughtful pause. He watched the candle flame flicker, listened to the cars whistle by outside. 'I've spent a lot of time living in the past. I thought I'd lost something, but I'm not sure I ever had it.'

'Melissa?'

'It's been more than a year.' He almost laughed, twisting a napkin through his hands nervously. 'Silly really. I don't know why I let her get to me the way she did. I'm usually stronger than that.'

'Silly doesn't even begin to describe it,' Karen said. 'She left you. She doesn't deserve any more of your time.'

'I suppose . . . I don't know, I guess I always thought she might come back.'

'Is that really likely?'

'I thought you, of all people, would be a champion for the lost cause.'

She dipped her eyes, folding her hands on the table. 'I just think

34

it's a waste.'

'Why do you say that?'

'Never mind.'

Ethan refilled her wine glass, then his own. 'You're right, of course,' he conceded, unnecessarily. 'I shouldn't still be hung up on her, not after all this time. I imagine she has quite happily got on with her life without me.'

'Does that help? Imagining she's happy?'

'No.'

'Then why do it?'

He repositioned himself, attempting to find some way to ease the uncompromising discomfort in his lower back. The painkillers were in the drawer by the sink. He resisted the urge to get them. 'She never gave me a reason,' he said, distractedly. 'She just left one day. Left the engagement ring on the bedside table, and walked out. When something like that happens, you tend to want to fill in the blanks. At least understand what the blanks were.'

'She didn't leave a note?'

'I don't think she had anything left to say. We hadn't been getting on so well for a while. Guess she just had enough.'

'And you never saw her again?'

He looked deep into his wine, almost as if he might conjure an image of Melissa's face there. 'No.'

'That's a sad story.'

'Everybody's got one.'

'And what about happy stories?'

'Those are harder to come by.'

'But not unheard of.'

He raised his glass. 'A toast then. To happy stories.'

Glasses chinked. Hot wax bubbled and dripped, forming hard, white tentacles along the length of the candle. 'Happy stories,' Karen agreed.

Her mobile phone started ringing. 'And that would be the next chapter in yours,' Ethan said. 'You can take it in the lounge.'

Karen moved through to the lounge, closing the door behind her. Even then, Ethan could still hear her voice. He gulped his wine, looked at the drawer by the sink.

Painkillers.

'Jamie, hi . . . Yes, the flat's fine. Obviously nothing like what you're used to, Mr Big Shot, but it suits me . . . Yes, of course. Ethan helped me move in, he's been just an absolute gem the whole time. He wouldn't let me carry any of the heavy boxes, even though he's . . . Oh, never mind.'

Ethan shook his head ruefully. Ethan, the gem, the nice guy, the loser. Just another one of the world's punch bags.

He drained the last of the wine from the bottle.

'Be serious.' Karen sounded frustrated. 'He helped carry a few boxes and he made me dinner . . . Jamie, stop it. What do you mean? I'm at the flats, where else would I be? Yes. I'm in Ethan's flat. I told you, he made me dinner.'

Ethan stood, winced. God damn. The muscles down his side were being systematically replaced with lead weights, and there was no allowance for being an apprentice. He eased his way across to the sink, opened the drawer.

Painkillers.

'Jamie, this is silly. Ethan is an absolute gentleman, he's actually a big fan of yours. He's seen you in the weighing room a few times, but he's never spoken to you before. He's really looking forward to it . . . No. Why? Why would I be lying? Stop it. I'm not going to talk to you while you're being like this.'

Ethan crunched two tablets, ran his mouth under the cold tap. Instantly felt better.

The lounge door opened. Karen stamped across to the table and snatched her wine glass, downing the contents.

'Jamie?' Ethan asked, innocently.

'Silly, pig-headed man.' She didn't look at him as she spoke, instead picking up the empty wine bottle, examining it, shaking it hopefully. 'We need more alcohol,' she said.

'Are you okay?'

'You won't believe what he thinks. He thinks that . . .' She finally looked at Ethan. Her expression softened considerably. 'You know what? It doesn't matter.'

'He's not too keen to meet me, is he?'

'He'll be fine. Once he's met you, he'll be fine. He wasn't happy about me moving out this way anyway.' She giggled. 'He certainly won't be happy I just hung up on him.'

'I don't want to make any trouble.'

'It'll take more than one bottle of wine to get us into trouble.'

'Just as well that was my last one then.'

She grinned playfully. 'I think I may have another bottle upstairs. You interested?'

Ethan blinked, analysing the question carefully. Several glasses of red wine and the dose of heavy-duty painkillers were already doing a good job of scrambling his senses but, even so, that question definitely sounded like a come-on. Couldn't be though. Wouldn't be. She was in love with another man. She didn't even know Ethan. Had only met him a few hours before. Couldn't possibly be suggesting what he thought she was suggesting.

'Interested?' he asked, dumbly.

'The wine?'

'I'm not sure that's such a good idea.'

She laughed, and there was a harsh edge to the sound. 'Oh, really,' she said. 'Sky diving isn't exactly a good idea, that's what makes it so much fun.' She opened the front door. The cold light of the hallway glared sickeningly, casting her delicate outline in silhouette, obscuring her face. 'I thought being a jockey was all about taking risks?'

He looked from the door to the table, at the empty wine bottle

37

and the guttering candle.

'Risks?'

He turned back to the door. She was already gone.

He swallowed, checked his watch. Nearly nine o'clock.

The telephone in the lounge chirped aggressively, cutting through the encroaching haze of prescription drugs. He answered it on the fourth ring, just before the answer-phone kicked in.

'Yes?'

'Hey, Ethan, what's the score?'

Ethan screwed his face up, tried to place the voice. American accent, deep intonation, a false air of superiority. 'Jason,' he said. 'The great Mr Montoya. How are you?'

'You've forgotten, haven't you?' Jason's voice was crackling and distant, distorted by a metallic twang. He was calling from a mobile phone. If he was calling from a mobile, that meant he was at a bar. Ethan could hear women in the background. Slowly, the pieces of a half-remembered jigsaw began to slot into place. 'I can't believe you've forgotten.'

'Sorry, Jason. It completely went out of my head,' Ethan said.

'Sorry doesn't cut it, Ethan. I've got two girls here waiting to meet my famous jockey friend.'

'You told them I was famous?'

'I told them I was a multimillionaire oil tycoon. So what? Now get your ass in gear and get over to the club.'

'Sorry, no can do.'

'Sorry? Sorry? This is supposed to be a double date. What am I supposed to do now?'

'You've got two girls there who think you're fabulously rich. Use your imagination.'

'And what are you doing that's keeping you so occupied?'

Ethan looked over his shoulder at the open door and the harsh light of the hallway. 'Sky diving,' he said.

*

The second bottle of Merlot was emptied a little faster than the first. Most of Karen's furniture, what little she possessed, had not yet been delivered, so they sat on the carpeted floor of the awkwardly shaped lounge among a stack of boxes, with only two candles for illumination. It did nothing for Ethan's complaining back, but he suffered silently, enjoying every moment of the exquisite torture of Karen's company.

'What's it like being a jockey?' she asked.

'Apprentice jockey.' The correction was automatic, self-deprecating when his current status was absolutely nothing to be ashamed of. As far as apprentice jockeys went, he was a good one. He had quickly proved himself in the saddle, trimming his seven pound weight allowance to five pounds within his first year, and another three first places would break the fifty wins limit and drop that allowance by a further two pounds.

'What's it like being an apprentice jockey?' Karen tried.

'Busy.'

'Do you get scared?'

'You can't be scared. Horses have a sense for the condition of their rider. They don't like taking orders from somebody scared out of their wits. If you lose your cool, the horse loses his.'

'Doesn't the idea of the jumps bother you?'

'I'm an apprentice, not a conditional jockey.'

'No jumping? Like Jamie?'

'No jumping.'

'What about your parents?'

He watched her closely, attempting to gauge the true nature of the question. 'What about them?'

'Where are they? What do they do?'

'Why do you ask?'

'Because I'm interested.'

'Why?'

She crawled towards him across the floor, stopped by his feet, swept the hair out of her face. 'Because you don't want to talk about them.'

'Aren't you going to allow me to keep any of my mystery?'

She wiggled between him and a box marked 'kitchen utensils', so they were sitting shoulder to shoulder, both looking out of the open window at the black, silver-speckled curtains of the night. 'What's the use of mystery?' she asked. 'Mysteries are just secrets. Secrets only ever hurt.'

He breathed deeply. She smelled of summer. 'You're right, of course, but they are interesting.'

'Only when they're shared.' Her open smile, brimming with perfect teeth, was dangerously alluring.

'You realise, I would probably tell you anything?' he said.

'I know, it's a gift.'

'My parents are in Africa. They have a small stud farm out there and a number of very respectable horses.'

'Why Africa?'

'It's a long story.'

'We best open another bottle of wine then.'

He tried to protest, or at least he meant to try and protest, but Karen was already on her feet. He leaned back against the wall and closed his eyes. There was banging and thumping from the kitchen as various drawers opened and closed.

Minutes passed. He floated weightlessly in an alcoholic bubble.

'Here you go.'

His eyes flicked open, examined the glass being waved under his nose. 'Thanks,' he said.

'So, this story . . .'

'My grandfather was a rich man. He loved horses, and they breed some of the most brutish bloody horses you'll ever see in

Africa. That's what he loved the most, horses all about strength. So, he went out to Africa and established himself as something of an expert in breeding.' There was definite pride in Ethan's voice, an inability to disguise how much he truly admired his grandfather. 'While he was out there he picked up a wife, a white African citizen raised on a horse farm and as rugged and bloody-minded as he ever was.'

He sampled the wine. It wasn't too bad. He listened to Karen breathing beside him. That wasn't too bad either.

'How did your grandfather make his money?'

'Not something he ever wanted to talk about, but I heard one or two rumours. He was a soldier, a good one by all accounts.' He paused uncertainly. 'But being good doesn't make you rich, and after the war he was a rich man.'

'So how did he do it?'

'There are . . . certain items, items belonging to Hitler, Nazi treasures. Very collectable, and very easily obtainable for the right soldier in the right place at the right time.'

'That's . . .'

'I know. My grandfather may have founded his stable on blood money. I think he believed he deserved to get something back from the war, something more than the arthritis and weak lungs he got from trench fighting.'

'And what do you believe?'

'I believe if he hadn't help lift those treasures, somebody else would have. Those were different times, people were just doing what they had to, to get by. Maybe he was wrong, but I can't judge him.'

Karen touched Ethan's hand. He couldn't be certain, but she seemed closer than she was before. He could almost feel her breath on his neck.

Could almost feel her lips . . .

'So,' he said, abruptly. 'My grandfather and grandmother had three children, one of which was my father, before eventually being forced to leave the country.'

'Why did they go?'

'They were rich, they had land, and they were white. They were supposed to set an example.'

'What example?'

'My grandfather lived through a war. He saw what harm prejudice could cause.'

'So they left?'

'You either live by the regime or you die by it. They always wanted to go back though. They didn't sell off the farm, they leased it to a black family they were friends with and that kept the place ticking over. Unfortunately, my grandfather never got the chance to take back his property.' He sipped wine, swirled it around his tongue. Tried to remember his grandfather's face. 'It was the lungs. They were never right when he came back. One day they just stopped. By then my father was married and was working for military intelligence as a translator. I must have been about six. I don't really remember much about it.'

'And what happened to the stables?'

'My grandmother returned. She wanted to be there. She said it was easier to remember my grandfather when she was with the horses.'

'Your parents?'

'They didn't go. Not straight away. But eventually my grandmother fell ill and they went out to take care of her. By then I had been offered my apprenticeship here with Mr Lesterton so I stayed.' He sighed heavily. 'Over a year ago now. Grandmother died, my parents took on the farm.'

'Why didn't you go out there with them?'

'I belong here.'

'With Melissa?'

'It wasn't about her. I needed to stay for me, to prove I was capable of looking after myself.'

'And you can honestly say you didn't stay for her?'

'I needed to prove I could make it on my own. I didn't want everything to be given to me by my parents.'

'But she wouldn't go with you, would she?'

He emptied his wine glass, looked sadly down the stem. 'I didn't ask. She had too many other commitments. College, things like that. I couldn't ask her to give all that up for me.'

'So you didn't even give her the chance?'

'She never gave as much as she took. I knew what her answer would have been.'

'You would have done anything for her, wouldn't you? Given up everything?'

'I believe in doing whatever it takes to make love work.'

A sad and thoughtful look passed across Karen's features. 'I believe the same thing, but at what point should you give up and start again?'

'I never give up.'

'But that was then. What's stopping you from going now?'

Black wisps of cloud stretched across the crescent smile of the moon. 'The only thing I've got left,' Ethan said. 'The belief one day she'll come back.'

'And if she does?'

'Then I get to go to Africa with the woman I love.'

## CHAPTER 5

Awake.

Ethan jolted violently into consciousness through several thick layers of dense sleep. Sat up. Cold sweat shivered down his back and chest; breath reverberated threateningly through every bone of his skeleton. The room - his room - was only darkness.

The bed seemed impossibly large. Didn't know how he had got there. Head was thumping violently.

Red wine.

The clock told him it was seven thirty-five. He was late for another day at the stables. Lesterton would be thoroughly annoyed.

Instinctively, stupidly, like every other morning for the past year, he reached over to the other side of the bed for the girl he knew wouldn't be there. His shaking hand touched soft skin, withdrew uncertainly.

Slowly, achingly slowly, he became aware of breathing that was not his own.

Christ. She was there.

He reached out again, touched a smooth shoulder, a bra strap. This wasn't a dream. She was really there.

Then, a voice in the darkness. 'Ethan? What are you doing?' He retracted his hand as though he had been stung. It was not Melissa's voice.

Of course it wasn't Melissa's voice.

'Sorry,' he whispered hoarsely, trying to keep the aching loneliness from his voice. 'I was dreaming.'

Karen rolled over to look at him. Considering she had drank as much as he had, she didn't look half bad. 'You look like shit,' she said.

'It's taken years of practice.'

Her gaze worked over his chest, abdomen, shoulders. He was suddenly aware of how naked he was. His bruising, the evidence of that bloody silly accident, was fully visible. 'You never said it was that bad,' she said, seriously.

'It's not as bad as it looks,' he lied, attempting to pull the duvet around him. 'It's much better than it was.'

She traced over a pale scar on his forearm. Even that slight touch was like electricity on his skin, jolting his libido into life. 'How did you get this one?'

'In a fight.'

'Really?'

'No. I fell out of a tree.'

'You fall down a lot, don't you?'

'I always get back up.'

She ran a hand through her mussed hair. Ethan tried to be as gentlemanly as possible and not stare at her breasts. Being a gentleman had never been something he was particularly good at.

'Are you going to the stables today?' she asked.

'Yes.'

'Do you think I would be able to come?'

45

'Not straight away. I'd need to clear it with the Governor first. He doesn't like people just turning up.'

'Right.' She clambered over Ethan, breasts pressing against his chest for the briefest and most exciting moment and hopped out of bed. She started rummaging around for her clothes. 'Could you switch on the lamp?'

He did so. Warm, muggy light blazed across the room, setting fire to Karen's pale skin.

'Thanks.'

He watched her as she darted around in her underwear, without even trying to disguise the devil in his eyes. Eventually she found her skirt and put it on, then the rest of her clothes.

'Right,' she said. 'You clear it with your boss and give me a ring when I can come round.'

'I don't have your number.'

'It's in your top shirt pocket. I put it there after you fell asleep.'

'Oh.'

'I'm expecting a delivery of furniture this morning but I should be free all afternoon.'

His head throbbed savagely, the taste of stale wine in the back of his throat was nauseating, yet this girl seemed entirely unaffected by the events of the preceding evening. He could not help but be envious as she bounced around energetically pulling on her boots.

'Why do you want to come to the stable?' he asked.

She was already at the door, full of bubbles, full of vitality, smiling and being everything Ethan could have possibly hoped she would be. 'Sorry?'

'Why do you want to see the stables?'

'Horses. I love horses.'

He glanced down at his numerous wounds. 'So do I, sometimes.'

She opened the door.

46

'Karen?'

'Yes?'

'Did we . . ?' He gestured suggestively.

'What do you think?'

'No.'

'No.'

'Then why are you here?'

Her grin flashed in the lamplight like a diamanté knife-blade, indescribably beautiful, terrifyingly deadly. 'My bed hasn't been delivered yet,' she said.

'Oh.'

The door shut. Only then did Ethan allow his disappointment to show.

*

The fresh air helped. By the time Ethan had walked down to the yard, a brisk wind had whipped away the larger part of his hangover. Small mercies. The last thing one needed, when preparing themselves for the onslaught of one of Lesterton's furious tirades, was a banging head and a gradually blossoming urge to introduce breakfast to the world.

He pushed open the main gates to the stables, which were never locked, and trudged painfully across the gravel forecourt. His bruises may well have been getting better but his body was a multitude of awkward, stiff plates, grinding against each other with every movement.

It was ten o'clock and the yard was in full swing. The second lot, an expansive range of resting thoroughbreds, was being put through the motions by a string of chatting lads. There was shouting and jeering and snorting, clumping hooves and the occasional curse. Sounds Ethan had grown to love.

He stopped in the middle of the drive, watched the parade of horses moving in an organised manner out to the gallops. The same gallops on which he had fallen. Same silly, damned gallops.

He looked away, looked instead at the house, a conservative two-storey building with small, unobtrusive windows, an efficiently tiled roof, and a smokeless chimney.

A glass conservatory to the rear of the premises unfolded onto an expanse of decking with commanding views of the woodland sprawling wildly in the bottom reaches of the valley, where, tucked away tastefully among the trees, a compact sauna house and gymnasium was hidden.

There was nothing flashy or garish to the house, it was, much like the rest of the stables, entirely practical; a perfect reflection of its inhabitant, the noisy, obnoxious, and totally brilliant Charles Lesterton. The man who was, even now, barrelling towards Ethan across the drive.

'You,' Lesterton said. He did not waste energy with pointing or waving his arms around. He didn't need to. In truth, that single word would have been more than enough to make most people wish they had stayed in bed. 'Where the bloody hell have you been? You get stepped on once and what? You need a month off?'

'A few days, Governor,' Ethan said.

'It's just a few bruises, boy, you need to toughen up.'

Ethan fixed Lesterton's gaze with his own. Lesterton's face was a mask of outrage, red and fat and half-concealed by a rampant grey moustache. He didn't tower over Ethan - he had been a jockey once and was no more physically imposing than anyone else in the business - but he gave the impression of a well-disguised giant. When he was truly angry, he could uproot trees. 'I'll try not to break so badly next time,' Ethan said.

'You could have been of some help to someone,' Lesterton went on.

'I could barely move.'

'And I could barely give a shit.'

'You always did have such a caring nature.'

'I'm being reincarnated next time round as a social worker.'

'I doubt it, you're too much of a stubborn bastard to die.'

Lesterton's dark expression was suddenly illuminated by a dashing smile that was always there but very rarely put on public display. Ten years instantly evaporated with his scowl. 'What are you doing here?'

'I know how this place has a tendency to fall apart if I'm not around for any length of time.'

'You're a cheeky little shit, boy. Come on up to the house and we'll fix you a drink.'

'I think I'd rather just get on,' Ethan said. He glanced across to the gallops. The sun licked the hillside, turning green fields yellow. His mouth straightened out considerably.

'You don't scare easy, do you?' Lesterton said, placing a hand on Ethan's shoulder. 'But sometimes being brave is a lot like being stupid. We'll put you back on a horse when the time's right.'

'And when will that be?'

'The same time it always is. When I say so.'

'If people see me off the horse, they'll start asking questions. It could look bad.'

'Let me deal with the questions.'

Ethan allowed himself to be led up to the house. 'You know,' he said, 'I can't afford to be out of the saddle.'

'I know,' Lesterton said, opening the front door. 'We'll sit in the study. Have a drink there.'

Ethan followed dutifully as Lesterton moved through the modest hallway and an equally tasteful reception area. The rooms were dressed much as the old trainer was, in muted colours, neat and low key. There were no pictures, no photographs, no family portraits.

No family.

'It's not too early for you, is it?' Lesteron asked, pushing open the door to the study and heading straight for the discreet, folding, drinks cabinet.

'The way I feel at the moment, it could never be too early.' Ethan looked around at the rows of trophies, Lesterton's only noticeable excess. Statues, cups, goblets, silver photo frames. All manner of rosettes and medals in regimental lines along the walls. For a study, there was a distinct lack of any books.

'How do you drink your whiskey?'

Ethan moved to the wide window looking out on the colts' quadrangle. He could see the distinctive white blaze and pointed parrot-like features of Counterfoil, poking inquisitively from the nearest box. He was a beastly creature, prone to crib biting, champing, snorting, pulling, pushing, jerking, shaking, and prolific sweats. The owners were reluctant to call it a day, but Ethan wouldn't even have ridden the bloody thing against donkeys at Blackpool. It was as ungenuine as they came.

He shuddered as dark memories surged restlessly at the back of his brain.

Muscular limbs were jack-hammering only inches from his mind's eye; hooves were pumping relentlessly, chewing the earth into black mulch. He could still feel the ground tumbling beneath him.

The world was unhinged, free-falling.

He gripped the windowpane, hard. After a few moments, the sensation passed.

'I drink straight from the bottle,' he said, distractedly.

'Straight up it is. Here.'

Ethan turned, accepted the tumbler Lesterton was holding out to him. 'You shouldn't be encouraging me to drink.'

'You're young. If I need to be encouraging you, there's something wrong. Take a seat.' He indicated two high-backed leather chairs beside the desk.

Ethan sat, sampled the whiskey. Ice-cold fire flushed through his body. Feeling better already.

'So, what happened?' Lesterton asked, sitting opposite.

'When?'

'When you fell. What happened?'

Ethan shook his head uselessly. 'I thought we already had this conversation?'

'Let's have it again. What happened?'

'Your horse threw me.'

Lesteron sipped whiskey. His face, his solemn expression, his straight, unforgiving mouth, let Ethan know there were no secrets here. 'You let the horse throw you.'

'Why would I do that?'

'Because your mind wasn't on the game.'

'My mind is always on the game.'

'But you still fell.'

'I was thrown.'

'That's a matter of opinion. You know Counterfoil as well as I do. The horse is a monster, put here to cause me, and everybody else, as much heartache as possible. You should have been prepared for what happened.'

'Are you saying I'm not fit to ride?'

Lesterton reclined comfortably, taking another sip of whiskey. 'I would never suggest that. But maybe now, while you're out of the saddle for a few days, you should ask yourself how fit you think you really are.'

'Just cut the smooth talk, Governor, tell me straight. Are you dropping me from the team?'

'Wouldn't dream of it.'

'Then what is this all about?'

Lesterton tutted, in the same way any disappointed teacher might. 'This is about one of the most talented jocks I've worked with in the last ten years letting himself hit the gallops during a simple exercise because his horse got a little skittish. You can't blame me for being concerned.'

'Concerned about what? Your investment?'

'About your safety, boy. Don't think you aren't expendable, I've never met a man yet who wasn't, but I do care about your well-being.'

'You don't need to worry about me. I'm fine. I'm always fine.' Ethan drained his glass with one hard, slightly over-ambitious, swallow. 'You know that.'

'I'm not so sure these days.'

Ethan set the glass on the desk with slow deliberation. 'And what, exactly, does that mean?' His voice was low, verging on a defensive growl.

'You look tired, boy. Dog tired. You sound tired too. The last couple of weeks, especially. Are you sleeping?'

'I'm sleeping. Standing up sometimes.' He laughed hollowly. 'Do you really want to know about my nocturnal activities? Is that why you called me up here?'

'I want to know what's going on in your head.'

'You'll have to join the queue behind me and any girl I've dated in the last year.'

'I don't want you losing your edge.'

'I'll be fine.'

'How can I be sure of that?'

'You'll have to trust me.'

'How am I supposed to trust you when you won't even talk to me?'

'I'll get through this.'

'Get through what?'

'Nothing . . . Nothing I haven't dealt with before.'

'Ethan?'

Ethan stood, returned to the window. He could feel the hot tears brimming in his eyes, threatening to reveal how fragile he truly felt. 'It's nothing.'

52

'Damn it, boy, I'll bust your silly head if you don't tell me what's going on.'

Ethan drew a slow, deliberate breath; strangled enough words into submission to articulate his despair. 'She left me exactly one year after I proposed to her. One year to the day.' He rested his hands on the windowsill. 'Our bloody anniversary, Governor. She left me on our anniversary. You can't tell me that was an accident. That was an intentional blow.'

Silence.

'The anniversary of the day we said we would spend the rest of our lives together.'

'Ethan?'

'That was a year ago tomorrow.'

'This is about Melissa?' Lesterton was unable to keep the genuine confusion from his tone.

'Pathetic, isn't it? She hurt me bad, worse than anybody ever hurt me before. I can't simply forget that, no matter how hard I try. Right now, the last week, it's been playing on my mind a little more than usual. It'll pass though, I'm sure of that. I'm not going to let her ruin my career.'

'Glad to hear it.'

'I don't even remember why I loved her so much. I can't even remember why I'm sad.' A tremble passed through his hunched shoulders and his fingers clenched the windowsill hopelessly. 'I just remember I should be.'

'You need to get over this.'

He kept looking out of the window as the empty tears coursed down his cheeks. 'I'd bought her this huge, stupid teddy bear, a dozen roses. I'd booked dinner at a restaurant, somewhere I couldn't really afford.'

'Oh for pity's sake, boy, snap out of it. You let a horse step on you because you were having some soft moment about a girl who left you in the lurch? You can't afford to go losing your head that

53

way. Not over a woman.'

'I won't. Not again.'

In his stable, Counterfoil snorted and jerked his head. His glistening mane bobbed. Two lads walked by, chuckling quietly over some private joke. Ethan was sure the joke was about him, and who could tell him any different?

'Right.' Lesterton stood. 'That's that then. Take a few days, let those bruises finish healing, then come see me again. I'm going to overlook this little mishap on the gallops, put it down to some bad beef, but mark my words, I don't overlook mistakes a second time. Get it together.'

Ethan finally found the courage to face Lesterton again. 'Thanks, Governor. After tomorrow, I'll be fine.'

The beginnings of a grin fluttered around the edge of Lesteron's moustache before he carefully concealed it again. 'You're a good boy, Ethan, you just care too much. The world is full of things that would like to step on you, people and horses alike. Always keep your eye on the prize.' He clapped Ethan's shoulder, a little harder than Ethan's fragile muscles appreciated. 'Keep your head about you or you're going to get yourself killed.'

'I know, Governor. I don't want to feel this way.'

'It's easier than you think, you know? To stop caring? If they want to keep hurting you, direct your focus elsewhere.' A knowing look passed across Lesterton's face. 'Stick to horses. Horses won't let you down.'

'I got through this once. I didn't think I'd have to get through it a second time, but I will.'

'And how do you intend to do that?'

'The same way everybody always gets over a woman. Get a new one.'

Lesterton fixed another two shots of whiskey at the drinks cabinet. 'Anyone in mind?' he asked.

'Funny you should mention that. There is someone.'

'Pretty?'

'As pretty as they come.'

Lesterton's calculating gaze fixed at some point outside the window beyond Ethan's shoulder - out in the quadrangle - as he handed over one of the whiskey glasses. 'Good dress sense? Nice pins?'

'Yes and yes.'

'Plenty of wiggle in the walk?'

'Absolutely.'

'Auburn hair?'

'How did you know that?'

'Because,' Lesterton's voice was level but full of menace, 'she's snooping around Counterfoil's stable right now.'

## CHAPTER 6

'Hey,' Ethan called, hobbling across the compacted earth of the quadrangle. 'Hey, Karen.'

Karen looked up and, for the briefest of moments before her immaculate smile illuminated the world, it appeared as though an expression amounting to something like panic twisted her features. 'Ethan,' she said. Then, more confidently: 'Ethan. There you are.'

'What are you doing here?' Ethan demanded.

'Just looking around.' Karen appeared to ignore the stoniness in his voice. Somehow, he was grateful for that.

'I thought you had a delivery of furniture to wait in for?'

'I did. It came early.'

'You were supposed to wait for me to call you. I told you Lesterton doesn't like unexpected guests.'

'I know.'

'I'm not exactly in his good books as it is.'

'But I got tired of waiting. I wanted to come and see the

horses.' Her lively gaze darted towards Counterfoil's angular head. The horse was gazing at her with a masterfully concealed intelligence. 'He's beautiful,' she said.

'You don't know a lot about horses, do you?'

'I know all I need to know about them.'

'This is the ugly monster who bucked me. Wretched thing couldn't win in a walkover.'

'Walkover?'

'One horse race.'

'Oh, that's mean. I think he's lovely.'

Karen moved to stroke Counterfoil's nose. Ethan snatched her wrist. 'Please don't do that,' he said, sternly. 'You've got me in enough trouble today already.'

'What trouble?'

'Don't let the open gates fool you. Lesterton doesn't like the idea of any old person walking around his stables. Horseracing is a big-money industry. Plenty of room for sabotage. Being pretty doesn't put you above suspicion.'

Karen withdrew her hand, laughing awkwardly. 'Oh, how silly. Do you think I'm going to hurt this horse?'

'I don't, but the Governor might. I'm going to have to walk you off the premises.'

'Really?' Karen's eyes flashed wickedly. 'Manhandle me? I think I might be able to take you in your current condition.' Counterfoil snorted something that, if Ethan hadn't known better, might have been mistaken for laughter.

'Come on, Karen. Don't make this hard for me. You shouldn't be here like this.'

'I came to see you, I didn't think I was doing anything wrong. Surely I can stay if you're here with me.'

Ethan glanced heavenwards. Streams of cloud, like flutters of lambs wool, dampened the frustrated glare of the sun. 'I suppose,' he said, thoughtfully, 'I can trust you. After all, any saboteur worth

57

her salt wouldn't be wasting time with Counterfoil here.' He ran a hand down Counterfoil's blazed snout. The sharp face swung around to examine him. There was definitely some kind of recognition in the creature's huge eyes, something in its gaze. Got you, it was saying. I got you, Ethan. 'A little dope might actually improve this critter's temperament.'

'Why? What's wrong with him?'

'He's a pain in the rear, that's what's wrong with him.'

Counterfoil snuffed and nodded, proud of his reputation as the trouble in Lesterton's otherwise rather impressive stable.

'He seems okay now,' Karen said.

'He can be, when he feels like it, but don't let that fool you. He's not anywhere near as placid as you might think. I wouldn't want to partner him for all the coffee in Columbia.'

'So why doesn't Lesterton get rid?'

Ethan looked hard at Karen, tried to judge whether she was genuinely interested or a damned fine actress. Hard to tell. 'Unfortunately,' he said, 'not all owners see this as a business. To me, this horse is a few days out of the saddle, to Lesterton, it's a lost cause, but to the owners, this horse is a pet. They won't get rid of it. Believe me, we've tried to convince them to.'

'Another lost cause.'

'Every stable has one.'

'But you've given up on this one?'

'No. I never had any faith in this one to start with.'

'So, if I was planning on doping one of your good prospects, which horse would you suggest?'

'Not a horse you'd find over this side of the yard. You'd want to pick out our little madam.'

'Little madam?'

'Come with me.'

Ethan took Karen's hand and led her back across the quadrangle. He could see Lesterton watching from the study window, pretended he couldn't.

Lesterton shook his head despondently.

'Where are we going?' Karen asked.

'I'm going to introduce you to a friend of mine.'

Ethan crossed the stretch of decking at the back of the house and cut right, down a gravelled pathway that wound lazily through a dense cluster of slender trees. Startled finches shivered their wings and chirped, darting across branches excitedly.

On the far side of the trees, the ground once again opened up into expansive fields. More stables here, more horses.

There were several lads moving between the stables, hefting bales of hay, and chatting when they were within chatting distance of one another. When they saw Ethan and his guest they nodded politely. Didn't speak.

'Where are we?' Karen asked, keeping hold of Ethan's hand unnecessarily as he walked through the quadrangle, heading for a stable on the far side of the sun-blistered enclosure.

'Fillies.'

'Just fillies?'

'We keep them separate.'

'Poor things.'

'Horse sex isn't as fun as human sex, there's a lot more opportunity for injury.'

'You think?'

'I mean physical injury.'

'I know.'

One of the lads brushed past Ethan, mumbled an apology, kept his eyes down. 'Hey, Daniel,' Ethan said.

The stable hand stopped in his tracks. 'Yes?' Still not looking, his body angled away uncomfortably, and his eyes fixed on a vacant point in space.

'It is Daniel, isn't it?'

'Yes.'

'How's Emphatic coming along?'

Daniel chewed on his bottom lip. 'Not my horse, Sir. Sally does for Emphatic.'

'But you must know.'

'I . . .'

'How's she coming along?'

'Fine.'

'Has she been worked today?'

More frantic lip-chewing, enough to draw flecks of blood. 'I think you should ask Sally what -'

'Don't tell me you don't know whether she worked today.'

'I was . . .'

'It's Emphatic. I could ask anybody here what she's done and they could tell me.'

'She . . .'

'Has she been worked?'

'Pipe opener.'

'Everything okay?'

'Yes.'

'Do we know who got the ride?'

'I . . . Mr O'Hara.'

'That's good.'

Daniel remained motionless, clearly awaiting, and hoping for, some instruction to motivate him to carry on as before. Ethan was silent. Eventually, Daniel risked a half turn towards him. 'Sir?'

'You okay, Daniel?'

'Yes.'

'Carry on then.'

'Yes.'

Daniel scurried away, heading for the concealed pathway leading into the trees. He had disappeared from view within a matter of seconds.

'Who was that?' Karen asked.

Ethan was looking around the quadrangle. All of the other hands had also vanished. A number of inquisitive horses' heads were hanging out of their stables, dark eyes surveying their guests with a quiet understanding.

'Ethan?'

'Sorry?'

'Who was that?'

'Daniel, I guess.'

'You guess?'

'I'm not good with names. I picked that one out of the air.'

'You were lucky to get it right.'

'I probably didn't. Some of these folk tend to take the route that causes the least amount of fuss. They don't really like talking to me if they can help it. They certainly aren't too keen for me to find out their names.'

'Any reason?'

Ethan shrugged. 'I'm better with horses than people.'

'That isn't an answer.'

'It's the best one I've got. Come on.' He led Karen over to the last stable, where a magnificent brown horse was calmly studying the horizon. 'This is Emphatic, isn't she a beauty?'

The horse looked from Ethan to Karen and back again. Its ears were pricked up and alert, its eyes cloudless. When its lips peeled back they revealed rows of perfect teeth no sane man would argue with.

'She's gorgeous,' Karen said, resisting the urge to stroke Emphatic's mane. 'Do you ride her?'

'Sometimes, for training. I think she likes me, she tends to try hard, but she's not my ride.'

'Who rides her?'

'Mr O'Hara, usually.'

'Usually?'

Ethan raised an eyebrow. 'You can't really be this interested.'

'Why not?'

'I thought you'd get enough of this from Jamie. Or doesn't he like to talk shop?'

Karen lowered her head. The damp clouds continued their impossibly slow trawl across the face of the sun. 'No,' she said. 'We don't talk that much, about those sorts of things.'

'So what do you talk about?'

'I thought you were supposed to be telling me about this horse.'

Ethan sucked breath between his teeth, tried to catch Karen's eye with his own prying gaze. She was revealing nothing, telling him nothing. He filled in the blanks hopefully. 'You don't like talking about yourself much, do you?'

'Not often.' There was a definite resolution in the line of her delicate jaw, a determination not to let this become something about her. 'Why does Mr O'Hara get to ride this horse, rather than you?'

'Are you serious? O'Hara is a genius. He can do things with a horse I haven't even tried yet.'

'But he doesn't always ride her?'

'He got jocked off a few weeks back. Lesterton wanted to prove some point, or maybe he just wanted to see a different rider partnered with Emphatic. Whatever the reason, O'Hara lost the run.' Ethan laughed quietly. 'O'Hara may be a genius, but he is a little . . . emotional, sometimes.'

'He got mad?'

'He didn't take to the idea of an outsider taking his ride. Didn't help that the other jock placed the horse and has been looking to secure a few more runs with her since then.'

'Who was the other jockey?'

'Man called Dalton. Nasty piece of work. Too keen on the whip for my liking.'

'Is he good?'

'He may just be better than O'Hara, that's the problem. O'Hara gets the next ride, but this is a competitive business and Dalton isn't going to sit on his laurels if something goes wrong tomorrow.'

'What's happening tomorrow?'

'Newbury. Just a little bit of a sprint, but enough competition to make Emphatic work. I may even get to go and watch.'

'And what about me?'

'What about you?'

'You weren't thinking of leaving me behind, were you?'

'Would you let me?'

Karen slipped her hand into Ethan's. 'Not likely.'

*

At the top of the driveway, Karen suddenly pulled away from Ethan. There was a Bentley parked up on the gravel. A diminutive man, who could only be a jockey, was leaning on the bonnet and rolling himself a cigarette with sure, confident fingers. The suit he wore was immaculate and tailored to his lithe physique. The handsome, dark features were unmistakable.

'Jamie,' Ethan said, quietly.

Jamie's small, perfectly formed, head rose. The hand-rolled cigarette found the corner of his mouth, where it hung expectantly, unlit. His steely gaze flicked from Karen to Ethan to Karen again. From this distance it was not possible to see any discernible emotion in his expression.

Karen looked at Ethan. Ethan smiled despondently.

'Go,' he said.

Karen ran across the drive, and threw her arms around Jamie's neck. 'Jamie,' she said, kissing his cheek. 'You never said you were coming down.'

From where he was standing, Ethan was unable to make out any response from Jamie. Karen's embrace was not returned.

Ethan drew a deep breath, shoved his hands into his pockets, and walked over to the Bentley. Each footfall jolted pain into his lower back, as though the ground itself was rising up to stab him in the spine, but now, more than any other time, he masked his pain expertly.

'Jamie,' he said, offering a hand.

Jamie looked at the hand, didn't accept it. Instead, he untangled himself from Karen's arms and reached into his jacket pocket, removing a lighter. A blue flame sparked into life and touched against the end of his cigarette. White smoke obscured his face momentarily.

'You Ethan?' he asked, stonily.

'I am.'

Karen looked at Ethan, then Jamie. The air crackled with hostile energy, snapping and buzzing between the two jockeys like a swarm of locusts. 'Big lad, aren't you,' Jamie observed.

'What's your point?'

'You look a little on the bulky side.'

'I manage.'

Jamie dragged heavily on his cigarette, wrapped an arm around Karen's waist. 'I understand you're quite handy. Making something of a name for yourself in the business.'

'So I'm told.'

'You want to be careful. It doesn't always pay for people to know who you are.' His cold, calculated eyes - handsome and sinister in equal measure - jumped towards Karen momentarily. 'You understand?'

Ethan folded his arms across his chest. 'Maybe you should explain it to me.'

'Maybe I will.'

'That sounds like a threat.'

Jamie drew smoke into his lungs. 'I don't threaten, Ethan, and I'm not here to speak to you. I'm looking for your Governor.'

'Is he expecting you?'

'I wouldn't be standing here if he was.'

'What's it about?'

'Since when is that a matter for discussion with the hired help?'

Karen stepped between the two jockeys. 'What's got into you two?' she asked, sternly.

Jamie gulped smoke. A challenging smile spread across Ethan's face. Their gazes remained locked, wrestling for a psychological advantage, looking for a crack - a twitch, a nervous tick - in their opponent's outward composure. 'If you don't tell me why you need to see the Governor,' Ethan said, with pointed deliberation, 'I can't help you.'

'Then I'll find Lesterton myself.'

Jamie moved away from the car, pushing Karen to one side. Ethan stepped up to meet him, planting a hand on the smaller jockey's chest. 'I can't allow you into the grounds without an invitation,' Ethan said.

'You may want to remove your hand from my chest,' Jamie said.

'You may want to remove yourself from my yard.'

'Is that so?'

Without warning, Jamie shoved Ethan hard in the chest. Caught off guard, Ethan lost his footing and hit the ground awkwardly. A bolt of pain like a static discharge burst through his spine. Temporarily winded, he made no attempt to rise. Jamie stood over him triumphantly.

'You get that one for free,' Jamie said. 'But if you ever touch me again, I'll kill you. Understand?'

'Jamie,' Karen said, pulling at Jamie's shoulder. 'Stop this.'

Jamie sneered. 'You've got the girl fighting in your corner. You're lucky.'

Ethan quickly pulled himself upright, took a few steps back to make sure he was out of reach of a second assault. His face was a blaze of red anger. 'I still can't let you in without an invitation,' he snapped.

'Well, why don't you run along and get me one?'

'Give me one good reason why I should?'

'I have a business proposition. Could make your boss a lot of money. I'm sure he would reward you handsomely if you were the one responsible for smoothing the way for a little . . . transaction.'

'What kind of transaction?'

'You ask too many questions, kid. Are you going to let Lesterton know I'm here or do we do this the hard way? A diet of gravel wouldn't be good for your weight, if you know what I mean.'

Karen stood back slightly, watching Ethan intently. Did she know what this was about? Had she really expected Jamie's arrival? It was impossible to tell. Her face, innocent and beautiful, could have easily masked a hundred secrets, a hundred sins.

'I'll see what I can do for you,' Ethan said.

'You know it makes sense.'

'I can't guarantee he'll speak with you, he's very busy. Big race coming up tomorrow.'

'I know, I'm racing in it.'

'Is that what this is about? You know O'Hara is the head jock around here. We haven't got room for any more.'

Jamie snorted, a sound that could have been mistaken for a laugh if it wasn't for the disproportionate amount of malice permeating it. 'You have a suspicious mind, boy. I don't want O'Hara's rides. I don't want yours either. I don't want any part of this pathetic outfit. I have business of another matter to discuss.'

'Jocks don't make the best businessmen.'

'Some do.'

Ethan turned and headed back towards Lesterton's house. About halfway along the driveway, Karen caught up with him.

'So,' she said, 'you've finally met your hero. Was it everything you had hoped for?'

'He's a real charmer.'

'Did he hurt you?'

'No.'

'Do yourself a favour, keep out of his way.'

Ethan stopped, hunched his shoulders. There was a terrible ache in his lower spine.

Desperate shards of cloud pulled themselves across the bleached sky. The sounds of the yard ebbed and flowed melodically.

He drew a deep gulp of brittle oxygen into his lungs, waiting for the ground to swallow him.

No such luck.

'You do me a favour,' he said. 'Stay away from me.'

He walked the rest of the way to the house alone.

CHAPTER 7

Ethan, who was clearly neither wanted nor required during the discussions, left Jamie and Lesterton in the study. They were sharing a bottle of very old, very expensive whiskey, and talking like old friends, when Ethan pulled the door closed behind him. It was that friendliness, more than the secretive 'business arrangement', that made Ethan nervous.

Lesterton wasn't friendly to anybody, least of all unexpected jocks looking to make some extra cash.

Pride still dented from his confrontation with Jamie, Ethan crossed the length of the yard to where the office buildings, and, more importantly, the office staff, were located.

The buildings were tucked out of sight behind the quarantine sheds, where currently one horse was being looked at for a suspected cough that might prove disastrous to the stable if left unchecked.

Several stable lads passed Ethan as he moved through the grounds. They all grunted unwelcomingly at him without ever

68

actually looking up from what they were doing. It was only to be expected. Ethan had stepped on more than a few toes to get where he was. Most of those toes still chased around after the horses he now rode. Sometimes, he thought, he was probably lonely, but as he had almost always been lonely he didn't have a great deal to compare with.

There had been Melissa, of course, but maybe he had been just as lonely with her. Those nights when she had come back late, when she hadn't come back at all.

Ethan thrust his hands into his pockets and hunched his shoulders, shielding himself from the bitterness of memories sharp enough to draw blood.

The man who lies to himself is invariably the loneliest.

He reached the office block and pushed on the door. There was no give. He examined the electronic keypad by the jamb, hit a few random buttons, then finally managed to find the one to activate the intercom. A grainy female voice buzzed out of a speaker above the keys.

'Who is it?'

'It's the tall, dark, handsome stranger you ordered.'

'Why do I doubt that?'

'One out of four ain't bad. Come on, Anne, open up.'

The door thrummed mechanically and, when Ethan pushed, it opened on a small office. Desks, computers, humming machinery; all the usual office trimmings but with one outstanding feature: Anne.

She was sat at the desk with her feet up, and a calculator in one hand. Her delicate spectacles were balanced on her slender nose in such a way to finish off the horny school-teacher look her beige jacket and skirt began. Her blonde hair was tied back with a black band in a severe ponytail that radiated a sense of authority and command which Ethan found arousing on an uncomplicated level. She was well aware of how good she looked.

Ethan had slept with her only once. Neither of them ever spoke about it.

'How's it going?' he asked, pulling the door closed behind him and taking a seat.

'Same old, same old.' She put down the calculator, kept her feet up on the desk to maximise the amount of flesh on display. 'Take a seat, why don't you?'

'Does the boss know you're sat in here with your feet up?'

'You know he never comes down here among all this pagan computer technology.' She examined her red nails. 'Come to think of it, nobody ever comes down here except for you. And even you don't come as often as you used to.'

'I've been busy.'

'It gets so lonely in here, all by myself.' She leaned back in her chair; her skirt rode up a few inches, revealing enough thigh to make the muscles in Ethan's stomach tighten dramatically. 'Some days I just don't know what to do with myself.'

Ethan cleared his throat awkwardly, began to examine his own nails. The computers whirred dutifully. The seconds on Anne's desk clock ticked away. In the corner, the fax machine spat out a sheet of paper, stopped.

'So what do you want, Ethan?'

'That transparent, huh?'

'All men are, baby. Spill it.'

He formulated his words carefully. 'I'm going to need you to be my eyes and ears.'

'What do you mean?'

'I need you to keep your eyes peeled for any . . . unusual trans-actions.'

The feet came off of the desk. She leaned forwards. 'Really? That sounds exciting.'

'Maybe.'

'Unusual in what way?'

'I don't know yet. A big name jockey turned up at the stables today. Jamie Redthorn. He's in a meeting with Lesterton as we speak, some new business venture.'

'Since when have you been interested in Lesterton's business ventures?'

'Since they involved Jamie.'

'You've got a problem with this jockey?'

'I don't trust him.'

'You don't trust anybody.'

'I trust you.'

Anne smiled, and Ethan was well aware it was the same smile that had led to him sleeping with her at the last stable Christmas party, in this very office. It was an instantly sexual and fragile smile, a come-on and a warning. He had thought, after several drinks, he had fallen in love with that smile, but the morning sun, always so callous and intrusive, had thrown a slightly less romantic light on the situation.

Anne had been a distraction. She knew that as well as he did.

'You have any clues as to what I should be looking for?' she asked.

'Anything out of the ordinary. Large sums of money moving between accounts. Any faxes or memos that don't seem to add up. Invoices for items above and beyond what you normally handle. Anything at all.'

'Do you have any idea how many invoices I handle?'

'It shouldn't be too difficult to pick up on anything new.'

'Can't you be any more specific?'

'Not really. But I can guarantee whatever Redthorn is planning is going to involve him getting paid somewhere along the way. I want to know why.'

'Do you think Lesterton may be planning something illegal? Because if you do, you might want to think about not playing detective.'

'Not illegal. Lesterton's honest as the day is long. After all this time accounting for him, you should know that better than anybody. But something is definitely going on. It may be nothing, but I have a bad feeling about it.'

Anne laced her fingers together beneath her chin. 'You make it sound all so serious. Why don't you just ask Lesterton what's going on?'

'I don't think he'd tell me.'

'Have you tried?'

'I don't want him to think I'm interested. If he thinks I'm interested, he's going to be more cagey about what he does.'

Her amused eyes flashed. 'You really do think he's going to do something illegal. You are a bad boy, Ethan.'

'What I think isn't important. I just need to know that should something happen, should some deal be made, you'll let me know what it is.'

'Chances are, if this is something that isn't exactly above board, there isn't going to be much of a paper trail.'

'There'll be something. Some letter for you to type up, some telephone-call to make. I'd like to be kept up to speed, no matter how insignificant something may seem to you.'

'I'll see what I can do.'

'I knew you would.'

'But what do I get out of it?' The feet found their old spot back on the desktop.

'My undying gratitude?'

'I may need more than that.'

Ethan stood. 'See what you can find out for me first. Then we'll talk about rewards. And please, try to keep this quiet. Don't even mention it outside of the stables.'

'Any reason why?'

Ethan took Anne's hand, kissed it. 'Because I asked nicely,' he said.

In the corner of the room, the fax machine whirred, and chugged out another two sheets of paper. Both Ethan and Anne ignored it, but for totally different reasons.

CHAPTER 8

Jason Montoya, an American student who, on good days, could just about recall what Bath University looked like, and, on better days, could remember where it was actually situated, was waiting at the bar when Ethan arrived. He signalled to the barman for two beers, and then watched as Ethan ducked and weaved through the crowds towards him.

It had just turned eight-thirty, but this particular establishment, being only a few doors up from one of the best night clubs in town, was already full to the rafters. The excessive amount of attractive females, showing off a suitably provocative amount of fake-tanned flesh, was just one of the many reasons Jason liked this place so much. That the music - an eclectic collection of '80s and '90s nostalgia tracks - was kept at a level allowing normal conversation, was an added bonus.

The barman, who seemed, unsurprisingly, more interested in a girl in red hot-pants at the other end of the counter, clinked two bottles of Export in front of Jason, and hovered expectantly. Jason paid with a crumpled ten and told the bartender to keep the change. Ethan squeezed into the mob by Jason's right shoulder.

'You're late,' Jason said, thrusting one of the bottles at Ethan.

'Fashionably so,' Ethan responded. 'And you know I can't drink that.'

'Go wild.'

Jason sucked on his own beer, absentmindedly letting his gaze glide across the inconstant crowd. The blue lighting was subdued and hid a multitude of sins; it was almost impossible to tell who was attractive and who was just exceptionally adept at applying makeup. Jason failed to see why any such differentiation should be made in the first place.

'How have you been?' Ethan asked, trying his best to ignore the jolts and bumps from the encompassing elbows and knees. 'Sorry I couldn't make it out last night. Something came up.'

'Something came up?' There was a gleam in Jason's eye. 'I'll bet. Who were you with?'

'Someone moved into the flat one up from me. And before you ask, yes she is and no I didn't.'

'Are you going to?'

'She's engaged.'

'But are you going to?'

'Unfortunately we can't all be bastards like you, Jason.'

'Why not?'

'I haven't managed to drink enough to stunt the growth of my conscience.'

'Your what?'

'Exactly.'

'But you like this person right?'

Ethan shrugged.

'What's her name?'

'Her name's Karen, but why does it matter?'

The crowd shifted around them, morphing from several large

men with shaved heads into a group of giggling underage girls dressed like twenty-one year olds. Jason studied each one, with the eye of a connoisseur, before answering Ethan's question. 'Women always matter,' he said. 'And you do like her, right?'

Ethan looked down the neck of his beer bottle. 'Yes, I like her. She's gorgeous. Strange.'

'Strange?'

'Different.'

'How?'

'She makes me forget.'

'Yet you aren't going to go after her?'

The underage girls cleared a path to the bar with their underage but suitably well-developed breasts and ordered a round of blue sugary drinks, which seemed somehow fitting. One of the girls - blonde, with lashes that could blow down straw houses - looked at Ethan with eyes full of sexual desire. He caught her glance and smiled politely. Those eyelashes batted, Ethan looked away. 'She has a fiancé,' he said to Jason.

'Nothing's sacred these days, Ethan. If you like her, go for it. Go get her.'

'Your life is very simple, isn't it?'

'Life's as simple as you make it. Are you aware I haven't heard you talk about anybody this way since Melissa?'

'So?'

'So this is huge. You've slept with some absolutely gorgeous women since her, I know because I've usually slept with them first, yet none of them even remotely interested you. This one,' he adopted his best British accent, 'makes you forget.'

'So do drugs. That's not to say they're good for you.'

Jason laughed, drained his beer, and caught the attention of the barman with a folded twenty. 'Drink?' he asked Ethan. Ethan exhibited his full bottle. 'You need to loosen up,' Jason said, ordering two bottles and two Tequila slammers. 'We're going to have

76

fun tonight.'

'Our ideas of fun are fundamentally different.'

'Fun is fun, and you aren't at the moment. Now drink your beer. You said yourself, you won't be riding for a while.'

'Thanks for the reminder.'

'Drink, damn you.'

Ethan examined the bottle suspiciously. 'There's nothing funky in here, is there?'

'As if I would do that to you . . . again.'

The underage girls, fronted by a tall dark-haired thing with pretty eyes and a cruel barbed-wire mouth, ordered another round of drinks. There were five girls in total, four of them were huddled together and whispering, occasionally looking over at Ethan. Jason watched them interestedly.

'You know,' he said, 'if you really aren't going to go after this Karen woman, why don't you go get a piece of that instead? They look up for it.'

Ethan glanced over at the girls. The blonde with the eyelashes was watching him hungrily. 'Jesus, Jason, we're older than the five of them put together.'

'They're old enough to be here drinking, they're old enough for everything that comes with it.'

Ethan shook his head, sipped his beer. 'I'm sure there are a number of photographers who would just love to get some shots of me compromising my career with an underage girl.'

Jason drained his beer and started on the second one. 'Do you know your problem?'

'I'm sure you'll tell me.'

'You think too much. You never just let things happen. You keep going over stuff and worrying and obsessing.'

'Thank you, Doctor Montoya.'

'It's true. When was the last time you just went with something, did something without considering the consequences?'

'The Christmas party,' Ethan said, without hesitation. 'The night I spent with Anne.'

'And do you regret it?'

Ethan drank beer. 'No.'

'I rest my case.'

'So what, if you are right? I can't just change the way I am.'

'Why not?'

'You can't go through life not considering the consequences of your actions.'

'Why not?'

'Life isn't that easy.'

'Maybe not for you.'

The mass of encompassing bodies was transforming again, flowing seamlessly from girls to boys, young to old. Jason's twitchy gaze lighted momentarily on each new face.

'So how is the world of International Politics?' Ethan asked, in a vague attempt to change the conversation.

'Wouldn't know, haven't picked up the study notes yet.'

'Are you actually planning on passing this course?'

'It doesn't matter.'

'Why not?'

'My parents were pretty much expecting me to fail anyway, they only paid for me to come out here because they thought it might help if I saw a bit of the world and learned to stand on my own two feet.'

'And you intend to prove them right by failing?'

'If I pass, I pass. If I fail, I fail. Either way I go back home and work in daddy's print shop.'

'Is that what you want?'

Jason clapped Ethan on the shoulder. 'I want to party, Ethan. That's all I've ever wanted to do. I get to do that for two more years before I even think about working.'

Ethan watched as Jason drank the rest of his beer and then

turned his attention to the Tequila. One of the slammers was nudged across the bar to Ethan. 'Time to make a toast,' Jason said.

Ethan took the Tequila. 'What are we toasting?'

'Women. What else?'

'To women then.'

They knocked back their drinks and slammed the empty glasses on the bar. Jason grinned drunkenly. 'A few more of those and I reckon this party is going to get started.' He opened his wallet, taking a twenty from a bundle of notes, and tried his best to get served again.

The barman finally ambled round and took Jason's order. Two beers, two Absinthe.

Ethan politely accepted one of the beers. 'You planning on going on to the club?' he asked.

Before Jason could answer he was slapped on the shoulder by a large man who had bundled his way through the crowd with a combination of force and ignorance. He wasn't exactly tall, but what he lacked in height he more than made up for in width. There was a terrible aggression clearly evident in his dark eyes. 'Jason,' he said, with an intonation not so much heard as felt.

'Bobby,' Jason said, certainly sounding pleased enough even if he didn't look it.

Bobby glanced at Ethan warily. 'Who's that?' he asked.

'Friend of mine. Nobody really.'

'I'm Ethan,' Ethan said, offering his hand.

Bobby ignored the hand and turned back to Jason. 'Shall we go and have a chat?' he asked.

'Sure,' Jason said. 'Ethan, keep my place. This will only take a few minutes.'

'Everything okay?' Ethan asked.

'Everything's fine,' Bobby said. 'Now you just sit here like a good boy and finish your drink. Your friend will be back in a minute.'

Ethan watched as Bobby guided Jason off into the crowd. Thought about following. Rejected the idea. Concentrated on his beer. Barely audible above the buzz of conversations, a song came on he liked but couldn't remember the words of. He drummed his fingers. Waited. His beer tasted like warm metal.

'Hi.'

He looked up. The blonde underage girl with the immaculate eyelashes was leaning on the bar beside him. She stood up to closer examination surprisingly well. Her red smile was attractive, her wide eyes interesting and sexy. Ethan reminded himself he wasn't interested in her.

'Hi,' he said.

'You look fed up.' She was holding one of those blue drinks, twisting the bottle nervously through her fingers, picking at the label.

'I'm not really in the mood for drinks this evening,' Ethan said.

'Your friend seems to be getting through them.'

'You've been watching?'

She winced, flushed red. 'No.'

'Don't worry about it. He's been checking you out all night as well.'

'Have you?'

'Sorry?'

'Never mind. Do you party?'

'If you and your friends are looking to score, I can't help you.'

The girl looked puzzled. 'Really? We thought . . ?' She stopped, looked back over her shoulder to where her friends were gathered expectantly and silently. 'My friends and I are going across to the club in a bit, then we're going back to my friend's house.' She breathed carefully. 'Her parents are away until the end of the week. Do you and your friend want to join us?'

Ethan stared at his beer bottle. 'That's a very tempting offer. Would you be terribly offended if I said no?'

'Not really. We just thought . . . You know? It's okay. You have a good evening.'

'Thanks.'

Ethan turned back to his beer. The song that was playing had finished, and the next had started. The girl was still standing next to him.

'Can I help you?' he asked.

'No, I just . . . Your friend . . ?'

'Yes?'

'You don't seem very much like him.'

'I'm not.'

'Then why are you friends?'

'I'm not sure we are. I'm not even sure I like him that much.'

'Then why . . ?'

'You wouldn't understand.'

'Try me.'

'I'd rather not.'

'What are you hiding?'

'Your friends are waiting for you.'

'Is that the end of the conversation, then?'

'Sorry to disappoint you.'

The girl smiled. 'That's the funny thing,' she said. 'You haven't.' She dissolved back into the crowd.

Ethan finished his beer. People bumped around, writhing like eels in a blue-lit aquarium. The five underage girls hovered, not too far away, talking in whispers.

Jason returned, wearing a smile as phoney as his party-piece British accent. 'Ethan,' he said.

'That was short and sweet.'

'Short, but not exactly sweet. Here,' he picked up one of the previously ordered Absinthes and pushed the other one towards Ethan, 'another toast.'

'What are we toasting this time?'

Jason paused. 'Friendship,' he said.

'I'll drink to that.'

They swallowed back their drinks, neither one prepared to gag afterwards.

'Right,' Jason said. 'What's next?'

'Next, I go home.'

'Home?'

'Yes, home, the place where I live.'

'But . . .'

Ethan put a hand on Jason's shoulder. 'See those girls over there?' he asked, pointing. 'They want to party with you. I'm going to go home and get some sleep, but you have a good time.'

Jason grinned. 'Yeah, good idea. You run on home. I'll call you tomorrow.'

'I'm sure you will.'

Ethan pushed his way to the main entrance of the bar, where two mountains in black suits were standing facing the street. Before leaving, he looked back and saw Jason approaching the five girls. He stopped, watched as the girls swarmed excitedly.

A minute ticked away. Two minutes.

Jason could no longer be seen for the press of females around him.

Ethan stepped out into the cold evening.

There was rain in the air and, long before he was able to hail a cab, it was falling in hard, flat sheets.

*

He arrived back at the flat a little before ten o'clock, got out of his wet clothes, and dropped onto the bed, naked. He lay there, in the darkness, and waited for sleep.

Twenty minutes later, still wide awake, still staring at the criss-cross mesh of scars and cracks in the ceiling, he heard the front door open.

Two voices: one male, one female, both familiar.

Footsteps on the stairs. The rattle of keys. The door opening, closing again. Muffled laughter.

'Oh shit,' Ethan said.

The voices moved around before coming to a stop directly above him, in Karen's bedroom.

There was a rapid exchange of words Ethan was glad he could not clearly hear, then the impossibly loud sound of springs as two bodies hit the bed.

'Don't do this,' Ethan whispered, sitting up and switching on his lamp. 'Not tonight.'

Hushed words in the night.

'Not now.'

The springs creaked above him relentlessly, awkwardly at first, then developing a smooth, devastatingly obvious rhythm. Ethan clamped his hands over his ears, could still hear them.

He rose, threw on a night gown, and went into the kitchen. If anything, the sounds were louder in there. Voices, inarticulate groans, the creak-creak-creak of the bed being put through a rigorous road test.

Ethan opened the fridge, grabbed some milk, and drank straight from the bottle, the kitchen illuminated only by the tiny, shimmering bulb in the fridge door. He paced agitatedly.

Creak-creak-creak.

He pulled open one of the kitchen drawers and found some painkillers, something to help him sleep. He fumbled the cap off the bottle and swallowed two tablets. He examined the label closely.

Creak-creak-creak.

He took two more tablets.

Creak-creak-creak.

He walked into the lounge, the sounds from upstairs receded.

He shut the door and the sounds faded to silence.

He put his back to the door, closed his eyes. 'Damn,' he whispered. 'God damn.'

He sat in darkness, drank the rest of the milk, stood, checked his watch, paced for twenty-two seconds, checked his watch again, sat, stood, walked back to the kitchen door, opened it. The bed was still creaking, more frantically now, both the springs and the voices growing to a feverish intensity, melding together into a peculiar hybrid sound that was both compelling and detestable.

Ethan threw the empty milk bottle in the sink and returned to the bedroom. He sat on the bed, opened the drawer of the bedside cabinet, and removed a set of photographs. Photographs of Melissa.

He flicked through them with numb fingers, trying to find one where she was smiling.

'Hi,' she said, in that soft sultry way she always did when she had something on her mind that involved removing her clothes. 'I've been waiting for you.'

'Really?' Ethan slammed the door shut and shrugged off his raincoat.

'Come over here.'

He moved across to the couch where Melissa was reclining in a bathrobe. 'I thought you were supposed to be working today,' he said, sitting beside her.

'I was, but I was sat in that hot, sticky office,' she sat forwards and ran her hands over his chest, 'and I couldn't stop thinking about you and what I was going to do to you when you got home.' She kissed him hard. 'How was I supposed to stay at work with that on my mind?'

He found the belt of her robe and loosened it, feeling his own belt being unbuckled. 'You should have let me know,' he said. 'I would have been home sooner.'

Her robe slipped over her shoulders and dropped silently to the floor, her breath was hot against his face. 'You're here now. That's all that matters.'

He drew her into his arms, kissed her cheek, her neck. 'I'm always going to be here.'

'You promise?'

'I promise.'

'And what happens if, one day, I go away. What will you do then?'

'Wait here until you get back.'

'What if I never come back?'

'Then I'll be waiting for a long time.'

She giggled, lay back on the couch, and, for the first time, Ethan knew what it was to be happy.

But that had been a long time ago, in a place less cold than this dark flat.

*

When he eventually managed to fall into a fitful sleep, the photographs spread over his pillow, Karen's bed was still squeaking angrily.

CHAPTER 9

Ethan arrived at the stables a little after six-thirty, earlier than he had intended.

After waking at four in the morning, unimaginably exhausted, he had been unable to drift back into sleep, unable to forget the sounds of Karen and Jamie doing what couples do. Instead, he had risen, checked his nicely healing bruises in the mirror, bathed, shaved, and gone out to face the cold morning, battered but unbowed.

It took only seventeen minutes, journeying on foot through the last ribbons of a thinning mist, to reach the yard. Only one car passed during that time, a silver Bentley travelling from the direction of the flats.

Ethan hunched his shoulders, thought about Karen, about Melissa. He thrust his hands deep into his jacket pockets, grasping for a corner of warmth.

This morning, more than any other morning in his life, he was alone; an unusual and solitary figure of sadness cut from the white mist.

It had been a year ago today.

A year ago to the very day, he had woken, not from a nightmare, but from a dream. It was the last night, as far as he could recall, he had ever dreamed about the good stuff.

The funny thing was, he could no longer recall the details of that last dream. He knew he had been happy, but he had no recollection why, or whether his happiness had been real. He could not think back past his first waking memory: that rude departure from the dreamworld, as his eyes flicked open to swallow in the blackness of life.

All he could remember was he had awoken. That was the exact moment the nightmare began.

'Melissa?'

The room was in darkness, only a hard edge of daylight, like a splinter of glowing flint, showed through the crack of the curtains.

'Melissa?'

There was no response.

He reached out across the far side of the bed. No-one there. Only an empty space. Cold.

The space had been empty for some time.

Something was wrong.

Melissa liked to sleep late. She had never been awake before Ethan, had never been out of bed before he was already down at the stables.

He sat up, flicked on the bedside lamp. A swell of unnatural light blossomed into the shape of his bedroom, cutting out the clean outlines of the bed, the wardrobe, the bookcase, the desk. He was totally alone.

The wardrobe was open, the contents gone.

He rubbed his eyes, threw his legs out of the bed. Something was wrong.

The alarm clock said it was four-thirty.

Melissa wouldn't have had the faintest idea what four-thirty in the morning looked like if it camped in the lounge. Something was seriously wrong.

He stood.

Something reflected sharply on the bedside table: a small ring, like a shocked mouth. He picked it up, examined it. The engagement ring.

She had loved that ring. She had cried when he had given it to her. She had said it was like something out of a story.

The story went: a girl had been walking down the street one day, her doting boyfriend dutifully in tow, and she had passed a jewellers. In the window, sat on a fluffy plinth with a small light shining directly onto it, was a ring.

The ring, as far as the doting boyfriend was concerned, looked like any number of rings, but the girl fell in love with it. She said it was the one ring, the perfect ring, for her.

'What's so special about that ring?' the doting boyfriend had asked.

'It's just like the one my mother had,' the girl replied, and that seemed like explanation enough.

Exactly one week later, the doting boyfriend returned to the jewellers and bought the ring, and exactly one week after that, the girl agreed to marry him.

Ethan put the ring back on the bedside table. His fingers were shaking.

He had thought the story was over, that it had been drawn to a neat conclusion with a typical, yet highly satisfactory, 'they all lived happily ever after'. He had been wrong.

He stiffly moved through to the kitchen. He half-expected to see her sitting at the table eating a bowl of cereal, or drinking tea. It's okay, he half-expected her to say, I just took the ring off so I could clean it. That's okay, he half-expected to say back, you're still here, and that's all that matters.

The kitchen was empty. There was no cereal bowl on the table, no tea in the pot. The lounge was also empty. It was as if it had always been that way.

He sat in the kitchen, put his head in his hands. Could he have dreamed it? Could he have created another life while he was asleep? A life in which he had a fiancée?

His whole body trembled. Could it all have been a lie? And now he was awake, was this empty home all he had? Was this - this desolate world - all there was?

Suddenly terrified, he ran back through to the bedroom. The ring was still there, gleaming beside the alarm clock. But there was something missing, something he instinctively knew should be with the ring.

He looked on the floor, felt around the side of the bedside table. Nothing.

He pulled the bed away from the wall.

Nothing.

He checked the bookcase and the wardrobe, then every corner of the kitchen and the lounge and even the bathroom, but there was nothing.

There was no note.

The last page of his story - the story that began the day he met Melissa - was left completely empty, and the only person who could fill it in had simply decided not to.

'What have you done?' he whispered, and the ghost of that question, which still remained unanswered a year later, followed him through the mist as he walked the morning streets alone.

*

The stables were already alive, but not with the calmly paced orderliness with which they normally thrived.

As Ethan trudged up the drive, he could see people darting in and out of horse boxes, could hear shouted orders carried on the wind. No horses were out on the gallops, no horses roaming in the paddock. They were all stabled. All waiting.

Something bad was happening.

Ethan quickened his stride, and almost tripped over Lesterton as the trainer barged out of the house and headed towards the fillies' quadrangle.

Lesterton's usual, calm, demeanour had been replaced with a blustering panic. 'Ethan,' he said, without stopping. 'Have you seen anyone?'

'Seen anyone?'

'Leaving the stables?'

'No, Sir.' Ethan fell into step beside Lesterton. 'What's wrong? Are you okay?'

'No.'

'What's happened?'

'I don't know yet.'

They entered the quadrangle. More activity here: lads running around with blankets and buckets. There was shouting, cries of 'get out of the bloody way', banging and crashing from the far horse box. Emphatic's box.

'Governor?' Ethan pressed.

Lesterton grabbed the arm of one of the nearest lads, a half-asleep boy with an empty bucket in his hand and an equally empty head on his shoulders. 'What's happening?'

'I don't know, Sir. She won't stop.'

'Won't stop what?'

'She just won't stop.'

There was a crash from Emphatic's stable. 'Christ,' somebody shouted, 'don't open the bloody door.'

Lesterton let go of the lad's arm. 'Clear the other boxes, get the horses out into grass. I don't know what this is, but I don't want it

90

spreading.'

The lad nodded and dashed off to find a few able hands to assist.

'What's happening?' Ethan asked.

'Emphatic's done one,' Lesterton said, on the move again. 'Damned thing's started knocking itself about. Throwing itself against the doors.'

More shouting from the crowd of lads around the box. 'She's bleeding.'

'I ain't going in there.'

'You won't need to. She'll be out in a minute.'

Ethan and Lesterton reached the crowd, pushing through to the door. Hinges creaked and strained, the padlock bobbed and clanked and buckled. Emphatic bellowed, terrified and terrifying. Her pain was almost tangible.

'How long has she been like this?' Lesterton demanded.

'She just started up,' one of the lads explained. There were tears in his eyes. Confused, angry tears.

'When?'

'A few minutes ago.'

There was another bone-shattering crash as Emphatic smashed into the door, twisting the hinges.

'She's going to kill herself,' Ethan said. 'How did this happen? Where's Emphatic's lad?'

'Here.'

A plain girl in her early twenties was hanging back from the main press of bodies. Her eyes were huge and scared and bemused. She was clearly distressed, chewing her way through an already ragged set of fingernails. Her left hand was bloody across the knuckles; her orange hair was a mess.

'Name?' Ethan asked.

'Sally.'

'What happened, Sally?'

'I . . .' Her horrified gaze moved towards Lesterton, as if she expected him to have some kind of answer for her. 'I don't know. I came down a minute ago and she was already bashing herself up like this.'

'What happened to your hand?'

'Never mind that,' Lesterton said. 'We need to get this beast calmed down before she kills herself.'

There was another scream from inside the box, another wet thud as the horse barrelled into the door. A choking, desperate gasp for oxygen. Silence.

'Oh no,' Sally whispered, backing further away from the frightened mass of stable hands. 'Oh no.'

'Shit,' Lesterton said. 'Who's got the key?'

Sally whipped her bleeding fingers through her hair, her eyes unfocussed, gaze darting rapidly between the faces of her comrades. 'I . . .'

'Damn it, girl, where's the key?' Lesterton snapped.

She pulled a ring of keys from her pocket with trembling hands. Ethan snatched the keys away, and frantically undid the padlock on Emphatic's box. 'Everybody stand clear,' he said. The nearest lads took a few steps back to make room. Ethan opened the door.

Emphatic looked up with wide, white eyes from where she was lying in her straw.

Her flank was rising and falling rapidly, her tongue lolling, fat and purple, from between her teeth. There was steam rising from her foaming, shivering body. Her legs were kicking spastically. The smell of blood and sweat - an excruciating death - was almost overpowering.

'What in the name of God . . ?' Ethan said, stepping inside and crouching by the horse, resting a hand on her neck.

Lesterton shouldered past a couple of girls who were holding back tears with hands clamped over their distraught mouths.

92

'Somebody got to her,' he said, matter-of-factly. The horse wheezed and convulsed, her hooves clattering on the stable wall hollowly. 'Where's Sally?'

'She's gone, Sir,' one of the lads said. 'Took off when you opened the door. Crying like.'

Ethan's hand smoothed over Emphatic's mane, ran down her heaving flanks. Her eyes rolled back in her head. He could feel her heart thundering.

'You poor bloody thing,' he said, and suddenly, like a light switch being turned off, the thundering stopped.

CHAPTER 10

Lesterton waited for Ethan to close the study door before he allowed himself to slam his fist on the desk, an outward show of emotion that anybody who knew him well enough would have been shocked to see. 'Damn it,' he said. 'What just happened out there? Can somebody tell me what just happened out there?'

Ethan glanced furtively at O'Hara, looking to the older jock for an answer. O'Hara, a gangly, rake of a man with impeccable dress sense and wisps of grey hair dragged over a balding pate, glanced back. His dull, almost lifeless, eyes said nothing.

'What a bloody mess,' Lesterton went on. 'What a mess. Have either of you ever seen anything like this before? Tell me, have you ever seen anything like it?'

O'Hara, who had only just arrived at the stables expecting to do nothing more than check everything was in order with Emphatic for what should have been a good chance at Newbury in the three-fifteen, shrugged helplessly. 'She didn't look right. That wasn't natural.'

'Not natural?' Ethan asked.

The question fell on a stony silence punctuated only by Lesterton's heavy breathing as he glared out of the little window and across the colts' quadrangle. The lads were moving around a little slower than normal, clearly distressed at the loss of one of the stable's treasures.

There was no sign of Sally among the unhappy faces; no flame of brilliant orange hair in the crowd of black and brown heads.

The death of any horse was a bitter blow to anybody connected with it. Sally would be taking it the hardest of all. Nobody had seen her since. If she considered herself to be responsible in some way, they might never see her again.

'This is very bad,' Lesterton said, eventually. 'There's going to be an enquiry. The owners are going to want to know what happened. What can I tell them?' He looked over his shoulder. The two jockeys remained quiet. 'What can I tell them? There will need to be vets, an investigation. Something was clearly wrong with the horse, there's no denying it. The police will be involved.'

'That's not necessary,' O'Hara interrupted, his usually sallow features appearing even paler than normal. His tongue darted over his dry lips.

'Of course it will be necessary. A crime has taken place here. The owner's aren't going to settle for anything less than a full investigation.'

'You're talking about the Darabonts, Lesterton. This won't be that big a deal to them.'

'Do you have any idea how much that horse was worth?'

Ethan looked at his shoes.

'I have an idea,' O'Hara said, wryly.

'Darabont may not know the first thing about horseracing, he may not give a solitary damn what the stride of his horse might be, he may not even be able to tell which colours are his, but he knows an investment when he's got one. He knows that the death of a horse is not to be taken lightly.'

Ethan scuffed his heels on the carpet. 'I think you're giving the old fool too much credit.'

'It's going to look bad for the stable. We'll lose business. There will be scandal. Newspaper stories.'

'You're assuming foul play was involved,' Ethan said. 'Horses can be temperamental things at times.'

'Emphatic? Temperamental? That horse was as genuine and level-headed as you could hope for, and you know that. Someone got to her. The vet will be able to confirm that.'

'The Darabonts will need to be informed,' Ethan said.

'How can I tell them?' Lesterton asked.

'Would you let me do it?'

'Why?'

'Because I don't think we need to let the media find out about this.'

'What are you thinking?'

'The owners don't need to know someone tampered with the horse, not straight away. We don't even know if someone tampered with the horse ourselves. There's no need to cause a panic.'

'We can't sweep this under the carpet,' Lesterton said. 'It would leave a suspicious horse shape.'

'I don't suggest we pretend this never happened, but there isn't any need to tell the owners everything, and there certainly isn't any need to get the police involved. Not yet.'

'The owners will want an investigation,' Lesterton said. 'Even the likes of Darabont will want to know where their money's going.'

'Maybe, but maybe they'll settle for something less than a police investigation. Horses die all the time, we don't need to tell them Emphatic beat herself to death in her box, do we?'

'That's true,' Lesterton said. 'But the truth has to come out sooner or later. If Darabont had the horse insured, by tomorrow there will be more black suits flapping round here than buzzards on a carcass. They aren't likely to be the type who will just take our word for what happened.'

'They won't have to.'

Lesterton smoothed a hand through his moustache, wiping beads of cold sweat from his lip. 'What, exactly, are you suggesting?'

'I don't know. I just think, if we can make some time for ourselves, give ourselves a chance to find out what really happened before the cameras start flashing, we might be able to control this situation.'

Lesterton clenched his hands on the windowsill, his brow furrowed thunderously. He looked like a cornered rat, bearing its teeth to the world. 'How do we keep it quiet?'

'Let me talk to the owners. I'll play it down, say Emphatic died in her box but it will take a few days for the vet to come back to us with a reason.'

'What does that achieve?' O'Hara snapped.

'It buys us time. It gives me an opportunity to do some investigating of my own before we need to let anybody else know about this.'

'You?' Lesterton said, flatly. 'What makes you think you're Columbo all of a sudden?'

'We need to keep this in house. Think about it, would you rather the investigation was undertaken in public view, with every move questioned, every false accusation published on the front page, or would you rather everything was kept behind closed doors until we had an answer to go to the authorities with. What would be the least damaging to the stables?'

'We can't stop this from hurting us. Whatever we do, we're going to lose business.'

'But I may be able to limit the damage caused.'

'And if you can't?

'It isn't going to hurt to let me try.'

'If it looks like we tried to cover this up . . .'

'A few days, that's all I'm asking.'

Lesterton sighed heavily, closed his eyes. Eventually, he seemed to come to some kind of decision. His voice was trembling when he finally spoke. 'You've got two days.'

'That's all I need.'

'What's your plan?'

'First, we need to get a vet in who we can trust not to talk to the press until we want him to. Do you know someone?'

Lesterton's back straightened visibly. He turned, and there was a simmering anger clearly evident in his expression. For a second the study seemed impossibly small, impossibly full. His voice was a low grumble of rolling storm clouds. 'What are you suggesting?'

'We need a vet who can tell us, and only us, what happened out there today . . . And maybe, just maybe, if he has to, make sure nobody else is ever able to discover the truth.'

Lesteron tried to loosen his shoulders, let some of the tension drain out of his arms. 'Yes, of course. But I'm not sure I know any vets who wouldn't be morally obligated to let the owners know the results of any autopsy they might undertake. I've never had the need to be dishonest.'

There was silence, pressing in claustrophobically.

Ethan waited.

'I know someone,' O'Hara said reluctantly. 'He'll check the horse over, no questions asked.'

'Good,' Ethan said. 'Contact him, get him out here as soon as possible. Tell him this in an emergency, but make sure he keeps his mouth shut.' Ethan turned to Lesterton, the light of an exciting adventure beaming in his eyes. 'Governor, I need you to talk to the lads. Make sure they don't tell anybody about this, but leave Sally to me. I want to talk to her alone.'

'Sally?'

'She knows more than she's letting on. I have some questions I would like her to answer.'

'You'll have to find her.'

'That's easy enough. There are only so many places a scared girl can go around these parts.'

'And what about the owners?'

'I'll talk to them too. If I don't raise their suspicions, if they think we are doing everything in our power to find out what happened, they shouldn't question our activities too much. As long as they don't talk to their insurance company straight away we should have enough time.'

O'Hara rose steadily to his feet, speaking as carefully as he moved. 'I'll go and phone my friend.'

'Ethan,' Lesterton said, once O'Hara had left the room. His voice was hard and unpleasant.

'Yes, Governor?'

'Why do you want to undertake this investigation yourself?'

'I think it makes sense, Sir. I can ask questions without making people feel nervous. They won't even think I'm investigating. Plus, the owners know me and like me. They'll trust me.'

'Is that all?'

'Yes.'

'Not because you think that Karen girl might be involved in some way?'

'Karen? She wouldn't be.'

'She was sneaking around here yesterday, poking her nose into a couple of the horse boxes. That's something of a coincidence, wouldn't you say?'

'Jamie was sneaking around here too.'

'Oh really?' Lesterton leaned forwards over the desk, a wide and vicious snarl cutting across his features. 'You think it might be Mr Redthorn, do you? Or are you just planning to pin this on him?'

'I intend to find out what happened, that's all.'

'I certainly hope so, because if I find out you're using the future of my stable to exact some petty revenge on Redthorn, I'll take you apart piece by piece.'

Ethan stood calmly. The certainty in his voice was nothing to do with bravado. 'You give me two days to investigate, I'll make sure you come out of this looking like you could eat sugar and shit candy floss.'

'And what happens if you haven't sorted this out in two days?'

'A lot can happen in two days,' Ethan said.

# CHAPTER 11

So much to do, so little time. So many places to go, people to speak to, but where to start?

Ethan checked his watch as he headed across the back of the stables and down the steep incline of the valley towards the woods. Just gone nine, already several hours since Emphatic had thrashed herself to death. Maybe already too late.

The bleary morning sun was spraying Ethan's elongated shadow in a contorted design before him. It was impossible to walk somewhere where his shadow had not gone before.

The grass was wet with dew, sparkling. Minute spider webs glistened intricately.

He took out his mobile phone, tapped in a number.

Waited.

Emphatic had been got at. Ethan didn't need a veterinarian to tell him that; he had seen it in the poor creature's eyes. But killing the horse hadn't been the intention.

Nobody would purposefully cause a horse to die so obvious

and horrible a death. There would be too many questions asked, too many connections wanting answers. Whatever had happened had clearly gone wrong, killing the horse rather than . . . than what? The vet might be able to help with that, but until then, Ethan only had one supposition to work on. Whoever had got to Emphatic had made a mistake, and that one detail was going to be critical over the next few hours. The sooner he could speak to people, the less time he gave people to recover from the horrors of the morning, to formulate believable alibis, the more chance he had of nailing the perpetrators of this unforgivable crime.

There was something else too, another reason why Emphatic's tragic death filled him with confidence in his ability to get to the bottom of this. Only amateurs made mistakes.

He held the mobile phone to his ear.

Karen answered after the third ring. 'Hello?'

'Karen,' he said, stopping just short of the green-black belt of woodland trees that concealed Lesterton's gymnasium and sauna room. Beneath the foliage, it was dark and grim. Lifeless. 'It's me, Ethan. I need to talk to you.'

'I thought . . .'

'Never mind that, can you see me?'

'After yesterday, I didn't think you wanted to see me anymore.'

'Forget that. I need to talk.'

'Okay. When?'

'In an hour, meet me at the café.'

'Okay.'

'And, Karen . . .'

'What?'

'Is Jamie there?'

'He's already headed off to Newbury.'

'Good.'

Ethan switched off the phone and pocketed it. Jamie could easily have got to Emphatic on his way out to the racecourse. He could easily have . . .

Ethan's breath caught as the memory of morning fog rolled back in his mind to reveal a shining silver Bentley. A Bentley that had been driving towards the stables, haze-smeared lights hacking through the early precipitation of the day and Ethan's equally smeared recollections of Melissa.

Jamie had been there.

Earlier that morning, Jamie had drove to the stables.

'You bastard,' Ethan whispered.

Checking his watch again, he moved around to the east, to the spot where the swollen mass of trees parted welcomingly to allow the admittance of a well-kept path into their clustered tangle of limbs. Set away back down the path, the gymnasium brooded quietly. Sitting on the gymnasium porch, Sally brooded with it.

As Ethan approached, she looked up, and he could see the shimmer of tears in her eyes. She made no attempt to bolt. Perhaps she simply had nowhere else to run.

'How's it going?' Ethan asked, sitting next to her but keeping his gaze directed towards the twisted trees. The question hung expectantly in a fog of his silvery breath.

'How did you know I'd be here?' she asked.

'This is the quietest place on the grounds. I like to come here myself when I need some time to think things through.'

Sally sniffed, and rubbed her nose in her sleeve, a strangely endearing action. She looked so fragile and innocent. Just another victim. 'I couldn't stand to be around everybody, not with them all watching me and staring. I know what they're all thinking of me. I had to get away.'

'But you didn't want to go too far?'

She lifted her head sadly. 'No.'

'You go too far and it gets difficult to turn back, doesn't it?'

She sniffed again. Said nothing. The cool breeze rattled the leaves, causing them to chatter like old crones.

'And you do want to turn back, don't you?' Ethan pressed.

'I need to see the Governor.'

'To resign?'

'I can't stay here now, can I?'

'I guess not.' Ethan paused, looked up into the muddled leaves of the powerfully oppressive trees. The woodland held its breath, awaiting the devastating question he had no choice but to ask. 'What did you do, Sally?'

'I don't know.'

'You did something to Emphatic, didn't you?'

A terrible sob escaped between Sally's lips and she seemed to fold in on herself, shrivelling before Ethan's gentle attack. 'I don't know what I did. I just. . .' Her trembling hands fretted at each other. 'I just did what I was told.'

Ethan resisted the urge to put a comforting arm around her shoulder. The last thing he wanted was for her to feel comforted. 'What were you told to do, Sally?'

Silence.

'Sally?'

'I was given a syringe. I wasn't told what was in it. I was told to inject Emphatic at the first available opportunity, that it was good for her.'

'And you believed that?'

Her hands continued to writhe and spasm. 'No, not straight away. I . . .'

'How much were you paid?'

'I . . .'

'Sally?'

Her head sunk, her fingers wrapping up around the back of her neck defensively. 'I said I couldn't do anything without Lesterton's say so. I told them I didn't want to do it.'

'So what convinced you?'

'They told me Lesterton didn't need to know about it. They said it would be okay, that it would be good for the stables. They told me it wouldn't hurt her.'

'They were wrong.'

'They gave me some money. I really needed that money.' She gasped, trying to hold back the tears. 'God. I've really made a mess of things this time, haven't I?'

'Did you know what was in the syringe?'

'No.'

'But you knew it was something bad, didn't you?'

'No. That wouldn't have made any sense.'

'Why not?'

'I mean . . .'

'Who gave you the syringe, Sally?'

'I can't say.'

'Why not?'

She began picking at a fingernail nervously. 'You know why.'

'Tell me.'

A shuddering sigh passed through her hunched shoulders. 'My father is ill. He has a brain disorder that means he can't look after himself anymore. He's in a home now. He sits in this chair by the window, looking out at the same street day after day. It doesn't matter to him, he doesn't remember things. He doesn't even know who I am when I visit. He just keeps staring out of that window. I did this for the money, to help him.'

'Sally, who gave you the needle?'

'Every day, it's the same street, but he watches it like he's seeing everything for the first time.'

'Sally?'

'If something happens to me, who's going to look after my father?'

'If something happens?'

She jumped up, full of frightened energy. 'I have to go and see Lesterton,' she said.

'Sally?'

She looked at Ethan as he stood. 'Don't chase this,' she said. 'Whatever your reasons are for trying to find out what happened, just let it go.'

'You killed a horse today.'

'I know, and I have to live with that. But if you tell anybody what I've said today, it will be bad for you.'

'Are you threatening me?' Ethan scoffed.

'Not me.'

'Then who?'

Sally was already heading off down the path, back towards the stables. 'Believe me,' she said, 'you don't want to know. Things will be worse if you do.'

Ethan trotted after her, grabbing her arm and spinning her around. Her sadness was almost immediately replaced with fear and anger. Primitive, animal instincts.

'I can't let it go at that,' Ethan said. 'You can't tell me you killed a horse and then just walk away. It doesn't work that way.'

Sally jerked aggressively, her lips peeling away from her teeth in an aggressive snarl. Ethan's grip tightened.

'I don't think you're listening to me,' he said. 'Now, tell me what's going on.'

'I can't.'

'You know I'm going to tell Lesterton what you've just told me.' He let go of her, and she took a cautious step backwards. 'I'll tell him everything you just told me, and then the police will want to speak to you. Are you prepared for that?'

She shook her head. 'You can't do that. If Lesterton finds out, they'll come looking for me. And they'll know you know too. We'll both be dead.'

'I don't buy into melodrama, Sally.'

'You don't have to. You just have to believe that they do. These people have too much to lose. They won't let you walk away. It's been happening too long.'

Ethan looked into Sally's eyes, and he saw there the truth of her words, melodramatic as they might have seemed. This girl wasn't lying, wasn't trying to cover her tracks. This girl was genuinely terrified.

'It wasn't meant to be this way, was it?' he asked.

'No.'

'They wanted to give Emphatic a little kick, make sure she won today. Is that about the sum of it?'

'I think so.'

'So who got it wrong? You or them?'

'I'm not sure.'

'Are they going to think it was you?'

'Maybe.'

'Are they going to try and hurt you?'

'I . . .' Sally's voice cracked horribly, fresh tears glittering the edges of her petrified eyes. 'I don't know what they'll do to me. I never wanted any of this to happen. I just wanted to help my father.'

'It's okay,' Ethan said, putting a hand on her shoulder. 'I'll talk to Lesterton for you. Just get out of here. Write to me in the next few days, let me know where we can pass on your papers. I'll make sure Lesterton gives you a good reference. Nobody needs to know about Emphatic or your involvement.'

Sally laughed emptily. 'People will find out, Ethan. People always do.'

*

Ethan pushed open the door of the café, barely registering the soft ting of the welcome bell suspended above the hinge. He stepped inside, and shook rainwater out of his hair. The waitress at the counter - not Liz - smiled pleasantly.

He looked around, searching for a familiar face among the assorted customers.

Karen was sat at his favourite table, nursing a cup of coffee, and looking out of the window.

He sat opposite. Said nothing.

She kept staring out of the rain-patterned window, watching the tumultuous skies as they were sundered by the first flashing claws of a storm that had already darkened the day. Eventually, her gaze strayed towards Ethan.

'You're late,' she said, humourlessly.

'Perhaps you were early.'

'What do you want, Ethan?'

'Where's all this hostility come from?'

The waitress shuffled over with a notepad. Ethan ordered coffee. The waitress shuffled away.

'Hostility?' Karen hissed. 'Weren't you at the stables yesterday?'

'As I recall, I was there being pushed around by your Neanderthal boyfriend.'

'And taking it out on me.'

'I didn't mean to do that.' He grinned boyishly. 'Guess I'm not too good at the ritual humiliation stuff.'

'This is another pride thing, right?'

'I'm a man, of course it is.'

The waitress returned with an almost-white cup of almost-coffee, putting it on the table and nodding her mousy head politely.

'I'm sorry that had to happen,' Karen said, when the waitress was out of earshot.

'That I had to be served coffee?'

'You know what I mean.'

'It's okay, I have a very short memory.'

'I don't know what got in to him. I was really angry.'

'You didn't sound angry last night.'

108

Karen caught the flare of bitterness and stale humour in Ethan's expression, pretended she hadn't. 'Sorry?'

'Never mind. I didn't come here to talk about what happened yesterday. Something more important has happened.'

'Oh. I thought you wanted to talk about . . . I thought you wanted to . . .' She wrapped her hands around her cup. 'You were so angry with Jamie, with me. I thought everything was ruined.'

Ethan reached across the table and touched her hand impulsively. 'It's okay. We're . . . friends. Jamie taking something of a dislike to me doesn't change that. It wasn't you that caused the trouble. We're still cool.'

'Really?'

'Really. I was feeling a little bruised and battered yesterday. I never meant to take anything out on you. If it felt that way, I'm sorry. Besides . . .' Ethan withdrew his hand, clenching it in a fist on the tabletop. 'Something happened this morning that put any petty squabbles I might have with Jamie into perspective. One of the horses died.'

'Which one?'

'Emphatic, the one that was supposed to race today.'

'That's terrible.'

'I know. We went to see to her this morning and she was . . . dead. In her box.'

'What . . ?' A moment's hesitation. Brief, revealing. 'What happened? Do you know why she died?'

Ethan sipped his coffee. The rain continued to run in jagged lines down the window, cutting the world into shimmering, warped shards of distorted beauty. The café suddenly seemed very quiet, only the hiss of burgers behind the counter alleviating an almost unnatural silence.

Ethan drew a long breath.

What if Sally hadn't been overreacting? What if knowing too much might be more dangerous than he could possibly imagine?

109

What if the beautiful woman sitting opposite him was merely attempting to gauge how much he knew in order to determine whether he would need to be dealt with? What if somebody, somebody who was just waiting for the perfect opportunity to take him down, was watching, even now?

He shuddered, put his cup back on the table.

'We don't know anything yet,' he said calmly. 'We haven't been able to get a vet out to her. It's . . . delicate, at the moment.'

'What do the owners think?'

'We told them the horse couldn't race today, that the going was likely to be a little too soft for her now that the rain's come in. We got one of the temp staff to ring, to avoid a lot of awkward questions, told them that someone would come out to explain everything . . .' He paused, breathing calculatedly, thinking how best to verbalise the terrible deceit he had helped to orchestrate. 'We haven't told them the horse is dead yet.' He checked his watch. 'They're next on the list though. I'm going to drive out there and break the news to them myself.'

'They'll be devastated.'

'I know. The whole yard is devastated. Somebody might as well have gone in there and shot one of the stable hands. That's what it feels like.'

'What do you mean?'

Ethan's teeth snapped closed, trying to swallow back a statement that was far too revealing. 'Nothing. I just mean it's a terrible loss to the stable. It's like losing a family member.'

'I'm sure. Will there be an . . . investigation?'

Ethan shrugged. 'I doubt it. Horses die in their boxes all the time. We don't suspect foul play.'

Karen physically relaxed, slouching in her chair and aimlessly stirring her coffee with a stained spoon. Ethan looked out across the stable grounds. Some semblance of normality had returned to proceedings, and staff members were moving about in their waterproofs with buckets and brushes. Working hard. Keeping things ticking.

Trying not to think about what had happened.

'Is this what you wanted to talk to me about?' Karen pressed.

'Not exactly.' Ethan sipped his coffee, tried not to look at her directly. 'I was just wondering if you knew why Jamie came to the stables yesterday.'

'Jamie?'

'Why did he want to speak to the Governor?'

'I don't know. Why don't you ask Lesterton?'

'Lesterton has other things on his mind right now with this business with Emphatic. Besides, I'm not sure he would tell me.'

'And you think I will?'

'I think so, yes. We're friends, after all.'

'I'm afraid I can't tell you anything. Jamie doesn't talk about business with me.'

He laughed quietly, shook his head. 'Quite.'

'Are you okay, Ethan?'

'Absolutely.'

She looked at him over the rim of her cup. He examined his fingernails. The hamburgers sizzled. Other people had conversations about nothing.

'Do you find me attractive?' she asked.

'I beg your pardon?'

'It's not that complicated a question, is it?'

'More complicated than you think.' He focussed his concentration on folding a paper napkin into a swan. 'If I say yes, I run the risk of damaging our friendship. If I say no . . .'

'What?'

'You'll know I'm lying.'

She revealed her teeth in a brilliant and mischievous grin. 'How interesting.'

Ethan stood. 'I have to go.'

'To see a man about a dog?'

'About a racehorse.'

He threw some money on the table to cover the coffee, aware of Karen's hard gaze burning into him.

'You're breaking my heart, you know,' he said, without looking.

'Really?'

'Every time you smile.'

He left the café, the bell over the door jangling merrily as he stepped out into the swallowing howl of the storm.

'Good,' Karen said, to herself.

## CHAPTER 12

Lord Darabont was very rich, very old, and just a touch senile. He had, like many Lord Darabonts before him, been born into money, and he had never really learned to appreciate exactly what that money was or how hard it was to come by for most people. His wife had also been raised by the landed gentry, and they made a perfect couple, living in a small but very expensive bubble where the rules of the common man did not apply.

Ethan stood out on the seventh hole of Lord Darabont's flamboyant and overly expensive golf course, with the collar of his raincoat turned up. The storm raged on, heavy blades of rain slashing down in diagonal sweeps from a blackened sky. The clouds piled up on the horizon in frightening walls of incomprehensible fury before overbalancing and rolling in grey waves across the treetops. Thunder boomed like cannon in the distance.

'Invigorating, don't you think?' Lord Darabont said, eyeing up his putt through rain-specked glasses, his shoulders hunched defensively against the wind.

'Very,' Ethan shouted. 'But isn't it a touch dangerous? With the lightning and everything?'

'Probably.'

Darabont putted; the ball splashed into the waterlogged seventh. 'Good shot,' Ethan ventured.

'Thank you.'

'Do you think we might go inside now?'

Darabont took off his glasses, wiping them thoughtfully with a stubby thumb as he looked up into the teeth of the heavy clouds with squinty, yellow eyes. The raindrops stabbed angrily at his crinkled, upturned face. 'I think it's going to blow over,' he said, somewhat optimistically.

'I'm not so sure about that,' Ethan pressed, hopping from one foot to the other uncomfortably as the persistent claws of rain ran down his neck and soaked through his trousers. 'And I really need to talk to you. It's quite serious.'

'More serious than golf?'

'Yes.'

Darabont's ageing brow wrinkled. There were so few things that were more important than golf. 'Your friend on the phone explained everything to my wife. He said the horse won't be able to race today.'

'The horse won't be able to race ever again.'

'My wife wasn't too concerned, she guessed it would probably be something to do with the rain. Your man on the phone said he didn't have any further information and somebody would be out to explain everything in person. My wife said it wasn't necessary, bless her. She didn't really think we had a chance at Newbury today anyway, despite what all the pundits and the bookmakers and your old boss said. She wasn't even going to go and watch, you know? I said she'd be better off staying home.'

'Lord Darabont, didn't you hear me?'

'Of course, I never really go and watch. Horses aren't really my thing. More of a golf man, myself.' He swung the putter triumphantly over his round head. 'Real sport of kings, a true noble art.'

'Lord Darabont?'

'Yes?'

'Didn't you hear me? The horse isn't ever going to race again.'

'Really? Well, that is a pity. My wife really did like that horse, but we've always trusted Mr Lesterton to do what's right by her and if he says -'

'The horse is dead.'

Darabont stopped speaking for all of a second, digesting this new piece of information like a well-done steak before responding. 'Really?'

'Yes.'

'Dead?'

'Yes.'

'Now, that really is a shame. Poor thing. Do you know why?'

'We're looking into it.'

'Jolly good.'

'Jolly good?' Ethan's voice was almost completely obliterated by an angry percussion of thunder. 'Jolly good? Is that all you can say?'

'What would you like me to say?'

'I don't know. Something. Anything.'

'The horse is dead. What can I say? It was my wife's anyway. I'll buy her another one.'

'I'm sorry?'

Darabont retrieved his golf ball. 'I said, I'll buy her another one. Hell, I'll buy her two. It's only money, isn't it?'

'We've organised a vet to look the horse over, but that's just routine. We're more than happy it was down to natural causes. We'll keep you informed, obviously.'

'Very kind of you, but not really necessary.'

115

Ethan clenched his hands into fists, swallowed back his anger. He couldn't possibly be having this conversation. If Lord Darabont had been there, had seen the horse die, frothing at the mouth with terrible, staring eyes, he wouldn't be having this conversation. Nobody who had been there, who understood how horrific the loss had been, could be so blasé.

'Aren't you at all interested to know what happened to Emphatic?' he asked, through tightly drawn lips.

Darabont wiped a liver-spotted palm across his hooked nose before sweeping silver-white hair back from his obviously bemused face. 'Should I be interested?' he asked. 'Animals die. It's a bloody nuisance, but that's how things go.'

Yellow lightning licked the golf course, strobing the old Lord's features into stark, angled contrasts. Thunder followed. 'Don't you want an investigation?' Ethan pressed, unable to comprehend Darabont's complete disinterest in the death of the expensive and extremely talented thoroughbred.

Darabont shrugged his thin shoulders. 'My dog died last month. I didn't have an investigation into that.'

'But this is different.'

'She was a lovely Golden Retriever. Ever such a good-tempered thing. I woke up one morning and she was just lying in her basket all curled up and not breathing.' He chuckled with an ugly humour Ethan could not understand or condone. 'She still had one of those squeaky rubber newspapers in her mouth, like she had been about ready to go out and play. She always was a silly bloody thing. She was probably dead ten minutes before she knew it.'

'Lord Darabont?'

'Now that was sad. She was almost part of the family. We miss her, but she was just a dog.'

'But . . .'

'Animals are animals. Horse, dog, cat, whatever. If you want to talk to my wife . . .'

'No. That's okay. I wanted to come out here to let you know what happened, to apologise for your loss. That's all.'

'Then consider your job done.'

'More than that, I consider my job to have been totally point-less.'

'Sorry?'

'Nothing. I just need to know . . .' Ethan stopped, breathed, continued in a more conversational tone. 'I just need to know if you took out any insurance on the horse.'

'No, I never really saw the point in that sort of thing. I don't even think my dishwasher is insured. When something breaks, you buy yourself a new one.'

Ethan sighed, his relief masked by the rain running down his face. 'And one other thing . . . You don't hold Mr Lesterton responsible for the death, do you?'

'Should I?'

Ethan paused. 'No.'

'Then I don't.'

'A vet will look the horse over. Nothing too serious. We'll make sure you get a complete report.'

'That's really not necessary.'

'We insist.'

'Of course. You have to do what you think is right. I will leave everything in your capable hands.'

There was a clash of thunder, a hanging silence. The two men looked at each other wordlessly.

'Why did you buy a horse?' Ethan asked, shortly before the silence became unbearable.

Darabont shrugged his gnarly shoulders. His head bobbed comically. 'Why not? You have money, you spend it. Isn't that the point?'

Ethan smiled thinly. 'Perhaps.'

Darabont looked into the tumultuous skies. Spiralling clouds boiled in rumbling flashes. 'Right, well if that's everything, I'm going to go inside for a stiff drink. Would you care to join me before you head back?'

Ethan ran his hands through streaming hair. 'I'll pass,' he said. 'I want to get back to the stables as quickly as I can.'

'Get back to your lovely fiancée, I expect. Right?'

The rain fell harder.

'Fiancée?'

'Yes, that lovely girl . . .' Darabont waved his hand absent-mindedly, as if to pluck a name right out of the air. 'Melissa. That's it, Melissa. Last time I saw you, she was hanging off your arm, and flashing that ring at anyone and everyone.'

'Oh. Her.'

'She's a lovely girl. And she's obviously head-over-heels in love with you. You're very lucky.'

'Well, actually we . . .' Ethan stopped himself. 'Yes. I am. Thank you.'

'You must pass on my regards to her.'

'I will, yes.'

'Good lad. Tell your Governor I'll be in touch in the next few days to discuss the purchase of a new horse.'

'Of course.'

Darabont nodded politely, ducked into the seat of his golf buggy, and trundled, with the whine of an electric motor, towards the white walls of the house. Ethan watched him for a moment, feeling the giant swell of heartache bubbling up through his chest. The rain seemed to stab at him ever more persistently.

Melissa.

With everything that had been going on, he had almost forgotten about her. How could he have done that? How could he have forgotten? Today, of all days.

He pulled out his mobile phone, jabbed at the luminous keys

with numb fingers.

Jason answered on the first ring.

'Ethan. Hi.'

'Do you want to go for a drink tonight?' Ethan asked.

'Sure. Where are you?'

'Doesn't matter.'

'What have you been doing?'

Ethan sighed. 'I have absolutely no idea.'

## CHAPTER 13

During the First World War, Newbury had been turned into a prisoner of war camp before going through several other reincarnations as a hay dispersal depot, and a munitions inspection centre.

Later, in 1942, the course had become a supply depot for American Allies, and was buried, by necessity, beneath concrete and railway lines.

Sat in the fabulous owners' enclosure with a brandy, those times must have seemed a million years ago for most people, perhaps even beyond their comprehension, yet today, those other lifetimes of the course were heavily rooted in O'Hara's mind.

Watching the blaze of coloured silks streaking by, listening to the tinny commentary from the loud-speakers, encapsulated in the blur of excitement that was the crowd, he could not help but think of this place as a prison. This was a place of utilitarian design, choking life and beauty beneath crate upon crate of deadly weaponry and trainloads full of an enemy who had no deeper comprehension of what it was they were fighting for than their captors. This racetrack was saturated with a history of death and despair, and, watching each race finish, waiting for the race Emphatic should have won, O'Hara could almost smell the blood.

He sipped his brandy.

The work that had been done in this place, all those years before, had resulted in countless lost lives, for causes both good and bad, purposeful and meaningless. Somewhere, on a foreign shore, there were rows of tombstones, jutting out of black earth like teeth, reminding the future of the cost of human life. O'Hara could only wonder if anything had changed.

There were other rides he could have taken, something promising in another race, but he knew better than that. Being a jockey didn't just mean sitting on a horse. Being a jockey meant being a partner for that horse. If you couldn't be part of the team, you couldn't win, and today, O'Hara could barely think straight. Whatever he rode today would lose.

He hated to lose.

He sat back, stretching his legs, and flicked through the official race programme. On the front cover was a particularly gushing welcome from the racecourse chairman, complete with a publicity photograph of the man himself standing out by the starting stalls. Nothing much of interest there, only the usual 'isn't our racecourse great?' stuff. O'Hara was sure it was true; Newbury was, on the surface, exceptionally beautiful. Just not today.

Not for him.

He skipped through to the tote tips section. No surprises there. Emphatic had been at the forefront of everybody's thoughts. She would have blown them away.

She would have blown them away if . . . He closed the programme, and pushed it away across the table. Finished his brandy. The man sitting opposite - tall, with a waterproof Mac' belted over a hand-woven wool jacket - peered out of the window with a pair of binoculars. 'They're going down,' he exclaimed, to nobody in particular.

O'Hara examined his brandy glass, wondering whether he should get it filled up again. He was already feeling moist and warm inside, his consciousness floating slightly above his head. His motions felt awkward, even if they weren't.

He spun the glass between his forefinger and thumb, watched the man with the binoculars.

'Number one doesn't look happy,' the man said.

'Why's that?' O'Hara asked. He didn't care, it just seemed proper to respond in some way.

For a second the man lowered his binoculars. His face was strangely angular, like it had been cut out rather than grown. His eyes were small and peculiarly bright, his hair, by contrast, mousy and dull. He seemed genuinely thrilled. 'He doesn't want to go in the stalls.'

O'Hara stood. 'Sometimes they don't.'

Outside the window, a bustle of raincoats and umbrellas jostled around expectantly. Inside, an equally anxious collection of dripping bodies edged closer for a better view of the course.

O'Hara imagined the turf, carpeted beneath concrete. The crowds didn't carry umbrellas, they carried guns. They were not awaiting horses, they were awaiting a train. Their anxiousness had nothing to do with excitement, it was all about fear.

He pushed his way through the crowd, careful not to upset anybody, and put his glass on the bar. The bar staff all smiled and gravitated towards him.

'Fill that up, please,' he said, against his better judgement.

'Of course,' one of the staff said, a young man, barely more than a boy.

O'Hara turned and rested his elbows on the counter. From here, all he could see were the backs of people's heads. Somehow, that seemed better.

He loosened his tie a little, reached into his pocket for a

cigarette. A full glass clattered on the bar behind him.

'Is that everything, Mr O'Hara?' the boy asked.

O'Hara handed over some money without looking, suggested the boy keep the change, and lit his cigarette. For a moment white smoke obscured his view.

The boy behind the bar went back to cleaning glasses.

The horses were running, O'Hara could almost feel the ground rumbling beneath him. Rumbling as the munitions train rolled in with its cargo of destruction.

'I should have been racing today,' he said, swirling his brandy glass. He could sense the boy behind the bar look up from what he was doing. There was no reply. 'I was supposed to be riding the best horse here.'

There was an awkward clearing of throats. 'We know, Mr O'Hara.'

'Well,' he sucked on the filter of his cigarette, 'it's all gone to shit now, hasn't it?'

'You can't be responsible for the weather though, can you, Mr O'Hara?'

'Weather?'

'The rain. That's why Emphatic isn't here, right?'

O'Hara closed his eyes, listened to the raindrops drumming on the roof. 'Yes, of course. The rain.'

'I would have had a little bet on you myself, if things had gone to plan.'

O'Hara turned, thumped his glass on the bar. 'Plan? What do you mean by plan?'

The boy paused, startled, a dishcloth wedged in the top of a hi-ball tumbler. His colleagues suddenly found something to occupy their time at the other end of the bar. 'I mean, if you had raced. If the weather had been right.'

The crowd roared as the horses hammered by, including the skittish number one. O'Hara smiled carefully, sipped his brandy, smoked. 'Of course.'

His mobile phone jangled merrily in his jacket pocket. 'Excuse me.'

He answered the call outside, sheltering beneath a drooping canopy. Excited punters moved around him, dashing off to the stands to claim their winnings. Two men in wax jackets and Indiana Jones hats marked names in their official programmes and shook their heads and tutted.

'Hello?'

'O'Hara,' Lesterton said, sounding distant and fractured over the phone. 'Where are you?'

'I'm at Newbury, where do you think I am?'

'Are you stupid?'

'My teachers always said so.'

'What are you doing there?'

'Watching the race.'

'Why in the name of God are you doing that? Are you not aware how serious this is?'

O'Hara watched the men in the wax jackets as they trudged off towards the stands. As they walked, one of them knocked into someone in the crowd - a middle-aged gentleman with thinning hair - who turned slightly, touched one of the wax jackets on the shoulder apologetically, and moved on.

'I know how serious this is,' O'Hara said. 'I thought it would look odd if I wasn't here.'

'You should have let me know.'

'Why? Would that have made a difference?'

'I would have known, that's the difference.'

O'Hara dropped his cigarette, and crushed it under the toe of his boot. 'Why are you ringing me?' he asked.

'Your vet friend has been.'

'And?'

'He looked shifty.'

'I thought you wanted somebody shifty?'

There was a pregnant pause on the other end of the phone. 'Are you alone?'

'About as alone as you can be at a racetrack.'

'Can anyone hear you?'

O'Hara looked around. There were people nearby, but they were all involved in their own conversations. The wax jackets were no longer anywhere in sight. Opened umbrellas obscured a good deal of his view. 'I don't think so,' he said.

Another pause. 'Are you sure we can trust this vet?'

'No.'

'What do you mean, no?'

'I mean, no. He's dishonest, that's why you wanted him to come and take a look at the horse. He'll keep quiet as long as he thinks there isn't any financial gain to be had from speaking out. Did you pay him?'

'The amount we agreed on.'

'We should be okay then. What did he say?'

'He said this is a complete mess, one of the worst attempts to dope a horse he has ever seen.'

'And did he tell you anything we didn't already know?'

'A little, but I don't want to talk to you about it over the phone. He's going to get back to me with the results of some more tests by tomorrow.'

'Okay. Let me know if you hear anything more.' The metallic voice began bleating over the speakers around the track, listing the runners for the next race, the race Emphatic would have won if she had been here. 'Lesterton . . . You didn't have anything to do with the horse dying, did you?'

'Absolutely not.'

'This wasn't supposed to happen, was it?'

Lesterton sighed. 'I don't know.'

The phone went dead; O'Hara put it back in his pocket. He

125

turned his jacket collar up, and walked out into the rain, down to the course. He leaned on the rails, bowed his head. In 1942 this had been a munitions depot, there had been no turf, no horses, no jockeys. There had been weapons.

He closed his eyes, let the rain run over his face. There had been weapons.

*

Down in the weighing room, waiting to be called into the Scales, Dalton was reading the newspaper when Jamie Redthorn came over to speak to him. Both men were already in their colours, Redthorn in green with yellow epaulets, and Dalton in red with double black hoops on the arms and a black Cross of Lorraine on the chest.

'What's happening in the world?' Jamie asked, sitting on the bench next to Dalton and leaning over his shoulder to get a look at the newspaper.

The headline read, 'Three Die In House Fire'. The accompanying picture showed a gutted building with a terribly sad-looking fireman picking over the remains. It was one of those pictures just screaming out for a stuffed teddy to be positioned somewhere in the blackened remains, for emotional emphasis.

'I don't know,' Dalton said. 'I was just reading the funnies.' He folded the paper and put it on the bench. 'Is there anything I can help you with?'

'I don't know, is there?'

'Mysterious as always, Redthorn. I take it you didn't come over here to talk about tactics?'

'Not exactly.'

'So . . ?'

'You've heard, I take it, that Emphatic isn't going to be running today?'

126

'Of course.'

'Well, that tends to put a little bit of a dynamic twist on the race, don't you think?'

'It certainly opens up some avenues of opportunity.'

'Indeed.'

Dalton picked at a fingernail. 'What do you want, Jamie?'

'You know what I want.'

'Well, you don't need to worry about me. This isn't my race.' He stopped, looked across the weighing room at a jockey in the far corner who was still pulling on his silks. 'Pickering's in with a shot, I should think.'

Jamie stood, slapped Dalton on the shoulder. 'I wouldn't be so sure of that,' he said.

Dalton watched Jamie leave, then took out the business card his visitor had given him the other day. He flicked the card through his fingers thoughtfully.

The doors to the Scales opened. They were being summoned.

*

O'Hara was still leaning on the rails when the two wax jackets reappeared. He did not look up as they approached, did not even acknowledge them when one stood on either side of him. He kept his gaze focussed on Newbury's immaculate turf. He could smell the damp wax.

'You look upset, Mr O'Hara?' the one on his left said, in a tone that was half conversational, half threatening.

'Or angry,' the one on the right said.

'Perhaps I'm both,' O'Hara said. 'Do I know you two gentlemen?'

'No,' Mr Right said. 'We're big fans of yours, though. It's such a shame you couldn't ride Emphatic today, but she'd die out there under these conditions. Too much cut in the ground for her.'

127

'For sure,' Mr Left said.

O'Hara was silent.

'Maybe you'd rather not talk about it?' Mr Right suggested. He put a hand on O'Hara's arm. 'Maybe it kills you just to think about it.'

O'Hara remained quiet. The hand on his arm seemed heavy, not friendly.

'You don't talk much, do you?' Mr Left said.

'Sometimes,' O'Hara said. 'Did you know that Newbury used to be a prisoner of war camp?'

'Actually, yes,' Mr Right said. 'It's nice to think the course played its part, wouldn't you say?'

'I don't know. It depends on what you think of the war, I suppose.'

'And what do you think?'

'I think, sometimes death can be avoided. Sometimes people would rather it wasn't.'

The wax jackets scratched their noses in synchronisation, looked at each other over the top of O'Hara's head, then glanced at the grey sky.

'Why don't we go up to the bar and watch the race over a drink?' Mr Right suggested.

O'Hara straightened. 'Okay,' he said. 'Let's do that.'

\*

Dalton's ride, the relatively successful two-year-old Brecon's Ridgeway, moved into his stall with the minimum of fuss and waited patiently beneath his hood. Occasionally he would huff and paw the turf, but beyond that he was as calm as anyone could hope for. He certainly looked in good shape for the race, a trip running a little over one mile, but Dalton could not imagine the horse making a first place in this company.

He looked over towards Jamie Redthorn, on the inside rail. He was riding for a trainer with a bad reputation these days, a man who had been involved in, and subsequently exonerated from, more than his fair share of scandals. Just the type of man Dalton himself might have approached for work.

The horse Redthorn was partnering was something of an unknown quantity, a horse called Dancing Shy, with little exposure in Britain. Rumour had it she was a star in the making, and had enough in store to make the pace and hold off all but the most resilient opposition. She certainly looked in good health from what Dalton could see of her.

He reached over to pat Ridegway's shoulder. The horse flicked its head; Dalton shortened the length of his reins.

The last horse slotted into its stall beside him, and the jockeys waited, trapped in their little metal coffins. For a second the tension was like static in the air. Then the doors of the stalls sprang open with a metallic clang, and the horses bolted.

Dalton deftly drew off Ridgeway's hood and discarded it, took one last look at Redthorn, tucked in his knees, stooped in the saddle, and he was away.

The crowd roared. Hooves ripped through the mulched earth. Black clods of mud sprayed up as the ground exploded beneath the passage of the horses.

The finishing line drew nearer.

*

Sitting alone in his lounge, watching the racing on the television with the sound turned down, Lesterton drank his third whiskey in as many minutes, and awaited the inevitable in perfect silence.

He watched as the stalls opened silently. He watched as the silent horses rushed out onto the course in a crazy muddle of multicoloured silk and watery splashes. He watched as Jamie

Redthorn silently moved to the front of the pack, riding confidently. He watched as the other horses silently fell out of contention.

He watched, helplessly, as Redthorn silently crossed the finishing line in first place, his riding whip waving in silent triumph above his head.

Lesterton examined his empty whiskey glass.

Somehow, the room seemed even quieter.

*

O'Hara finished his brandy just as Jamie crossed the finishing line. The two wax jackets waited for him to say something. He wasn't exactly sure what they might be waiting for him to say, so he settled for, 'Well.' A surprisingly empty word.

'Well, what?' asked one of the jackets.

'Well, that's that, then.'

'That's what?'

O'Hara stood. 'That,' he said, and walked away.

The wax jackets watched him go, then removed their racing programmes, scratching notes in the columns by various horse names.

The crowd milled around aimlessly, perhaps looking for someone to congratulate them.

'Did you really know this place used to be a prisoner of war camp?' one wax jacket asked.

'Didn't have a clue,' the other said.

Behind them, on a wall-mounted monitor, a smiling Jamie waved his whip.

It was still raining.

## CHAPTER 14

Ethan was drunk. He was well aware he was drunk, but he ordered himself another beer anyway. The handsome bartender served him efficiently without so much as a second glance, took the money, returned change, and sauntered off to the other end of the counter where two middle-aged women were quietly discussing their day at the office.

Ethan studied his watch face, mildly horrified to see it had only just turned seven. Far too early to be this drunk. The mirrored wall behind the bar reflected his image back at him; he tried not to pay it any attention.

One of the women laughed theatrically and flicked her hair in a way that suggested she wanted to be noticed. Ethan did his best not to, inhaled half his pint, waited. Watched bubbles forming on the inside of his glass. Watched the bubbles burst.

Out of the corner of his eye he could see the women, the only other customers in the bar, lean together, talking quietly.

He snorted a wet laugh through his nose. They were talking

about him. Look at that, they were saying. Isn't that Ethan Hunter, the jockey? Look at the state of him. Surely he shouldn't be drinking like that. What would the papers think?

'To hell with the papers,' Ethan slurred.

'Sorry?'

He looked up, smiled stupidly at the bartender. 'Nothing mate,' he said. 'Just talking to myself.'

'First sign of madness,' the bartender said happily, walking away.

'No,' Ethan whispered. 'Not the first.'

He slurped his beer, and let the world blend into a beige kaleidoscope around him. Music from the jukebox ebbed and flowed through his conscious thought. He allowed himself to slump more comfortably on the bar. His eyes grew heavier, his beer glass got emptier. He could only imagine how dishevelled and unattractive he must have appeared.

The bartender, young and bored-looking, prowled up and down the other side of the counter like a caged tiger. The clock on the wall ticked monotonously, its large hands counting down the seconds to the moment when Ethan would have to return to his flat.

His empty, lonely flat.

'Ethan, sorry about that.'

Ethan glanced over his shoulder at the sound of Jason's familiar American voice: a slow Texan drawl, half-buried under a New York twang.

'Where the hell have you been?' Ethan demanded.

'Making a few calls. You look like shit.'

'I'm not used to drinking this way.'

'We can rectify that.' Jason clambered up on a stool next to Ethan, and slapped the palm of his hand on the bar. 'Service,' he said, cheerfully. 'It's an emergency. This man runs the risk of becoming very boring. He needs bourbon.'

'I need sleep,' Ethan said.

'Sleep when you're dead.'

'I think I am.'

Jason reached into the pocket of his designer jacket, and pulled out a roll of cash. The bartender hovered expectantly. 'Two bourbons,' Jason said. 'Over ice.' He slapped Ethan on the shoulder. 'Lots of ice for this man, he's only an apprentice. And whatever the women over there are drinking.'

The bartender nodded and swaggered off to the optics. When he returned he had four glasses: two bourbons, two vodkas. 'Would you like to take the drinks over yourself?' he asked.

'You do the honours,' Jason grinned.

'Little old for you, aren't they?' Ethan said, through a mouthful of beer, as the waiter stalked off with the vodkas.

'Nobody's too old, nobody's too young. Women are women.' The laughter in Jason's eyes was playful yet telling. 'Speaking of which, have you managed to have any luck with this girl who's moved in upstairs yet?'

'Not yet.'

'Mind if I have a go at her?'

'You and I may well fall out, Jason.'

'All's fair in love and war.'

Ethan shook his head. Over Jason's shoulder he could see the two women sipping their vodkas and occasionally shooting provocative glances across the bar. Jason would probably end up taking them both home if he got the chance. Ethan could not deny they were attractive.

'But it's never love with you, Jason, is it?' he said.

Jason drank his bourbon, and watched the women. A cruel smile crept into the corner of his mouth, and spread malignantly. 'Why are you here, Ethan?' he asked.

'Because I felt like getting drunk.'

'Why?'

'Bad day at the office.' Ethan took a beer mat from the polished bar, and began systematically shredding it into a metal ashtray. 'Very bad day.'

'This isn't about the horse, though, is it?'

'Probably not.'

'Horses have died before. You've never needed to drink it out of your memory.'

'This is different.'

'Why?'

Ethan sighed heavily. 'I don't know.'

What else could he say? That the horse had been killed? That the horse had been killed by a member of staff? That he thought the woman he had recently become infatuated with might be involved? That Jamie Redthorn was almost certainly behind the whole incident? That he couldn't even tell Lesterton what he suspected for fear he might wind up dead?

He let his head sag.

What else could he say? That despite everything, despite all these terrible events, the very mention of Melissa's name by a senile old lord had almost brought him to tears? That today, one year ago on this very day, he had woken to find his engagement ring lying on the bedside table, and a tragically empty space in his bed? That one year ago today, his life, which before had always seemed so complete, had been utterly destroyed without even one word of explanation, without one single reason why?

What else could he say?

What could he possibly say to explain that?

'I just don't know.'

'What do you think happened to the horse?' Jason asked, without diverting his gaze from the far end of the bar and the women sitting there.

'The vet said . . . The vet said it was natural causes. One of those things.'

'Will there be further investigations?'

'Why are you so interested?'

'I'm not.'

'You sound interested.'

'Those women want us.'

'Is that so.'

'They keep looking at you, man. Reckon they must know who you are. You interested in the type of ride you won't get at Newbury?'

'You aren't funny.'

Jason searched his jacket for more money. The bartender magically appeared beside him, almost as though he had always been there. 'Yes, Sir?'

Jason ordered two bourbons. Ethan stared into the bottom of his empty pint glass. The clock kept ticking, seeming louder now.

'So why are you really here?' Jason asked.

'I can't race, I figured I might as well have a few beers while I had the chance.'

'Seems as good a reason as any.'

'The best reason. Why are you here?'

Jason looked around the deserted bar, the empty booths, the flashing fruit machines, the harsh glare of fire escape lights. Given a few hours, this place - tidy but not quite classy enough to be clean - could well be busy. Right now, it was a tomb. 'You rang me,' he said. He sucked the inside of his cheek thoughtfully. 'You've never rung me before.'

'But why are you here?'

'Because I've got nowhere else to be.' His perpetual grin widened. 'Besides, some friends will be stopping in later.'

'What sort of friends?'

'The kind that keep me rich.'

Ethan ran a hand through his hair, and examined one of the glasses of bourbon dubiously. He understood all too well the kind of people that kept Jason rich. 'This isn't something I want to know about, is it?'

'Not really.'

'You're going to get in real trouble one day.'

'Only if they catch me.'

Ethan laughed emptily. 'Everybody gets caught sooner or later.'

*

Ethan was conscious. He was conscious, but everything was in darkness.

Everything was in darkness because he was blind . . .

No, not blind. His eyes were closed, heavy. So very heavy. Arms were leaden, legs were somewhere else altogether. Face was pressed against something hard and wet.

This was the shadow world, the limbo between asleep and awake, the place where he was aware of his body but unable to control it. This was a place that had all the stuff of reality, but was steeped in shadows.

Bouncing around in those sickening shadows, there were voices.

'Is he okay?'

'He's fine. Come on, Ethan, up you get.'

Ethan's eyes flicked open. He was in motion. He was being hauled backwards, away from the bar. 'Hey,' he mumbled as his stool toppled over beneath his flailing legs with an impossibly loud clatter. 'Hey, what's going on?'

The world swooped around him in disorientating waves of black and colour, dark and light. Fruit machines jangled and chugged change. Amused faces swam in and out of the chloroform haze. Laughing. People were laughing.

Voices buzzed through his bunged up head: one female, another he recognised to be Jason's.

'He looks in a bad way.'

'He doesn't drink much.'

'Will he be okay?'

'He's not the first person to fall asleep on a bar. I've phoned him a taxi.'

'Aren't you going to go with him?'

'He's a big boy, he'll be fine.'

'But . . .'

'It's okay. Why don't you go and order us another round of drinks. I'm going to get him outside in the fresh air.'

The universe was on the move again, crowds of people shimmering past in a blur of excited motion as Ethan was pulled inexorably away.

'Come on,' Jason was saying. 'I'm not going to drag your ass all the way. Try and get those legs working.'

'What's going on?' The words were thick in Ethan's throat, sticking together in unnatural clumps that tasted like vomit. 'What happened?'

'You drank too damned much, that's what happened. You're in a right mess.'

'But what happened?'

'You crashed. Fell asleep on the bar. Come on, I'm getting you out.'

'Crashed?'

'Yes. Stand up, damn it.'

'I love her, you know?'

'I know.'

'I really, really love her.'

'If you say you love me I'm going to leave you here.'

'No, I think you're a bastard.'

'Yes, I know. Come on, try and stand up.'

The ground heaved underneath Ethan's wobbling legs as he tried to support his own madly fluctuating weight. His head had gained about three hundred pounds and kept dragging forwards onto his chest. His breathing was heavy, each expulsion of air churning the contents of his stomach.

'I think I'm going to . . .'

'Not here. Not on me. I'm on a promise and puke never impresses the ladies. Come on, this way. Outside.'

Suddenly brilliant cold enveloped Ethan, and that was all the invitation his lunch needed. He heard, rather than felt, the horrendous gush of vomit escape his throat and splutter across the pavement.

'Christ, that's it. You're on your own. I suggest you walk, try and sober up. You'll never get a taxi like that, anyway.'

Receding footsteps behind him.

'Jason?'

No answer.

'Jason?'

Ethan took a few staggering steps, eventually finding a wall to cling to. After a few moments he was able to focus on the shimmering halo of a nearby streetlight. There was the hushed whisper of passing cars. Bright headlights hacked through the sludgy darkness of the night, occasionally glaring in his face and shimmering the street into stark, white nightmares.

'Jason? When did it get so late? How long was I sleeping?'

No answer.

He took another faltering step, and the wall that had been his only support vanished from under his hand. Dustbins clattered as he sprawled across the wet pavement. A cat hissed and darted away from his clumsy intrusion.

'Jason?'

For a while he was unable to do anything except lie there on his back, upturned face spattered by the inconsistent flurries of rain that continued to spiral from the arching purple sky. Footsteps went by, accompanied by quiet voices.

'Look at that.'

'It's sad.'

'It's pathetic.'

Ethan smiled.

Sad, yes. Pathetic, yes. Stupid, definitely. So why couldn't he stop? Why couldn't he stop feeling this way? The tears streamed down his cheeks, mingling with the rain. Why was he feeling this way? Who was he crying for? Melissa? Karen?

'Damn it,' he whispered, forcing himself to stand. 'Look at yourself, Ethan. You're pathetic. You don't even know what you want.' He laughed, and the bitter sound contorted into a fitful cough. 'That isn't true. You know what you want. You want what you've always wanted. You want the things you can't have. You want her.'

Her?

Her?

Who the hell was he talking about? Who did he want? Did he know? Did he care? Did it matter? Did he just want somebody, anybody?

He pressed his back against the wall. The darkness crowded in.

'Now come on feet, walk me home.'

After a little persuasion his legs began to move in the direction he hoped would take him back to his flat. A walk of three miles.

One step at a time.

'That's good.'

One awkward, drunken step at a time.

Without warning, the night came alive around him, and something pounded into his stomach. He doubled up in pain, but there was no time to register what had happened before he was being slammed back against the wall. The numbing shock smashed the breath from his lungs. He caught movement in the corner of his tumbling vision, then something hard and flat was cracking across the left side of his face. It could have been a fist, it could have been anything. Under the circumstances, he didn't really care what it was, all he cared about was making sure it didn't hit him again.

He lifted his hands to fend off further blows but something hammered into his lower abdomen instead. His legs crumpled beneath him, and he dropped to the floor.

A shadow towered over him.

'You were seen today, Mr Hunter,' the shadow said. 'Let this be a warning. Next time, we make sure you never ride again. Understand?'

Ethan scrambled to his knees, trying to find something to focus on in his crazily spiralling world. All he could see was somebody's leg. Somebody's leg was all he needed to see.

He lunged forwards silently, pushed upwards, and threw himself with as much force as he could muster in the general direction of his assailant. His body thudded against somebody else's and everything collapsed in a jumble of limbs. His angry clutching fingers found the soft parts of a face and began to dig into the flesh.

Someone screamed.

Screaming was good. Screaming meant someone was hurt.

He bunched his hands, and began clubbing at his assailants head, feeling the warm wetness of blood on his knuckles, not certain whether that blood was his or not. 'Die,' he screamed. 'Die, you son of a bitch.'

Suddenly, terrifyingly suddenly, the world snapped into perfect focus, the darkness drawing back like a curtain to reveal the stage of this macabre contest in all its bloody glory.

He looked down at what he was pounding, looked at the face of a man who had already lost consciousness. Not the face of a man he recognised.

'What am I doing?' he whispered.

Then something thundered into his right temple, and the waves of darkness crashed back in.

Of course.

He slumped into the night, certain that never again would he see the daylight.

Of course.

There were two of them.

## CHAPTER 15

Ethan woke to the sound of raindrops drumming on a tiled roof, and quickly drew together enough strands of reality to determine he had been dumped on the doorstep of his home.

Over the next twenty-four hours he would frequently wonder why his assailants had done that, almost as often as he would wonder who they were, but the best reason he could ever think of was simply they hadn't wanted him to die on the street. They had wanted him to live, and to remember the warning he had been issued.

He could not help but be comforted to a certain degree by that thought. It meant these people didn't really want to kill him. Not if they could help it.

He sat up, then used the front door handle to pull himself to his feet. His head was throbbing, the world was floating in disorientating swells. His breathing came in rasps. Every movement fired fresh spikes of pain through his body. His clothes were drenched with rain and, to a lesser but far more frightening extent, blood.

He probed his chest awkwardly with frightened fingers. His lungs howled in protest.

'I think they broke my rib,' he laughed, fumbling his key into the lock. 'They broke my damned rib.'

He staggered down the wildly rocking corridor, bouncing off the walls, losing his footing once and falling against the stairs. Small thunderclaps of agony popped frenziedly around his tightening muscles. He gritted his teeth and refused to scream.

It took what seemed an eternity, an age of terrible nausea, before he finally pushed inside the door of his own flat and pulled the bolts behind him with shaking hands. He dropped to his knees, let pain and fire envelope him totally, hands splayed on the cold tiles, consciousness fluttering into shadowless tatters.

His eyes closed.

His eyes were heavy, they had to close. But if they closed he would sleep. If he slept he might never wake again.

'No,' he muttered, hauling himself to his feet and slamming through the door to the bathroom. 'Not yet.'

He fell asleep sitting on the toilet while he ran a bath, woke in a wreath of gagging steam, carefully removed his bloody, ripped clothing.

Resting on the edge of the bath, barely able to focus on the numbers of the keypad, he made a phone call.

By the time he clambered cautiously out of the bath, twenty minutes later, Anne, God bless her, was already pulling up outside in her battered four-by-four.

Ethan let her in gratefully. She told him he looked like shit. He didn't argue.

*

Pain had sobered Ethan, more quickly than the coffee Anne had made. By two-thirty in the morning, sat on the couch in the lounge, he was able to feel every irritating twinge of discomfort as she treated his wounds.

As she worked, from the light of a single lamp, efficiently putting right the hurt of an evening's abuse, he watched her seriously. There was a great deal of worry in her eyes, more worry than he had ever expected to see, even in the eyes of a friend.

'They didn't break any of your ribs,' she said. 'I think you'll live.'

'Anne?'

She scrabbled through Ethan's medicine bag, found a bottle of sterilising fluid.

'Anne?'

'What?' She didn't look up from dabbing disinfectant on his grazes.

'Anne, look at me.'

She bowed her head, concentrating on some minor abrasions on his hands. The knuckles were all split open, and, as Ethan watched them being treated, he became increasingly aware of an uncomfortable memory nesting at the back of his brain, a part of the evening he could not clearly recollect: a pulped human face crushed beneath his pounding fists. When he tried to focus on the memory, bring it into sharper focus, it dissolved like a shadow on the face of the moon. Perhaps he should have been grateful for that.

He reached out and touched Anne's cheek. She flinched away from his fingers, turning slightly so her face was no longer in the lamplight.

'Are you scared of me?' Ethan asked.

'A little,' Anne said.

'Why?'

'Look at you. You ring me at two in the morning and ask me to come over, and look at you. You look like death.'

'I don't feel too good either.'

'What happened?'

'I told you. Two guys took a dislike to me and they jumped me outside the bar, gave me something of a beating. Things like this happen all the time.'

Anne took his right hand and began to apply plasters. 'And what about this?' she asked.

'I tried to defend myself. Isn't that what anybody would have done?'

'This looks like you did more than defend yourself.'

Ethan snatched his hand back, snapping his teeth on a yelp of pain. 'Are you accusing me of something, Anne?'

'No.' He could see the tears simmer in her eyes. 'I'm scared, Ethan. Something happened to you tonight, something more than a random mugging, and you won't tell me what it is. You could have been killed.'

'They didn't want to kill me.'

'It doesn't look that way.'

'Anne, this is nothing to worry about.'

'Nothing to worry about?' She stood. 'How can you say that? They almost broke your ribs. What if they had done more? They could have punctured your lung or anything.' She threw her arms up uselessly, and Ethan saw the simple truth in that one motion. 'You could have died.'

'You're not scared of me, are you? You're scared for me.'

'Of course I'm scared for you, Ethan. You turn up at the office asking me to keep a look out for any suspicious account transactions, then our best horse turns up dead. One of the stable lasses leaves without even asking for her P45. Now this happens. Are you going to tell me that none of these events are related?'

Ethan grinned in the gloom. 'Would you believe me if I did?'

'How can you laugh about this? You could have died tonight. What would I have done if . . ?' She stopped suddenly. Ethan's eyes widened.

'What would you have done?' he said.

Anne screwed her hands into fists. 'Can you just forget I said that?' she asked.

'I'm not sure. Why don't you come and sit down?' He patted the couch.

'I'm just tired and afraid,' Anne said, sitting beside him.

'Is that all?'

'Yes.'

'Why did you come over tonight, Anne?'

'Because you asked me to.'

'But why did you come?'

'We're friends. You said you needed my help.'

'You live thirty minutes away. You got here in twenty.'

'You sounded bad.'

Ethan touched her hand. This time there was no flinching. 'Really?'

Her fingers entwined with his. She drew a deep, shuddering breath of resolution. 'There was something today, at work. Lesterton pulled a lot of funds in.'

'Where from?'

'Different accounts, some bloodstock. Nothing obvious, and no great sums, but lots of transactions between accounts. Looks like he was trying to scrape together as much money as he could without drawing any attention to it.'

'Anything like this ever happen before?'

'No.'

'So how much, all told?'

'Enough.'

'To do what?'

'Whatever you wanted to.'

'Like bribe a vet?'

'Perhaps.'

'And all the money ended up with Lesterton?'

'He made it difficult to track, but yes, Lesterton was definitely the only person who could actually get his hands on the cash.'

'Does it seem legitimate?'

'It's his money.'

'But he's definitely gone to certain lengths to conceal the withdrawals?'

'Definitely.'

Ethan leaned forwards on his knees, hands clasped together. 'Damn,' he said.

'Not the news you wanted to hear?'

'I don't know. Not the news I expected, at least.' He held Anne's hand again. 'Thanks for telling me. You're a star.'

'Do you think it will help?'

'We'll see.' He kissed her cheek. That close, he could smell her perfume, the soap she used. His !ips lingered on her smooth skin a fraction longer than he had really intended. When he finally pulled away she was watching him closely with eyes that glowed with the intensity of a stolen moment of opportunity. She had never looked more beautiful.

'Why don't we ever talk about it?' she said.

'What?'

'You know what.'

'You mean the Christmas party?'

'Yes.'

'I didn't think you wanted to discuss it. We'd both been drinking. As I recall, it wasn't particularly romantic.'

'Is that what you think?'

'In your office on the desk is hardly the stuff great love affairs come from.'

'Why not?'

'I was angry. You were angry.'

'So we were angry, so what? Does that negate any feelings we might have for each other?'

'Feelings?'

'What if anger was just the catalyst. What if we could have had something more?'

'I was alone, and your boyfriend had just cheated on you. We drank about a litre of vodka, and had a drunken fumble while nobody was paying attention.'

'It was more than that.'

'You were doing it to hurt someone, I was doing it to forget. There was no future in us, no commitment to be together, no need to talk about it again.'

'Do you really believe that?'

He fixed her with his stare. Her eyes were wide and open and gorgeous. He felt the chasm of emptiness open in his chest, threatening to swallow his heart. He didn't know whether he had any genuine feelings for this girl, he just knew she was right here, right now, and he didn't want to wake up alone.

He leaned closer.

'What are you saying, Anne?'

'I'm saying, maybe then the timing wasn't right. But now . . . Why can't things be different now?'

'Maybe this isn't such a good idea.'

'Are you really that ready to give up on us before we've even given it a chance?'

She moved forwards, pressed her lips against his. He allowed her to kiss him. He returned nothing. Eventually she pulled away, her hurt undisguised. Ethan's face was a white mask, devoid of expression, empty of emotion.

'Don't you want to try?' Anne asked.

'I can't make you any promises.'

'I'm not asking for any.'

The hard line of Ethan's mouth softened considerably. She was beautiful. She liked him. Could he be so certain she wasn't the one?

'I'd like us to try,' he said, cautiously.

One rogue tear mapped a delicate path down her cheek. 'Can I stay tonight?' she asked.

She was beautiful.

She liked him.

How could he be so certain she wasn't the one?

'Okay,' he said.

She moved closer, brushing against his left arm and firing sparks of pain into life. He winced, tried his best not to let it show.

'I guess sex is out of the question,' she said.

'I think so.'

She kissed his forehead. 'That's okay. I've waited this long, a few more days isn't going to hurt.'

## CHAPTER 16

Ethan sat on the edge of the bed, and choked back a handful of painkillers with swallows of cold water from a glass tumbler. It was still early, just gone six, and Anne was sleeping, her hair bunched attractively around her peaceful face. She had a smile like glass.

'Damn,' he whispered, as he listened to her breathing. The first narrow spikes of the intrusive morning sun were already beginning to illuminate that which pain and passion had previously sought to conceal. He licked his dry lips.

This morning she was as attractive as she had been last night, but this morning it wasn't enough.

'Damn.'

At least he hadn't had sex with her, maybe that would make things easier.

'Damn.'

She stirred, rolled over. He gazed at the smooth curve of her neck. She murmured something to her dream man, hugging a pillow to her chest. Maybe she wouldn't take it badly. Maybe she would feel the same way as he did in the cold light of day. Last night had been strange, full of emotions beyond their comprehension. People made errors of judgement in times of stress. She would understand that, surely? She had to understand that.

He stood, hobbled through to the kitchen. It was too hard to be in the same room as her, too hard to imagine the look on her face when he told her this had been a mistake. He didn't want to have to hurt her in that way. He wanted - needed - to love her. He needed to feel something more than he did. He just didn't know how.

Something inside of him was dead, and the type of love this girl had to offer wasn't going to revive it.

He wasn't necessarily looking to be hurt, but at least when love hurt he knew it was real.

Coffee steamed and hissed in the percolator, his angry ribs grumbled uncomfortably but less sharply than the previous evening. More daylight seeped into the world, bathing everything that had been dark blue in golden yellow. The chilly morning gradually began to thaw.

He sat at the kitchen table, and tried not to think about what it was he was going to do.

The clock ticked endlessly, tapping into his brain like a woodpecker into tree bark. Each second brought him closer to the moment he dreaded.

Every second brought him closer to . . .

A knock on his door.

The sound shocked him to his feet. He looked at the clock. Still only six-thirty. Too early for anything but trouble to come calling.

Another knock, timid, almost frightened. Not a knock on the front door of the building. A knock on the door of his flat.

His heart hammered against his ribcage agonisingly. His gaze swung across to the open bedroom door. 'Oh no,' he said. 'Don't let this be happening.'

He staggered back to the bedroom and looked in. Anne was still sleeping, thank God. But if he didn't answer the front door, she wouldn't be for long. If she woke up, and the person knocking was who he thought it was . . .

He quietly pulled the bedroom door closed, headed back into the bathroom. Checked himself in the mirror.

He was an explosion of cuts and bruises, far worse than when he had fallen on the gallops. There was nothing he could do to try and make himself look any better, he was just going to have to bite the bullet, answer the door.

Knocking. Louder this time.

He cringed and made his way to the door, undoing the bolts. He drew a deep breath, already knowing the worst had happened.

Karen was stood in the corridor, arms folded across her chest. She looked lost inside an oversized orange cardigan and faded jeans. Her eyes were red from crying, and they flared with alarm as they acknowledged Ethan's wounds. 'My God,' she said, almost stepping back. 'What happened?' The look on her face said more than words ever could.

'Little accident,' Ethan said quietly.

'Did somebody do this to you?'

'I was mugged.'

'That's terrible.'

'I'm getting used to taking a beating. It looks worse than it is.'

There was a moment of uncomfortable silence. Karen looked down at her feet, scuffing her shoes nervously. She looked like she was scrunching herself up from inside like a piece of paper with too many ink blots on it, desperate to talk, but too desperate to know what to say.

'Are you okay?' Ethan asked.

'Do you think I would be able to come in?'

He looked towards the bedroom. 'Well . . .'

'Are you not alone?'

'Well . . .'

'Oh.' Karen wiped the back of her hand across her nose, sniffing loudly. 'I'm sorry. I didn't mean to disturb you. I'll . . .' She pointed off down the corridor.

'Do you know what time it is?'

'Early?'

'It's not seven yet.'

'I wanted to . . .' She swallowed hard. 'I wanted to catch you before you went off to the stable.'

'What's happened?'

'I shouldn't have come here, I'm sorry.'

Ethan quickly glanced over his shoulder, then moved out into the corridor, pulling the door closed behind him. He rested a swollen, purple hand on Karen's trembling arm. 'Tell me what's happened. Is Jamie upstairs?'

She said nothing.

'Karen?'

'He's gone. We had an argument.' Her wide, brimming eyes looked up into Ethan's. 'He's left me.'

Ethan's expression remained unchanged. He tried the smoothest and most hollow lie he could manage, hoping the flutter of his heart would not betray him. 'I'm sorry.'

'I think he's gone for good this time.'

Ethan pulled Karen towards him, holding her close despite the protestations of his bruises. 'It'll be okay,' he whispered, kissing her hair.

For long moments, moments he hoped would never end, they stood that way, Karen sobbing quietly against his chest while he stroked her hair and said nothing. He felt only the slightest twinge of guilt that he should feel such joy over this girl's sorrow.

It had to end eventually. It was Karen that ended it.

She pulled away, looking him in the face. 'I'm sorry,' she said. 'I shouldn't have dumped this on you, not like this, not after what's just happened to you.'

'I'm glad you did.'

She wiped her face with her cardigan sleeve. 'I'm so selfish. Look at you, all beaten up, and all I have to worry about is my boyfriend.'

'Fiancé,' Ethan corrected.

'He's neither now.' A fragile smile played uncertainly around her mouth.

'We should talk.'

'Where?'

'Considering the situation, I would suggest your flat.'

Karen nodded and headed up the stairs, Ethan following carefully. 'So who is she?' she asked, as they moved into her flat, and sat in the lounge.

'Who?'

'Your visitor?'

'Does it matter?'

'No.' The response was a little too quick, a little too harsh.

'Then why ask?'

'Just wondered whether it was anyone I knew.'

'It's not. It's just a girl. But we didn't come up here to talk about me, did we?'

Karen nodded sadly, somewhat reluctantly. She had not applied any makeup, she looked like she hadn't slept. Had she perhaps known about Ethan's visitor? Had that been the cause of her argument with Jamie? Had she turned up at Ethan's flat because she wanted to interrupt what might be happening?

He thrust the questions to the back of his mind, unwilling to let himself get carried away on the dark wings of wild fantasies. Now was no time to go losing his head.

'He said he never wants to see me again,' she said.

'Why?'

'It was a bad argument.' She curled her legs up beneath her on

154

the couch. 'We've never argued that way before.'

'How bad was it?'

'Terrible.'

'Maybe it's not as terrible as you think it is.'

A lonely sigh, like the dying breath of summer, shuddered through her body. 'It is.'

Ethan stood. 'Right,' he said, as authoritatively as possible. 'I'm going to make you a cup of tea and you are going to tell me what all this is about.'

'It's not what you think,' Karen said.

'And what do I think?'

'It's not about the horse.'

'Emphatic? Why would I think this was about her?'

'You believe Jamie had something to do with it, don't you?'

Ethan stopped in the kitchen doorway. 'What makes you say that?' His tone was guarded. He forced himself to remember that, despite his feelings, he didn't know this girl, and she could be setting him up for another fall. If he told her what he thought . . . if he turned out to be right about Jamie . . . if she was involved in some way - God forbid, but if she was - maybe next time he wouldn't wake up from the beating. Maybe he wouldn't get the opportunity to fight back.

'I can tell you think Jamie's involved,' she said.

'The horse died of natural causes.'

'Play by the rules, Ethan. No lying, no passing, no phone a friend. Remember?'

'That was just a game, Karen.'

'Just a game?'

'This is serious.' He folded his arms defensively. She was asking awkward questions, second-guessing his actions. Even if she wasn't involved, if she could see through him, could somebody else? Somebody who might want to send him a little warning? He cleared his throat, tried to keep his cool. 'And the truth is we aren't

155

even certain what happened to the horse.'

'Yes you are.'

'You're making assumptions.'

'And you're still not as mysterious as you think you are.'

Ethan sat, the tea forgotten. 'I don't know what happened to Emphatic, and I don't suspect Jamie of anything. I certainly didn't think you showing up at my place this morning had anything to do with what happened at the stables or . . . Or . . .'

'Or what happened to you last night?'

'I wasn't going to say that.'

'You didn't need to.'

'Okay, so tell me, what was your argument about?'

'It was . . . He was all full of himself after winning at Newbury, brash and loud and . . . we didn't agree on one of his new business ventures. He doesn't like being disagreed with. Something of nothing really.'

'And yet your relationship is over because of it?'

She nodded. She could hardly believe it herself. 'I think so.'

'There must be more to it than that.'

'There isn't.'

'What was the business venture?'

'Nothing really. He'd come up with an idea to make some extra money.'

'How?'

'It isn't important.'

'Why don't you let me decide?'

'He's gone, that's all that matters. He left.'

'Is this to do with Lesterton?'

'No.' That same pained snap; a snarled answer almost before he had finished the question, as telling as the black glimmer in her eyes.

'Why are you protecting him?'

'I'm not.'

'I asked you, yesterday at the café, what he spoke to Lesterton about. You said you didn't know. Did you try to find out last night?'

'No.'

'Did you find out what he was doing?'

'No.'

'I think you're lying. I think, after we spoke, you came back here and asked him what he had talked to Lesterton about, and he told you. You didn't like what you heard, because whatever it is . . .' he gestured the rest of the sentence away. 'You told him to stop. You fought. He walked out on you. That's what I think.'

Karen drew her legs up to her chin, hugging her knees protectively. 'You think too much.'

'It's one of my more endearing qualities.'

'I can't tell you anything.'

'Try.'

'What do you want from me?'

'The truth.'

'And you think I know what the truth is?' The words were sneered venomously. 'I only know what he tells me, and he only tells me what he wants me to know. You're right, I asked him what his business deal with Lesterton was. He wouldn't tell me. He said the whole thing had fallen through but that was okay because another opportunity, a better opportunity, had arisen. He said winning at Newbury was going to put more money on the table than either of us could possibly imagine. He told me . . .' Her hands rung together, her face contorted with sadness. Ethan waited patiently. 'The horse didn't die of natural causes, did it?'

'I'm sorry?'

'It's okay, I know. Jamie knows too.'

'What are you saying?'

'I think Mr Lesterton has more to do with this than you might think.'

'What makes you so sure?'

'Talk to him yourself.'

'What would he tell me if I did?'

'He has a stable to protect, a business that dead horses can hurt. The truth is a high-value commodity, and keeping it buried can be just as costly as exhuming it.'

Ethan nodded, checked his watch. 'Okay,' he said. 'I think I'm beginning to understand. I'll talk to Lesterton.'

He stood.

Karen watched him. 'You're leaving?' she asked.

'I have to go and . . .' He pointed at the floor, to the flat below their feet. 'You know?'

'Is she someone special?'

'No.'

'One night stand?'

Ethan's insides contracted into a hard fist of granite, his heart pounded loud enough for the whole world to hear. 'I didn't sleep with her,' he said.

Karen smiled without softening the hard glister of her stare. There was something like victory in her tone when she spoke. 'Could we spend some time together today?'

'I'd like that.'

Ethan walked to the door, already trying to formulate the sentences he would need to break Anne's heart. His heavy footsteps caused the universe to tremble around him.

'Ethan?'

He looked back. Karen was still sat on the couch, legs pulled up into her cardigan, arms wrapped around her shins. 'Yes?'

'There's something else.'

'What?'

'Something else we argued about last night, besides his work.'

Ethan waited.

She strangled the words into submission. 'We argued about

158

you. You and I were seen at the café and he drew some conclusions. The wrong conclusions. The obvious ones.' She looked down at her fingernails.

'I see.'

'I think, perhaps, although I don't know for certain, you weren't mugged last night.'

Ethan laughed coldly. 'I know I wasn't,' he said.

By the time he returned to his own flat, it was empty. A pot of coffee had been prepared and then left. The bed was made.

There was a note on the kitchen table, written in Anne's smooth, looping script. It said, quite simply, *I understand.*

'So do I,' Ethan whispered. 'So do I.'

CHAPTER 17

For the next hour, Ethan worked quietly at the kitchen table, a mug of coffee close to hand.

In no real order, and with little to separate fact from fiction or proof from theory, he wrote down names, places, and times that had been called into question during his preliminary investigations. Sometimes he would cross items out, sometimes he would link two different items together with an arrow. Sometimes he would stop and suck the end of his pen. Sometimes he would scratch a question mark before or after a sentence, but always, always, the same name kept appearing. Jamie Redthorn.

Ethan's hero. The man Ethan had admired, had striven to be like. The man Ethan had wanted to be.

The pen danced across the notepad, leaving a spidery trail of possibilities in its wake.

Jamie Redthorn. Ethan's hero.

It wasn't just Jamie though. There were other names.

Charles Lesterton. Ethan's mentor.

O'Hara. Ethan's friend.

Anne.

Karen.

Maybe Karen.

He threw the pen down, ran shaking fingers through his hair. Damn it, he knew full well what he thought had happened, he just couldn't bring himself to write it down. If he wrote it down, that made it real. It made it possible.

He drained the last of his coffee. Stood.

He needed to speak to Anne.

*

Anne buzzed Ethan into the office wordlessly. She waited for him to close the door and sit at the desk opposite.

Her hair was pulled back aggressively, her glasses resting far forwards on the delicate line of her nose. She looked every inch as beautiful as Ethan knew she was. She kept her attention fixed on the pale glow of her computer screen, and didn't turn her head when she spoke.

'Business as normal, is it?'

'Anne . . .' He paused, running out of words a lot sooner than he had intended. This was as far as he had ever got in his head, when he had been deciding what to say. 'Last night was . . .'

'Don't bother, Ethan.'

'Anne, if I've hurt you, I didn't mean to. Last night I really thought . . .'

'You were vulnerable, I shouldn't have tried to take advantage of the situation the way I did.'

'But . . . I just need to say . . . I really like you, Anne. I like you a lot. I never would have slept with you if I didn't. But . . . It wouldn't be fair for us to . . .'

'If you say 'it isn't you, it's me', there will be bloodshed.

161

Understand?'

'I need you to . . .'

'Ethan, you clearly didn't come here to speak about us, otherwise you might have bothered to prepare a speech of some kind. Let's not kid ourselves.' Her narrow fingers danced across the keyboard of her computer. 'Are you going to tell me why you're really here?'

'I need you to know I'm sorry.'

The fingers stopped moving. For almost two heartbeats the office was in perfect silence. 'I'm sorry too,' she said, and the fingers blurred back into motion, filling the room with the click-click-click of accountancy.

'You're . . .'

'Enough, Ethan. You're sorry, I'm sorry, we're both sorry. This whole situation is sorry, so let's forget it ever happen and just carry on like before.' The clicking of the keyboard grew faster. 'How can I help you?'

'I needed to talk to you about Emphatic.'

'Then talk.'

'And I need you to listen to me carefully.'

'Why?'

'Because if something happens to me, I'm relying on you to blow this whole thing open.'

'If something happens?'

'You know as well as I do, I wasn't mugged last night. I was being sent a warning.'

For the first time, Anne's eyes flickered to focus on him. She did her best to mask the concern in her voice. 'Maybe you should listen to that warning.'

'You know me better than that.'

'Do you want to get yourself killed?' Her gaze switched back to the monitor, her fingers once again stabbing at the keyboard, bleeding letters across the screen.

162

'I think I know what happened.'

'You only think?'

'I can't prove anything yet. But I will. That's what I'm going to do today.'

'You make it sound very easy.'

Ethan leaned across the desk and placed a hand on Anne's wrist. To his surprise, she did not shy away from his touch. 'It isn't going to be easy, and I could be putting myself in danger. That's why I need to be sure that if I go missing today, you'll make sure something is done.'

She sat back in her chair. Her cold eyes admirably concealed her deeper concern. Anybody who didn't know better would have assumed she had no feelings for Ethan at all. 'You're really going to carry on this cops and robbers nonsense, aren't you?'

'Yes.'

'At the expense of everything else?'

'Yes.'

'Why?'

'Because I have to.'

'So tell me, then,' she said, clasping her hands together in her lap. 'What happened?'

'It's simple really, I don't know how I didn't notice it before.' He stopped, mentally backtracked. 'That's not true. I didn't notice it because I didn't want to. Karen was the key. She used me to get close to the horses.'

'Karen? The girl who moved in upstairs from you?'

'Yes.'

'How disappointing for you.'

'I think, once she realised who I was, she worked something out with her boyfriend, Jamie Redthorn. A way to make some money by using my connections.'

'This sounds a little bit like paranoia.'

'Think about it. Karen turns up at the stables, interested and

163

innocent. She likes horses, just has to come to the stables and see them. She walks around, unsupervised, until I point out the best horse in the stable and tell her when it's running.' He laughed bitterly. 'Suddenly, without warning, Jamie turns up with a 'business' venture for Lesterton. That's some coincidence as far as I'm concerned.'

'But that might be all it is. Coincidence.'

'You weren't there, you didn't see it. Karen ran off and threw her arms around Jamie's neck and -' God damn it if he couldn't almost see it happening '- she whispers in his ear. 'Emphatic, tomorrow.' I tell you, she was the point man. She had the whole thing wrapped up right under my nose.'

'Sounds like you seriously misjudged this girl.'

Ethan's head sank. 'I don't know how I let it happen.'

'I do.'

'She was so genuine. Fun, intelligent, interested in me.'

'Or interested in the stable?'

'Maybe.'

'Is that what you really think?'

'Honestly, I couldn't say. My mind is telling me there isn't any other possible explanation. She had to be responsible. I just can't . . .' He trawled through the last two days in his mind, desperately trying to remember something, something Karen had said or done, that might help this all make sense. Something that would put her above suspicion, where she should clearly be. 'I can't let myself believe it. She isn't like that. I know her. We've eaten together, got drunk together, we even . . .'

'You haven't finished your theory,' Anne interrupted.

He swallowed dryly. 'I don't know, maybe I'm wrong. She never would have had the opportunity to speak to Sally, not unless . . . Not unless she did it while I was introducing Jamie to Lesterton.'

'What's Sally got to do with any of this?'

Ethan looked over his shoulder towards the office door. It was shut, locked. The only way to get in was to enter the code into the electronic keypad from the outside or be buzzed in by someone already inside. Nobody could sneak up on him here. Not like last night.

'Ethan?'

'Do you ever get that feeling somebody's standing behind you, but when you look there's nobody there but you?'

'Sometimes.'

'I'm getting that a lot recently.'

'Ethan, what's this got to do with Sally?'

'Sally gave Emphatic an injection.'

'She what?'

'She wouldn't tell me where she got it from, but somebody paid her a large amount of money to make sure Emphatic was a little feistier than normal.'

'Why would she do that?'

'Her father is in hospital. She was trying to subsidise her income.'

'Is that why she left?'

'She was in danger here.'

'Your friends from the bar?'

Ethan gently probed the soft, fleshy bruise over his right eye with questing fingers. 'Perhaps. I don't know.'

'She was your only witness. With her you might have had a leg to stand on if this went to court.'

'I had to let her go. She was too scared. If something had happened to her . . . I couldn't be responsible for that. Not for someone else.'

'But this doesn't make any sense. Why would somebody pay Sally to make sure the horse was more charged up? If anything, surely they would want the horse sedated?'

'Not if they were planning on the horse being found out.'

165

'What do you mean?'

'Jamie would have known Emphatic would be spotted by the stewards. Anybody with half an eye could have told she was on something. That was the point. Jamie was racing at Newbury in the same race. By doping the horse he was forcing it out of the competition so that he would be able to get a better price on his own ride before the dust settled.'

'But he got the dose wrong?'

'I don't think he ever knew what the right dose was. I think there was a fourth person involved.'

'Who?'

Ethan looked over his shoulder again, almost as though he expected to see the shadow of his unseen adversary looming over him. 'Lesterton,' he said.

CHAPTER 18

Ethan knew he was playing a dangerous game, but the simple truth was, he didn't want to stop. If he stopped, he started thinking about the possibility he had been betrayed.

Melissa, Karen, Jamie, Lesterton. All people who had claimed, or had been believed, to be something they might not be. All people who might have played Ethan for everything they could get.

If he stopped, if he decided things had got too hot, then all he would be left with was the hurt, and the uncertainty. He didn't want the hurt, he didn't want to live the rest of his life not knowing if he had been used in some obscene chess game.

And it wasn't worth denying it; in some strange kind of way, he was having fun.

The smile on Ethan's face, when Lesterton ushered him into the study, was totally genuine.

'Ethan, what happened to you?'

Ethan took a seat without waiting to be offered, and waited for

Lesterton to sit next to him. 'I was mugged,' he said. 'I got jumped outside a bar.'

'You look terrible.'

'I get that a lot.'

'Have you seen a doctor?'

'No, but I have taken a lot of painkillers. What's the news with Emphatic?'

'Not in the mood for small talk today, then?'

Ethan tapped his watch theatrically. 'Pressing engagement at one. Can't miss it.'

'A girl?'

'Is there anything else?'

Lesterton's eyes twinkled playfully. There was smug superiority in that look, the misguided belief he was winning. 'Nothing quite so important.'

'So what did O'Hara's vet say?'

'What we already knew. Emphatic's heart gave out.'

'Why?'

Lesterton sniffed, as if something rancid had just passed under his nose. 'Traces of Ephedrine was found in her blood stream.'

'What's Ephedrine?'

'Like Amphetamine. Designed to increase the speed of the metabolism and reduce appetite. Emphatic was on one serious high when she went.'

'Any idea how she was got at?'

'There was a puncture mark in her jugular vein.'

'Jesus Christ.' Ethan put his hands to his forehead. 'Whoever did this, what the hell were they thinking? Were they trying to kill her?'

'The vet said the level of Ephedrine detected would have been considered a safe dosage for most horses. He said Emphatic would have been one in a hundred, an extreme minority. He said this was a very unfortunate and rare situation.'

Ethan shook his head in disbelief. 'How did this happen? How did we get into this situation?'

'I don't know.'

He sat back, gaze shifting along the rows of silver trophies and plaques on the shelves. 'How did the vet manage to get back to us so quickly?'

Silence. Ethan laced his fingers together. One question too far, perhaps. One step over a line that was already close to being invisible. Lesterton cleared his throat, and steepled his hands in front of his face.

'He was paid a substantial amount of money to fast-track the whole process. Why does it matter?'

'I'm curious. I thought it would have taken a few days to hear back from the autopsy.'

Lesterton shifted his weight uncomfortably. 'Well, there wasn't an autopsy, as such.'

'I'm sorry?'

'Sooner or later somebody else may need to look at the horse. Would look very bad if she was all cut up, wouldn't it? Bad for all of us.'

'Darabont hadn't insured the animal.'

'That doesn't mean he isn't going to want an independent body to come in and take a look.'

'So what, exactly, did this vet do?'

'Took some blood, drank a lot of weak sugary tea, and then got paid enough money to forgot he was ever here.'

'So there could be more to this? He could have missed something?'

'Perhaps, but at least we know more than we did before, and I wanted you to be working with all of the facts as soon as possible.'

Ethan tapped his foot against the side of the desk distractedly. 'I'm not getting very far.'

'Have you located Sally?'

Ethan's head jerked up. For a moment his expression betrayed him. 'Sally?' he asked, trying his best to keep the tremble he felt in his legs out of his voice.

'You went looking for her yesterday.'

'Yes, that's right. I didn't find her. I don't know if she was involved in this or not.'

'It seems very probable.'

'But I have no proof of that. I assume no needle was found in or around Emphatic's box?'

'No.'

'I'm afraid I'm not much of a detective.'

'You're a jockey. Stick to what you know.' Lesterton got to his feet and patted Ethan's shoulder. 'Lord Darabont has already been on the phone requesting that I look into purchasing him a new horse or two. Some real talent.'

'What are you saying?'

'Sally has vanished, one horse is dead. I would say that is all the evidence we need. There will not be another case of doping here now she's gone.'

'And Emphatic?'

'Any vet who examines her will find traces of Ephedrine, but not enough to point to that as the cause of death. Lord Darabont will remain a loyal customer and bring us some new horses. I would say there is little else to say on the matter.'

'So we're going to cover this whole mess up?'

'What good would it do to let the whole world know?'

'But I thought . . .'

'You think too much, Ethan.'

'A crime has been committed.'

'By Sally.'

'No, not by Sally.' Ethan jumped to his feet. 'This can't all be pinned on one girl. We have to take some responsibility for what's happened.'

'This little adventure is over. Go home to your girlfriend and learn how to have fun.'

'But . . .'

'Let this one go, Ethan.'

'And Sally?'

'Let her go too.'

'Don't you want me to locate her?'

Lesterton smiled, an action that seemed to draw the light from the room, and form cold shadows at Ethan's back. 'I don't think Sally will be causing us any more problems,' he said.

## CHAPTER 19

After the storms of the previous day, the sun had decided to resurface. By the time Karen and Ethan made their way down to the riverbank with a basket of sandwiches, a bottle of wine, and a blanket, most of the earth's damp had been burned away in wisps of steam like lost souls.

This particular location, a few miles from the flats, was a favourite of Ethan's. He had sometimes brought girlfriends here in the hope that wild flowers, and trees whispering of the things only they had lived to see, would spark an emotional chord that would, ultimately, result in him having sex by the end of the day. On the whole, it generally worked, but he hadn't been here for a while. Not for over a year.

This was where he had proposed to Melissa.

This time his visit wasn't about sex, or love. This was about evidence. This was about finding some means of proving Jamie was responsible for the atrocities of the last two days. If Ethan had to use Karen to do that, if she had to go down with the whole stinking bunch of dishonest bastards, then so be it.

He wasn't going to let Lesterton cover this up. He was through with being played.

The river was swollen, and the water babbled hurriedly over the remnants of a half-dam the children of the village had been working on over the course of the summer. The chatter and splash was, for a long time, the only sound.

'Are you okay?' Karen asked, eventually.

'Still a little sore,' Ethan said, being purposefully obtuse.

'That's not what I meant.'

Ethan topped up Karen's wine glass, making certain she drank a lot more than he did. 'What do you mean?'

'You seem distant. Have I done something?'

'I don't know, have you?' He immediately checked himself, forced a grin that indicated his question was only a joke. It was all so much harder than he had thought. Just being in Karen's presence was devastating. He loved her, he was certain he loved her, and to know he did . . . He took a bite out of a cucumber sandwich and packed his anger down tight in his stomach. This was no time for feelings of hurt. He had to be in control.

'Is this about this morning? The girl you were with?'

'No.'

'Then what is it?'

He sipped his wine, looked out across the rippling waters of the river. 'I think I like you more than I should,' he said, without really intending to.

'Is that bad?'

'I think so.'

'You don't want to like me?'

'I've been alone for a long time now.'

'I don't understand.'

'Eventually people get used to what they know, they come to appreciate the hurt. It's part of their life. It's part of mine.'

173

'Ethan?'

'When a man has no-one to break his heart for him, he ends up breaking his own.'

'Are you going to talk in riddles all day?'

'People form routines, that's how they live. You change the routine, you change the very fabric of their lives.' He sighed. This wasn't what he had come here to say. He had come here in order to determine what Karen's argument with Jamie had been about. He had come here to trap her, to find out the truth behind all the pretty lies. But the closeness of her body, the false innocence in those eyes, changed everything. Changed him.

But those things he could never hope to put into words. He didn't even try.

'You upset the balance,' he said.

'Balance?'

'I don't need you to break my heart too.'

'What makes you think I will?'

'You already have.'

She looked almost pained, as though this was some terrible accusation, far worse than being accused of conspiring to dope a racehorse. 'I never meant to,' she said, and Ethan could almost convince himself it was the truth.

'I've fallen in love with you,' he said.

Only the river, chuckling over smooth, round rocks, dared to respond.

'You do know that, don't you?' he pressed.

'I . . .' Karen looked down at her hands. 'I didn't . . .'

'I don't suppose that was ever supposed to happen, was it?'

'You . . .'

'Lust is easy to control, it's very simple, and that was what you were looking for, wasn't it? Staying in my bed the first day we met, but not sleeping with me.' He sneered at himself, at his own foolishness. 'You could see it in my eyes the moment we met. You knew I recognised in you something I'd lost.'

'What are you saying?'

'Has Jamie rang you yet?'

'I . . .'

'Or did you ring him?'

'We . . .'

Ethan clenched his hands into fists, anger seething behind every word. This was dangerous, silly dangerous. If Karen realised he knew the game, he was as good as dead. 'Is that the twist, Karen? He waits for your signal?'

'Ethan . . .'

His gaze scanned the tree line. There could be any number of people hiding out there. Maybe one of them would have a gun. And so what if they did? Would it matter? Would it really be any great loss to the world if he was to be executed right here, right now? He had already been murdered once before on this very spot, when Melissa had said 'yes'. So what if, now, somebody did to his body what that woman had already done to the rest of him?

'I just need to know why,' he said, straining to stop his voice from cracking. 'Why did you have to involve me?'

For several minutes Karen made no effort to answer. Her wide eyes filled with tears, blinked clear, filled again. The wind in the leaves rattled. The rushing river bubbled ever on, too busy to stop and wonder at Ethan's distress.

'I'm sorry,' Karen said. 'You weren't supposed to fall in love with me, you were just supposed to . . .' She gestured hopelessly. 'You were meant to make Jamie love me more. I do like you, that's why I wanted to be around you. I loved that you wanted me, I loved the way you made me feel better about myself, but I don't . . . I couldn't . . .' She choked back a sob. 'I love Jamie, and I wanted him to love me back.'

Ethan wiped the back of his hand across his mouth, licked his lips. 'That's it? This was all about making Jamie commit?'

Karen nodded.

'That's all? You do this . . . Jesus, you did all this, just to make Jamie care?'

'I didn't know what else to do.'

'Don't you get it?'

'Get what?'

'Jamie doesn't care about you any more than he cares about me. He uses people, that's what he does. He used you and you didn't even realise it. He couldn't possibly love you. The only person he loves is himself.'

'You don't know that.'

'Then where is he?'

'He . . .'

'What was your argument about?'

'I told you.'

'Well, tell me again.'

'No.' Karen tried to stand, but Ethan grabbed her wrist, holding it more tightly than was absolutely necessary.

'Tell me.'

'Let go of me.'

'Or what?'

'I'll scream.'

'Go ahead, who's going to hear?' Ethan looked off towards the crowding trees beyond the expanse of the river. 'Or is there some-one out there? Maybe Jamie's out there. Why don't we invite him over to join the party?'

'Stop this.'

'Hey, Jamie, come over here. Come on. You're more than welcome.'

'What's got into you, Ethan?

Ethan let go of Karen's wrist, and hauled himself up with the use of a nearby tree. 'You have. You've got in here.' He jabbed his forehead with two fingers. 'And I can't get you out. I need to get you out.'

Karen scrambled to her feet, beyond Ethan's reach. 'You're mad.'

'You did this, Karen. You made me into this, playing your little games. Didn't you even think of my feelings for one moment? Did I matter so little to you?'

'You weren't supposed to care,' Karen screamed. 'Why should you care when my own fiancé doesn't?'

'But I do.'

'Why? How can you possibly love me? Look what I've done to you. If you want to know what we argued about, I'll tell you. We argued because he paid someone to beat you up last night.'

Ethan's breathing was ragged, his entire soul laid bare. 'And why would he do that?'

'I don't know.'

'I don't believe you.'

'I don't.'

'Be honest, Karen. You haven't been honest with me since the day we met. Try it now, just once. See how it fits.'

Karen ran a shaking hand over her eyes. 'I . . . He saw us together and drew some conclusions he shouldn't have.'

'There must be more to it than that.'

'He got suspicious and went through my things while I was out. He found a journal, something I'd written.'

'What did it say?'

'Are you going to make me spell this out?'

'I think you should.'

'It was something I'd written about you.'

Ethan's stomach knotted into steel bunches. 'What had you written?'

'I'd written that while I was having sex with him, I was thinking about you.'

Ethan swallowed, his throat working rapidly. Air was getting

177

thinner, his breath shallower. There wasn't enough oxygen in the world. For terrible seconds he was floating, suspended from his hunched shoulders like a coat on a hanger. 'Why would you write that?'

'I don't know.'

'Why would you write that if you don't feel the way about me I feel about you?'

'I don't know.'

'Why won't you be honest with yourself? There's something between us, you know there is. Why are you trying to kill that? Why can't you just . . . let it happen?'

'You said it yourself. Eventually people get used to what they know, they come to appreciate the hurt. It's part of their life. It's part of mine.'

'But . . .'

'You don't know me, Ethan. You may think you love me, but that would change soon enough. Jamie knows me, knows me better than anyone. There aren't any skeletons he doesn't know about, but he still stands by me. I can't surprise him. We don't have a perfect relationship, but we can't hurt each other any more than we already have.'

'Listen to yourself. This is crazy.'

'You get so far down the road and it's easier to keep going rather than turn back. I can't go through all the pain again.'

'So that's it? You'll stay with this man and be miserable?'

'Yes.'

'News flash, Karen. He left you.'

'He's left me before. He'll get over it, he always does.'

'You can't be serious.'

'I am. Deadly.'

Ethan faltered, unable to find any argument in the face of such a stubborn and ignorant resolve.

Karen's mobile phone started ringing, shattering the silence.

'That's him,' she said.

'What are you going to do?'

She took the phone out of her pocket. Looked at it. 'The same thing I always do.'

Ethan turned away.

She answered the phone.

\*

After Karen had gone, Ethan remained in the clearing, watching the course of the river, and waiting for a long-expected lightning bolt to blast him off the face of the planet.

It didn't make any sense. Why would this girl insist on staying with someone who made her unhappy? How could she use someone else's emotions so callously in order to further her own doomed relationship? How could she stay with someone who had paid to have someone else beaten up?

He drank the rest of the wine straight from the neck of the bottle, and watched the clouds travel across a reddening sky.

When had it all gone so terribly wrong? He was supposed to be in control of this situation. He was supposed to be finding proof of a crime that looked all too likely to be swept under the carpet. He laughed to himself. How could he have been so wrong about so many people? How could he have let himself be put in the middle of this bloody mess?

He threw the wine bottle into the river, heard the flat splash. 'Should have put a message in it,' he whispered, closing his eyes, and leaning back against a tree.

Who would help him now? Who could he trust? He had trusted Anne, but he had ruined that alliance. He had trusted Karen, but she had . . . She had . . . What? His eyes snapped open. What had Karen done?

Karen had used him to make Jamie care more. She had

179

purposefully got herself close, even turning up at the stables. Turning up at the stables to be close to him, not to spy on horses. Never to spy on horses. She had argued with Jamie, not because she had discovered some plot, but simply because Jamie believed she was having an affair.

Perhaps Karen wasn't involved, and if she wasn't, could he really believe Jamie was? That he would be able to keep it a secret from her?

'No,' he hissed. 'No, I can't believe that. There is no-one else. No-one.' Except Lesterton, of course. Lesterton, who would be able to convince Sally that what she was doing was for the good of the horse. Lesterton, who had enough money readily available to be able to cover up his tracks quite neatly. Lesterton, who could get the only person who might question what had happened out of the way by letting him play detective.

Ethan's chin dropped to his chest. God damn it, what was he to believe? Who was he supposed to be chasing?

Was he supposed to be chasing anyone at all?

His breathing slowed, arms felt like lead. If he wasn't so damned tired, maybe he could think more clearly, maybe he could figure out . . .

Figure out . . .

Who . . .

Was . . .

He woke suddenly. His mobile phone was trilling angrily, demanding his attention as it vibrated in his trouser pocket. The world was in darkness, night wrapping everything but the river and the phone in a cloak of lonely silence.

Darkling shadows moved between the trees, where nocturnal creatures sniffed in the undergrowth for scraps.

Ethan answered the phone.

'Yes?'

'Ethan, I need your help.' Jason's voice, but not his carefree tone. The usual brightness had been replaced by something like fear. 'Can you come over here?'

Ethan sat forward, wiped his eyes groggily. 'Where are you?'

'At the flat.'

'What flat?'

'My flat. I need you to come over.'

'What time is it?'

'A little after eleven. Please, you have to come over.'

'What's wrong?'

'I'll tell you when you get here.'

'Why can't you tell me now?'

'Hurry.'

The phone went dead in Ethan's hand. He looked at it dumbly. Eventually, he got to his feet.

It was going to be an incredibly long night.

## CHAPTER 20

Jason lived in a small flat on the outskirts of Bath. It was a nice place, large enough for his needs but not too large to cause him unnecessary concerns when it came to things like housework. He had decorated in shades of purple, and accessorised with futuristic stereo-television home entertainment equipment and black and white prints of Gulf war correspondence photography by an award-winning daredevil who had spent the war dodging bullets and putting his head where wiser men wouldn't even put their beer. The photographs were relatively small, and scattered across the wall like a shotgun blast. They gave the impression somebody had peeled away the purple paint to reveal layers of death beneath.

The lounge was largely devoid of furnishings, with only two leather couches consuming a giant-sized bite of the available space, but the interior design was impeccable, suggesting the presence of a young jet-setter with a wallet full of platinum to keep him in essential labels.

The bedroom, also fitted out with only the barest but most

expensive essentials, contained a king-sized bed that looked very impressive and very used. One would think, for a lowly student, Jason lived somewhat beyond his means.

Of course, anybody who knew Jason well enough, knew he was a student by day, but a creature of an entirely different breed by night.

Ethan had known about Jason's sideline business since virtually the first day he had met him, and, while he had never condoned what Jason did, he had not considered it reason enough to disassociate himself from the man completely. It was a decision that, good or bad, largely bad, he had lived with. Tonight, when Jason opened the door, Ethan doubted that decision for the first time.

'What happened?' he asked, stepping inside and quickly pulling the door closed behind him.

Jason was dressed in clothes that had once been fit for a night out at a bar, but were now largely destroyed through a variety of sticky-looking stains and unsightly gashes. His hair was flecked with blood and mud, as though he had been dragged through a hedge that had taken something of a dislike to him. His eyes, usually uncomplicated, were wide and terrible.

He formed words soundlessly with pale lips somebody had obviously mashed up with a fistful of rings.

'What's wrong?' Ethan said, putting a hand on Jason's shoulder.

Jason pulled away from Ethan's hand. He appeared to lose his balance, half-slumped against the very expensive, very purple, wall. A grimace that had nothing to do with physical pain twisted the corner of his mouth. 'Don't touch me,' he said.

'Jason?'

Jason walked through into the kitchen, arms wrapped around his head, fingers laced behind his neck. 'It's bad,' he said. 'Really bad. You said they'd catch up with me and they have.'

'Who? What?'

Jason leaned against the kitchen sink. There was blood on the chrome-finished taps, more on the tiles and on a towel thrown over the cooker hob.

'Are you okay?' Ethan asked.

'Just bruised. Took a couple of hits in the chest and around my back. It's nothing.'

'What the hell happened?'

Jason swallowed, clutching at the kitchen counter until his knuckles bleached against the black marble-effect surface. His shoulders trembled.

'Jason?'

'It was an accident.'

'What?'

'It wasn't supposed to be this way. Christ, I'm not big time. I've never been big time. I just do what I can, when I can.' He paused, closed his eyes. The kitchen clock kept the rhythm of Ethan's heart like a time bomb, marking the passing of each hollow second. Tick-tick-tick.

Tick.

'Jason?'

Tick.

'Talk to me.'

Tick.

'Shit.' Jason turned and threw the full weight of his large right hand against the clock. Fragments of spring and glass ricocheted around the kitchen. Wire and cogs threw fragmented shadows across the cabinets. 'Shit.'

Ethan moved back into the doorway, watching in quiet horror as Jason pounded the remains of the clock into sparkles of glass sand. The ticking stopped. The only sound was Jason's heavy breathing as he slid down the wall and drew his legs up into his chest. His bleeding hands covered his face. His voice was shattered.

184

'I'm in trouble, Ethan.'

'So I gather, but I can't help unless you tell me what's happened.'

Jason gulped air hungrily. When he spoke, there was no single remnant of the bold, confident man Ethan knew. 'I want to tell you, but I'm afraid if I do, you won't understand. I need you to be on my side, and I don't think you can be.'

'Try me.'

'I've done something bad, Ethan. I've done the worst thing possible.'

Ethan moved into the kitchen, and sat on the floor with his back to the cooker. The ground flashed and spangled where the glass face of the clock had been powdered. 'What is it?' he asked, suddenly unsure whether he really wanted to know.

Jason moved his hands away from his face, and looked at the palms as if they were some alien appendages he could neither control nor understand. 'It was an accident, a mistake, you have to believe that.'

'What was?'

'It was just a routine pick up, a straight exchange. Hooper was -'

'Hooper?'

'My usual guy. He ran into a few problems at the airport the other week, and we've been a little dry in these parts. Demand outweighing supply, lots of dissatisfied customers. Bad for business.'

'Wait. Stop. I've told you before, if you want to make yourself some money selling that shit to street punks, that's fine by me, but I don't want to know about it.'

'You need to know this.'

'I warned you, Jason. I told you that sooner or later this stuff would come back to get you. Why didn't you listen?'

Jason wrapped his arms around the top of his knees. There were tears in his eyes, possibly for the first time ever. It was the

185

tears, more than the blood, that made Ethan realise what he was about to hear was beyond comprehension.

'Hooper set me up with a contact of his, someone who could get me out of a fix. I've got bills to pay, the same as everybody else. Look at this place.' Jason waved at the kitchen. 'I don't live cheap, and no product means no pay. I had to do it.'

'Jason? What did you do?'

'I'm a big fish in a little pond around here, but I had to move into deeper waters. Hooper's contact was something I've never dealt with before. I must have looked like a stupid kid when I turned up. I thought I could walk in there like it was a God-damned cash-and-carry. They chewed me up and spat me out.'

'What happened?'

Jason laughed, a bitter blast of acidic breath. 'They took every-thing I had.'

'Everything?'

'These people deal in cash, and they took everything.'

'And the blood?'

'I had every penny I had left with me. Rent, tuition fees, loans, grants. I emptied every account I have for this deal, and they took everything.' The tears gleamed in his eyes. Ethan had never seen a man so devastated. 'I'm going to lose this flat, I'm going to lose everything I have. Most of these things aren't paid for yet.' He picked up the wooden frame of the broken clock. 'Even this damned thing isn't paid for. And I was supposed to let it go at that? How could I do that?'

'It's just stuff, Jason. Things. Your parents will help you out.'

'Yeah, they'd love that. They'd love me to come running back. That's exactly what they'd expect.'

'So what's the alternative?'

'What I did.'

'And what did you do?'

'I fought back. There were three of them, but I was so damned

186

angry.' He rubbed his knuckles. 'They'd never seen anything like me before.'

'You sound proud.'

'Shouldn't I be?'

'You tell me.'

Jason let his head rock back against the wall. 'You're right,' he said. 'Of course, you're right. I should have let them take the money, but I wasn't thinking clearly. I wanted to hurt them. I wanted to prove they couldn't just take things because they wanted them.'

'What happened?'

Jason stared at the purple ceiling, arms and chest shaking with suppressed sobs. 'The biggest one, the one with my money, started walking back to his car, leaving the other two to give me a beating. He didn't expect me to be able to break free from them, to chase after him. He didn't even see me coming until I took him out.'

Ethan began picking at his fingernails, agitated by a bloody half-remembered face that lurked deep in his memory. His hands still throbbed from his own fight, still ached with the knowledge of combat. It was too close, too similar. Two consecutive nights, two friends, two brutal assaults. Too many coincidences.

Slowly at first, then gathering momentum, the memories started coming back.

'Did you hurt him?'

'He fell awkwardly. He . . . he's in the hospital.'

Ethan shuddered, wiped the sweat from his brow. This wasn't possible. This was too much. Last night's events, everything: it was all coming back in one impossible swell of bloody visions. He tried to force them out, but fragments of the previous night cut through the blackness of his consciousness, illuminating his mind with images of pain. 'No,' he said, quietly. New thoughts, maybe fabricated by guilt - a hand clutching at his shirt as he punched at

187

the wretched face of his assailant; a gurgled, choking plea - dropped neatly into the empty slots of his memory.

'No.'

He could hear the dull smack of his knuckles making contact with teeth, could smell the nauseating stink of the gore. Couldn't stop though. Couldn't stop punching. Too scared to stop, too scared to give his opponent the chance to fight back. He had to keep punching until he was sure the other man was dead. Even when the hands grasping at his neck went limp. Even when he couldn't hear the pleas to stop any more.

Had to keep punching.

He pressed his hands to his forehead, trying to crush the memories back into the dark pit from which they were emerging.

'No. That didn't happen,' he gasped.

Jason sat forwards. 'I didn't mean for it to happen,' he said. 'I just wanted my money back. He wasn't supposed to be hurt.'

Ethan closed his eyes, but he could still see the face of his attacker, bloodied beyond recognition.

Dead.

He wasn't supposed to be dead.

'He landed awkwardly.'

Ethan suddenly scrambled to his feet, vomited in the sink. Jason sank back into his hands.

'It wasn't supposed to happen.'

Ethan ran the cold water, splashing his face. 'Stop talking,' he said. 'Don't tell me this. I don't want to hear it.'

Too many memories. He couldn't be sure if any of them were real, but by God, they seemed real. The scrabbling, clawing, spastic hands on his face, the terrible sense of release with each satisfyingly meaty thud of each unrelenting blow.

He heaved, gasped for breath, let water sluice over his face and neck. 'For God's sake, Jason, don't tell me any more.'

'But I need your help.'

'My help? You put somebody in the hospital, Jason. You committed a crime.' He turned off the tap, let his head hang over the drain until he was sure his stomach would revolt no further at the constant bombardment of images flickering through his mind like an obscene slide show. 'I can't help you deal with that.'

'You have to.'

'No.'

'I need an alibi for tonight.'

Ethan's fingers retracted into tight balls. 'I can't help you. You can't expect me to.'

'You have to.'

Have to? Why? Why did he have to? Because he had done the same? Because he had done worse? That might not be true. He could barely remember the previous evening. These thoughts, these memories . . . fiction. They were fiction. Mind games, a terrible reaction to Jason's confession. A result of sleepless nights, stress, pain. Anything.

It wasn't real.

The memory of those wild, white eyes staring up at him as his hand smashed into an already shattered nose. It wasn't real.

'It's not real,' he whispered.

'Ethan, I know this must be hard for you, but it was an accident. He fell and hit his head. Jesus, I didn't want to hurt anyone. I was just protecting what was mine.'

Ethan put his knuckles to his temples, trying to force closed the floodgate that had allowed these images into his brain. Too late though, his mind was making connections, joining dots, piecing together the scrappy remnants into a terrifying picture of a night that might never have happened. Might never have happened if Jason . . .

Ethan's lips drew back in a snarl.

'You left me.'

'Ethan?'

'Last night. You left me in the street.'

'You were . . .' Jason stopped. 'You were getting into a taxi. You said you would be okay to get home by yourself.'

'Bullshit.'

'I waited with you in the rain. You must remember that.'

Ethan drew himself up. 'Look at me, Jason. You left me and I was attacked. They almost killed me. You left me and I had to . . .' He slammed his fist on the kitchen counter. 'You made me do something I didn't want to.'

'What?'

'You made me hurt someone. You made me have to fight, and you took enough of my senses away to make me not know when to stop.'

'I was forcing the drinks down your throat, was I?'

'You're cancer, Jason. You're the disease that fills our streets with degenerate, gang-banging murderers.'

'You don't mean that.'

'But I do. I hate you. I hate everything you are and everything you stand for. I hate you.' Ethan caught his breath. 'I hate you because I can't be you. I can't be that person who doesn't care, and you really don't care, not about anyone.'

'That's crazy, Ethan. We're friends.'

'When you want something.'

'We've always been friends.'

'When you want something.'

'I look out for you.'

'Like last night when I was having seven shades of shit kicked out of me?'

'Just remember, Ethan, you rang me. You came to me. I didn't take you anywhere you didn't want to go.'

'I know.' Ethan breathed heavily. 'I know, and that's what scares me.'

Jason paused, wiped his mouth. 'Ethan, please. I can't go to prison. Prison would kill me. I'm not like you, I'm not strong enough for that.'

Ethan laughed callously. 'Strong?'

'I can't go to prison.'

'Everything's eventual, Jason. Sooner or later the world bites you in the ass.'

'You have to help, I haven't got anybody else.'

Ethan looked at his wounded hands, at the zig-zag patterns of scar tissue. 'I guess you and I are in the same boat.'

'Then you'll do it?'

'I don't know. I'm not sure anybody should be helping us. We're animals. Violent, uncontrollable animals. And the worst thing is, I think we've always known it. We found each other because we saw some likeness.'

'We made mistakes.'

'We're angry. Angry at the world, everybody in it. We're self-destructive. We've always been heading here.'

'We can get through this.'

'But maybe we shouldn't. Maybe it's time we faced up to what we are.'

'We're human beings.'

'Who crossed the line. We're human beings who went too far, so far we couldn't even see where the line ended. But I don't want to be that angry, scared person running mindlessly into the teeth of the storm. I want out.'

'We can get through this.'

'I can't get through this while you're still around. I realise that now. Maybe you didn't bring me down to this place, but you're stopping me getting back up.'

'Ethan, please? I've never asked you for anything before, in all the time I've known you.' Jason's eyes gleamed like terrified lanterns. This wasn't a game, some fabrication. This was a man genuinely pleading for his life. Ethan couldn't walk away from that. 'You have to help me now.'

'If I give you an alibi, what happens then?'

'What do you want to happen?'

'I want to never see you again.'

Jason smiled meekly. 'That can be arranged.'

CHAPTER 21

Ethan arrived at the stables at nine o'clock, feeling a little less physically abused but a little more mentally cracked.

The night had been long, full of visions of a fight he could barely recall but implicitly understood had been brutal and largely unnecessary. A fight in which he may have killed someone.

At three o'clock he had started phoning hospitals, asking if anybody had been brought in with serious trauma to the face and neck. No luck.

Sleep had finally hit him at six, but the nightmares were just as bad as the reality. Painkillers he didn't really need to take, and scotch he probably shouldn't have drunk, weren't as much help as he would have liked.

By eight o'clock in the morning he had bathed and dressed. He wasn't ready to face the world, but hiding wasn't going to help. He needed to take action, to do something, anything, that would make him stop thinking about that fight.

And her.

He trudged up the driveway to Lesterton's house, aware of, but not acknowledging, the stable lads that moved around the place. The rain fell heavily, angrily. It seemed as if the whole universe had a bone to pick.

Karen, dressed in a long overcoat and knee-high boots, was standing in Lesterton's hallway. To her credit, she tried her best to look pleased to see Ethan as he walked in, shaking the raindrops from his hair. 'Ethan,' she said, but she could find no words to append to her initial exclamation.

Ethan shrugged off his soaking jacket, and draped it over one angular limb of the coat stand that stood guard by the front door. 'Karen,' he said, doing an admirable impression of a man who wasn't on the edge of a mental breakdown. 'I didn't expect to see you this morning. I assume Jamie is here.'

Karen nodded, looked away.

'It's okay, Karen. I'm not going to make this awkward. You made a choice. I hope you'll be happy.' He ruffled his hair. 'Are they in the study?'

'They're busy.'

'So am I.'

Ethan pushed by Karen, and walked down to the study. He stopped with his fingers resting on the door handle. Fear hatched a nest of spiders in his stomach, injecting silk threads of terror into his trembling veins. He could hear Jamie's and Lesterton's voices.

'It isn't enough, Lesterton.'

'These things take time.'

'You're running out of time. I need that money.'

'I've already pulled together everything I could, everything I had easily available.'

'That's not good enough.'

'It's the best I can do.'

'You knew the deal.'

'Oh, I knew the deal all right, but . . . is someone outside?'

Without knocking, Ethan thrust the door open and walked in. Lesterton was hunched at his desk, Jamie was towering over him like a bloated tarantula. As Ethan entered, they both stopped talking, and turned to watch him. The anger they had been exhibiting for each other was immediately switched to the new target.

'Good morning, Gentlemen,' Ethan said.

'You,' Jamie said, straightening.

'Me.' Ethan threw himself into a chair and slung his legs up on the desk. A theatrical smile blazed across his face and forcefully drove the shadows from under his sunken eyes. 'What are we talking about?'

'Business,' Jamie said, 'and we'd like to get on, if you don't mind.'

'I don't mind at all. You just carry on.'

Ethan made no attempt to move. Lesterton cleared his throat awkwardly.

Jamie's brow creased with anger and confusion. 'Alone, would be good,' he said.

'Three's a crowd?'

'Ethan, can we help you?' Lesterton interjected.

'I'm not sure.' Ethan put his hands behind his head and tilted his chair back. 'Can you?'

Lesterton leaned over, fixing Ethan with a gaze of stone. His words, expressed levelly, held in their midst the ghost of concern. Who that concern might be for was anybody's guess. 'What are you doing, Ethan?'

'Yes, Ethan,' Jamie added, like a startled rattlesnake. 'What are you doing?'

'I might ask you the same question,' Ethan responded. The tension in the room went up a notch, enough to cause the hairs on his neck to prickle.

'I might just throw you out,' Jamie hissed, slamming his fist on the desk.

Ethan shook his head and tutted. 'Really need to watch that temper, Jamie. Very bad. Get you in lots of trouble.'

'Looks like you've already been in lots of trouble.'

'You should see the other guy.'

'Are you okay?' Lesterton asked. His gaze flickered towards Jamie.

'I'm okay. I've not been sleeping too well recently, but then, you already know that. I think I might be taking too many painkillers, and there's a very good chance I have been drinking more than I should. I was seriously assaulted the other day, but beyond that, I think I'm doing okay.'

'I think someone knocked you a bit too hard in the head,' Jamie said.

Ethan expertly masked his gut reaction to get out before he did something really stupid. 'No, I'm fine. Do you want to know why?'

'Why?'

He took his feet down off the desk and moved forwards, whispering. 'I know who did it.' He quickly glanced at Jamie, secretly revelling in the jockey's look of mild discomfort. 'I know who got our horse.'

'I thought we'd decided to stop the investigations,' Lesterton said.

'You did. I thought I'd carry on. It's not like I had anything better to do with my time.'

'Would someone like to tell me what's going on?' Jamie asked.

'Not really,' Ethan said.

'Now hold on, you burst in here while we're having a business meeting and -'

'I don't give a damn about your little business meeting.'

'Excuse me?'

'Jockeys make bad businessmen. Didn't anybody ever tell you that? I can't imagine anything you say is going to interest Mr

Lesterton in the slightest.'

'You arrogant -'

'Shut up, Jamie. Just shut up.' Ethan turned his attention back to Lesterton, who was trying his best to conceal the part of a smug expression behind his stubby fingers that the flutters of his moustache failed to hide. 'Mr Lesterton, I know you think Sally was responsible for what happened, but you're wrong.'

'What makes you say that?'

'Because I've found the perpetrator.'

'Who?'

Ethan tapped the side of his nose conspiratorially. 'I can't say, but I have a plan for bringing them out into the open.'

'Bring who into the open?' Jamie asked.

'Are you still here?' Ethan said.

Lesterton clasped his hands together on the desk. 'What's your plan?' he asked seriously.

'I'm going to force their hand, make them expose themselves.' Ethan looked at Jamie challengingly. 'I intend to make them come after me.'

*

Karen was still standing in the corridor when Ethan left. She watched him as he walked by without a word, watched him put on his jacket, watched him open the front door, watched him walk out into the rain. Watched him.

Did not follow.

At the end of the driveway, Ethan was stopped by two men he did not know or care to know.

'Ethan?' the tallest of the two men asked.

Ethan examined the man's straight, hard face, the pinpoint eyes, and narrowly cut raincoat. He gave the impression of a stooped vulture, loitering hungrily around a car wreck. The

197

second man, more muscular, with a thicker neck and wider lapels, was more like a bull terrier. They both wore black. They had both been lured here by the smell of blood.

'You're police officers,' Ethan said. He did not necessarily mean for it to sound like an insult, but it sounded like one just the same.

The vulture flashed a badge-wallet. He looked into the tumbling blur of storm clouds, hunched his pointed shoulders. 'What gave us away?'

'The smell.'

'Sensing some hostility,' the terrier said. 'What do you think, Turner?'

Ethan's tired gaze ran over the vulture - who didn't much look like a Turner - before sweeping over the terrier in the same studious manner. 'If he's Turner, does that mean you're Hooch?' he asked, with a smirk.

'We've got ourselves a comedian,' Turner said. 'Is that what you are, funny man?'

'You're the policemen around here, why don't you figure it out for yourself?'

'Can we arrest him?' Hooch asked.

'We'll see.'

A yellow heartbeat of lightning sketched angry faces in the sky. Rainwater formed beige, swirling eddies in the gravel. The day grew more uncomfortable.

'How can I help you, Officers?' Ethan asked.

Hooch thrust his hands into his coat pockets, and hopped from one foot to the other, causing muddy splashes. 'We need to ask you a few questions,' he said.

'Just routine questions,' Turner confirmed.

'So ask.'

'Any chance we could go somewhere?' Turner asked. He sounded hopeful.

'No. Ask me here.'

198

'You don't like us very much.'

'I hardly know you. I'm sure you're both just lovely, and under different circumstances I might have introduced you to my Bridge club. But right now I suggest you ask your questions before we all catch pneumonia.'

Turner reached into his breast pocket and withdrew a leather-bound notepad. He flicked through several pages. Cleared his throat. Tried to present himself as professionally as his discomfort would allow. 'Just some routine enquiries, Sir, nothing serious. We need to establish your whereabouts last night between the hours of nine and eleven.'

'I was in a bar with my friend, Jason Montoya.'

Turner wrote something in the notepad, possibly a reminder to buy dog food for Hooch, who was looking increasingly restless. 'Can anyone vouch for that?'

'The other thirty or forty people in the bar, I suppose.'

'Anyone you know?'

'No.'

'That's a surprise.'

'Indeed.'

'But you are something of a celebrity. Easily remembered, I would think.'

'I'm very small. If people see me in a crowd the only thing they're going to remember is my hair.'

'Would the barman remember you?'

'I doubt it.'

'Why's that?'

'I don't have breasts.'

Turner nodded, and scribbled something in his soggy notebook. Squeaky toy, doggy treats, get well soon card for the postman. 'What time did you leave the bar?'

'After last orders.'

'And where did you go?'

'We went back to Jason's flat and had a few more beers.'

'But you're a jockey.'

'I am.'

'And you were drinking beer?'

'It's not unheard of.'

'And how long did you stay at Jason's flat?'

'Not sure, maybe until one o'clock.'

Turner lifted the collar of his coat and drew his vulture-like neck into his body. 'Are you sure we can't do this somewhere else?'

'Positive.'

'So you left at one?'

'Around then.'

'And where did you go?'

'Home.'

'You drove?'

'I got a taxi.'

'I don't suppose you would know which taxi company?'

Ethan shook his head.

'I'm not surprised. Okay, Sir, we'll leave it at that for now. Thank you for your assistance. We'll be in touch.' The notepad found its way back into Turner's pocket. It was unlikely that any of the pages of blotchy pencil marks would be even remotely readable.

'Can I ask a question?' Ethan said, wiping the rain out of his face.

'Certainly.'

'What's this all about?'

Turner smiled humourlessly. 'Last night someone broke into the home of one Samuel Hooper and beat his head in with a base-ball bat.'

'Hooper?'

'Name sound familiar?'

'I . . . No. No. And you say he was beaten up at home?'

'You look surprised.'

Ethan swallowed hard. 'Is he . . ?'

'Dead?' Turner's smile widened into a vicious sneer. 'Oh yes.'

## CHAPTER 22

It was four-thirty, and Ethan floated on painkillers, listening to the buzz of conversation around him.

The hay barn on the west side of the colts' quadrangle was a regular haunt for several of the stable lads, and when the weather was severe enough to drive them from the gallops they could often be found sat among the bales, discussing their charges, and drinking whiskey. Lesterton knew what went on, and he left them to it most days, although he would always make a point of confiscating liqueur from any unfortunate soul unlucky enough to be caught drinking.

Three of the more regular visitors to the hay barn were Daniel, Simon, and Roger, good strong lads with a passion for horses that was exhilarating to be around. Daniel was the ring leader, a tough old boy of fifty-three with a glint of steel in his eye, and granite in his jaw. He was one of the oldest workers on the premises, and there was very little he didn't know about the workings of the stable. He looked after the younger staff, and made it his business to keep his ear to the ground. If anybody had an idea as to who had got at Emphatic, it would be him.

The other two, Simon and Roger, were both hard-working types, dedicated to their profession, but prone to gossip as much as the other lads.

Surely, between the three of them, they would have heard or seen something to lend some credence to what Ethan had already decided was the only logical explanation for what had happened.

He joined them at three o'clock, with no expectations of a warm reception and no warm reception received, and had tried his best to blend into the wall ever since. It had taken a little over an hour, but the lads were finally beginning to forget he was there, and tongues, fuelled by alcohol and the taste of the juiciest gossip the stable had ever generated, were getting looser.

'I can't think it was Sally,' Roger said, with the simpleminded innocence his colleagues had grown to love. His open face was filled with insurmountable confusion at the very thought of a stable lass doing something to hurt a horse. 'She loved Emphatic. Once I said to her that I'd do for Emphatic, just once like, so Sally could get off for the day. She got so angry, I thought she'd claw me eyes out. She loved that horse more than anything else. That's why she run off like that.'

Daniel, smoking a hand-rolled cigarette with no regard for the stable's health and safety regulations because, quite frankly, he had been there long enough to ensure that any rules were no longer applicable, shook his head. 'You got a lot to learn, son. That girl was always out for what she could get. She clawed your face because she was worried you might do a better job than her and she might find herself looking after one of the nags.' He flicked ash on the floor, sending a shimmer of sparks dancing across the concrete. 'I remember what she was like when she first got here. You were too busy checking out her chest to see the look in her eye.'

'What look?' Simon asked, taking a hefty slug from a hip flask that had been waved at Ethan once, and never again since he had declined.

'She looked hungry, like the stable was a big pie and she was going to get the lion's share of it.'

'No.' Roger laughed to disguise his genuine concern that this most horrifying opinion might be proved to be correct. 'She weren't like that. We used to go out sometimes, when she wasn't on with her boyfriend from Up North. She didn't care about money and all that. She just wanted to look after horses and ride and have fun.'

Simon giggled and passed the hip flask to Roger. 'You had it bad for her, didn't you?'

'She was special.'

'Well I say good job she's gone,' Daniel spat, stomping his cigarette under one mud-caked boot. 'And I hope she never shows her face round these parts again. All she ever cared about was money. Why, if I ever saw her I'd do more than claw her eyes, I tell you.'

Roger sucked on the flask for a minute, screwed his nose up, and passed the flask on to Daniel. 'Well I think you got her all wrong.'

Ethan, lying on his back in the hay, able to feel the painkillers rushing around in his veins absorbing hurt he wasn't sure was real, smiled to himself.

They had all got Sally wrong. She hadn't done this for money, at least, not just for money. She had done this because she had thought it was her job.

If the governor told you to do something, you did it.

The rain pounded on the corrugated roof of the barn, and trickled through the bolted joins. Ethan closed his eyes and tried to focus on the conversation. If he could focus on the conversation then he didn't have to think about the other things. The bad things.

'But she wouldn't have done it if there hadn't been somebody offering up the green,' Simon said.

'Well, that's the point,' Daniel mused, fishing in his pocket for his tobacco and papers. 'Somebody paid her to do it, there's no doubt about that.'

'I don't think she did nothing,' Roger protested.

'Course she did,' Daniel continued. 'Only one reason why she would have taken off the way she did. Guilt. Means she either neglected the horse or was directly responsible for its death. Either way, couldn't stay round here, could she?'

'She had to leave 'cause folk like you would be saying like what you are. How could she come to work knowing what you were thinking?'

'She couldn't, because she knew what we were thinking was right. She killed that horse as sure as I'm sitting here.'

'So who paid her?' Simon said, screwing the lid back on his flask, and pocketing it. 'Who would want the horse dead?'

'They didn't want it dead,' Daniel chuckled. 'Jesus, didn't you see her? She was raring to go. They were trying to give her a little boost, make sure there was a little something in the tank for Newbury. Dosed her up a bit too much is my guess.'

'Lesterton ain't into nothing like that,' Roger said. 'He wouldn't never allow someone to go tampering with his horses.'

'Of course he wouldn't.' Daniel took out his lighter, and sucked his freshly rolled cigarette into life. For an exceptionally rare moment he was silent, breathing smoke. 'Lesterton has never done anything dishonest in all his days.'

Ethan put his hands behind his head and stared at the ceiling. If only he could be so certain of that. If only he could believe Lesterton wasn't involved in this mess in some way.

'So the question remains,' Simon said. 'Who paid Sally to get at Emphatic?'

'O'Hara.'

Ethan sat bolt upright, causing all three men to jump. 'O'Hara?'

he asked.

Daniel, realising he had probably said too much in front of a jockey, smoked quietly. Roger and Simon examined their hands as if seeing them for the first time.

'What made you say O'Hara?' Ethan pressed.

'It was just talk,' Daniel said.

'It's okay, whatever you tell me goes no further than us. What made you think it was O'Hara?'

Daniel shrugged and stubbed his cigarette on the ground. 'He was going to be riding the horse at Newbury.'

'That doesn't sound like a very valid reason.'

'And there was that Dalton fellow. He was snooping around again last week, trying to pick up some extra rides.'

'Dalton? The jockey who rode Emphatic for us before?'

'He's a nasty piece of work. He was just waiting for O'Hara to slip up so he could take on Emphatic full time. Reckon maybe O'Hara got a little jumpy, thought he might lose Emphatic for good if he didn't guarantee a win.'

'That all seems a little far-fetched,' Ethan said.

'There was the girl, too,' Roger said.

'Girl?' Ethan asked.

Everybody looked at Roger, whose skin turned a deep red. This was clearly a piece of gossip as new to the group as it was to Ethan. 'The girl you were showing around the stable the day before.'

'Karen?'

'If that's her name, yes. I seen her speaking to Mr O'Hara.'

'When was this?' Ethan pressed.

'After you took Mr Redthorn in to see the governor. They were talking all quiet like, whispering to each other, and they stopped when I walked by.'

Ethan's heart thundered in his chest, his nerves buzzed. 'My God,' he said, breathlessly. 'That makes sense.'

He was on his feet, heading back out into the rain.

When they were sure he was gone, Daniel, Simon, and Roger started talking about Karen's rather impressive chest proportions.

*

Just outside the flats, Ethan's mobile phone started ringing. It was Jason. Ethan switched the phone off without answering. He had said everything he intended saying to Jason, there was nothing left between them. He had lied for that man, risked his own freedom for some foolish notion of camaraderie, and he had been betrayed again. Lied to, as he had been lied to by everybody else.

Now, Jason was a murderer, and what did that make Ethan? Was he an accessory to murder? Or an accessory to perverting the course of justice? Could he ever go back to the police and tell them the truth, or had he ensured that this crime would go unpunished? Could he live with himself if that was true?

He put the phone back in his pocket, and went into the flats. He couldn't think about Jason now. Not now. He had to deal with one thing at a time.

Jason could wait.

He headed up the stairs to Karen's apartment, and knocked on the door.

No answer.

He knocked again, louder this time.

'Karen?'

The door jerked open, and Ethan was face to face with Jamie Redthorn. Behind Jamie, several other men were walking around, drinking from cans of beer, smoking, chatting, and laughing. There was no sign of Karen.

'You again?' Jamie said, unable to disguise his shock and more than a little amusement. 'You are determined to get your ass kicked, aren't you?'

'Is Karen home?' Ethan kept his voice level, patted down the fear that was twisting his stomach into painful knots.

'She is.'

'Can I speak to her?'

'What do you think?'

'It's about Emphatic.'

Jamie shook his head in disbelief. 'You really are something, Ethan. You really are. What could Karen possibly have to say about your dead horse?'

'I don't know. That's why I'm here.'

'Screw you.'

Jamie went to shut the door, but Ethan's foot was already jammed into the frame. 'Tell her I know about O'Hara.'

Jamie's brow creased, then Ethan removed his foot, and the door closed with a slam. Ethan let his breath out slowly between gritted teeth. That was probably a really silly thing to have done, but he could think of no other way.

He was not a detective, he didn't know how to accumulate evidence and reveal criminals for what they were. All he knew was he had to make these people come out into the open, and if that meant he was going to be the bait, so be it.

He wasn't a detective, he was a jockey. Sometimes jockeys gambled.

## CHAPTER 23

In the Weighing Room at Chepstow, O'Hara switched off his mobile phone and put it in his kit bag. It was not quite so easy to switch off Lesterton's voice in his head.

'We can't keep the horse's death buried,' the old trainer had said. It was a peculiar choice of words.

Buried.

It was rare indeed for that which was buried to claw its way back to the surface unaided, there almost always had to be someone prepared to exhume it.

Without thinking, O'Hara rummaged in his bag until he found a crumpled packet of cigarettes. One cigarette left. He lit it with the last match from a book he had taken from a hotel room in Catterick. There was a telephone number scribbled on the back of the book that he had never thought to ring.

Maybe he should have. Who knows?

Tomorrow, he could be dead. Worse still, he could be alive. Alive, with only the memories of missed opportunities to sustain him through a lifetime of nights.

The girl who had written her number down on the matches no longer had a face in his memory, and maybe she should have. Too late to change things now, though. Much too late to make the call. Too late to even know what the call might have been.

He drew heavily on the cigarette, leaned back, closed his eyes. His head throbbed incessantly.

Buried.

Lesterton had sounded frightened. He had never sounded frightened before in his life. Lesterton didn't know what it was to be afraid.

O'Hara spun the empty matchbook through his fingers. He could remember the girl who belonged to the phone number. Long legs, blonde hair, incredible breasts. Just her face was missing. He couldn't recall a single feature. Her nose, her mouth, cheeks: they weren't there, like somebody had opened up his head and erased that one single memory from his brain. Or maybe her face was still there, just buried deeper than he was prepared to go. A face waiting for somebody else to exhume it.

Her name had been Karen too, the same as the girl who showed up at the stables the other day looking for Ethan. 'Have you seen him?' she had asked.

'No,' O'Hara had said. 'But maybe I can help.'

She had looked at him strangely, as if seriously contemplating whether he really could.

She had been beautiful.

O'Hara shook his head for no particular reason, and crushed the matchbook. Ethan was certainly a lucky man to have a girl like that asking after him.

In the Weighing Room, the other jockeys talked among themselves. Leading from the off? Definitely. Got a horse with a rocket in its hind quarters. The dirt is really going to fly when this colt starts. Fine grey, noble look in his eye, lots of stamina. So on, so forth.

O'Hara stubbed out his cigarette, and concerned himself with his silks. The horse he was riding was a flighty young thing called Pointy Bird; no real muscle to speak of, but fast, and with a good action. Not much of a chance, but still worth a little each-way bet, according to numerous pundits.

He pulled on his colours.

'We can't keep the horse's death buried,' Lesterton had said. 'Ethan has uncovered something, and I don't think he will keep quiet about it.'

It was impossible to bury things these days. There was always some do-gooder with a shovel waiting for his moment in the spotlight.

Emphatic's death had been buried directly under Lesterton's stables. Digging it all up now was going to seriously shake the foundations, perhaps bring the whole yard crashing in on itself. Lesterton was running a good chance of losing everything he had, and if he was sunk, the chances were O'Hara's reputation would end up stained as well.

Ethan was risking more than he could possibly realise by poking around in the dirt.

O'Hara fished a newspaper out of his bag and flicked through the pages. Same old news. Doom and gloom. The police were looking for the perpetrator of a vicious assault. Someone had been beaten to death. The crime had been 'cold and calculated'. There were a number of promising leads.

There had been a terrible crash on the M4 motorway. A maintenance truck carrying red traffic cones had lost control and turned over. Three other cars had been involved. Five bodies in total; one dead, four severely injured. Road-works had been delayed for several hours due to the non-arrival of the aforementioned cones. The truck driver had been talking on a mobile phone, and he had been drinking. He was still alive.

The dead person was a two-year-old girl.

A Member of Parliament had been photographed leaving the house of a known prostitute. He was refusing to make any comment other than to say the lady who owned the property was an old family friend. A neighbour, and frequent 'visitor' of the property, who wished to remain anonymous, claimed to have seen the Member of Parliament on numerous occasions.

O'Hara scanned through a couple more stories, looking for something on a lighter note. It seemed that the world was largely as depressed as he was.

'You're reading the wrong paper,' said a voice by his left ear. It was an incredibly crisp and British voice; so perfectly upper-class that it could have been mistaken for a parody of the stereotypical British accent used by Hollywood movie stars.

'Hello, Dalton,' O'Hara said, without looking away from his newspaper.

'In my paper there's a story about a bag of kittens being washed up on the riverbank.'

'Really?'

'Six kittens in total. All alive.'

'Am I supposed to care?'

'Not really.'

O'Hara folded his paper and put it to one side. 'So what did the reporter say about these cats?'

'Not cats. Kittens. They were only kittens.'

'Is there a difference?'

'Only in stature. They're being found new homes now, places where they will be looked after.'

'That's nice.'

'Do you realise that, under normal circumstances, the kittens would probably be put down?' Dalton's eyes were as lifeless as ever, his true purpose shrouded in their black depths. 'It's true. They would have spent a couple of weeks being pampered at a cat shelter somewhere, then, when nobody took them away, they would have been given a lethal injection.'

'What's your point?'

'My point is simply that now they've been in the paper, nobody would dare bump them off, would they? Can you imagine the scandal? Miracle kittens killed off due to lack of funding for the local cat shelter.'

O'Hara scrutinised his fingernails. 'You're going to have to spell this one out for me.'

'All I'm saying is that the newspapers have a lot of sway over the hearts and minds of the population. It's far easier to make nuisance animals disappear when you don't have to worry about what some reporter is going to print.' He smoothed a wrinkle out of his trousers. 'Don't you think?'

'What is it you want, Dalton?'

'Nothing. Not any more. I'm not sure there's anything you have I'd be interested in taking.'

'Just shooting the breeze, then?'

'Something like that.' From his pocket, Dalton took a creased business card, straightened out one crumpled corner, and studied it quietly. 'There was something else I wanted to mention,' he said, quietly.

Between the chrome pegs, the other jockeys walked up and down, chatted, laughed, and paid Dalton and O'Hara no attention at all. Their attention was focussed on the upcoming races, the thrill of the cheering crowds.

'If it's a story about puppies, I don't want to hear it,' O'Hara said, agitatedly.

'He came to see me, you know?'

'Who?'

Dalton handed O'Hara the card. 'He turned up at my house before the race at Newbury.'

O'Hara looked at the card. The gold leaf print was peeling but still readable. 'He seems to get around,' he said.

'So he came and saw you too?'

'Maybe.'

'What did he say?'

'Maybe I should be asking you that?'

Dalton scratched his neck, stared at the pegs on the other side of the room. 'I think I'm going to come in under weight today. I hate carrying dead weight.'

'Everybody has to sometimes.'

'My Governor hates it too. We're of the same mind. A horse reacts better to live weight. Lead blocks slapping around in a weight cloth never did anybody any favours.'

O'Hara flicked the business card from hand to hand. 'I expect you're right.'

'I guess that's why he came to see me.'

'What did he say?'

'He came to make sure he was going to win. He had nothing to fear from me on that score, but you were a different matter. Emphatic was a star.'

'She is, you mean.'

'Of course, she is.' Dalton drew a slow breath, gathering together the words he required. 'It's interesting she didn't show at Newbury. Even with the rain like it was.'

'We can't control the weather.'

'And when it rains it rains. I know that. But perhaps it was more than the rain that got to Emphatic.'

'What are you suggesting?'

'Nothing. I'm just thinking out loud. I'm thinking I had a visitor. He'd shown up because he thought I was riding a very good horse with a lot of potential. He was wrong, of course. You were riding the horse. I'm thinking my visitor then came to visit you. I'm thinking he made you the same offer he was going to make me. I'm thinking, you accepted that offer.'

214

'Maybe you think too much.'

'That's a possibility. Maybe I should run it by the police, let them do the thinking for me.'

'And what would you tell them?'

'I wouldn't have to tell them much. I'm sure they'd be able to draw their own conclusions. You have to admit, it doesn't look very good.'

The Weighing Room suddenly seemed very quiet. A gut-wrenching breath reverberated through O'Hara's body. 'There's no point,' he said.

'In what?'

'Trying to blackmail me.'

'I've tried no such thing.'

'But you're going to, aren't you?'

Dalton sat back, put his hands behind his head. His mouth curled slightly. His eyes remained empty. 'I don't know,' he said, honestly. 'I thought I'd just see how things played out.'

'You really are a weasel, aren't you?'

'Why don't you tell me what happened to Emphatic? Is she still alive?'

The card trembled in O'Hara's hand. 'I'm not going to tell you anything.'

'That doesn't matter, I think I know the answer anyway.'

'I suggest you get up and walk away now.'

'Why's that?'

'Because if you don't walk away now, you might never be able to walk again.'

'That sounds awfully like a threat.'

'It does, doesn't it?'

Dalton's mouth straightened out again. He stood. 'Just remember, I know the truth. I can pull the plug any time I like, and wash you away.'

'Any time you like,' O'Hara grinned.

Dalton stalked away.

O'Hara continued staring at the business card in his hand. The business card that had put him at Dalton's mercy. The business card that had probably ended his career.

Jamie Redthorn's business card.

CHAPTER 24

Ethan chewed the last of the painkillers he had in the drawer, and drank quarter of a bottle of scotch, before finally drifting into an uncomfortable dream.

In the dream, he was on fire. He could feel his skin blistering, cracking and peeling away. He could feel his muscles blackening, fusing to his crumbling skeleton. He could feel the blood congealing in his veins.

The pain was incredible, beyond endurance, yet he was unable to lose consciousness. He had to endure every excruciating second of his torment.

He was not alone, in this nightmare; Melissa was there, and Jason, and O'Hara, and Lesterton, and Jamie.

And Karen.

They all watched him, with blank, lifeless eyes, ignorant to his pleas for help. Then, all together, they began pouring petrol on him.

The flames went higher.

He woke, several hours later, to the sound of knocking. It was dark, still early, the flashing digits of the alarm clock illuminated only the hard edges of his bedside table. His curtains flapped at an open window like banshee's hair. Everything was silent, then: the knocking again. Someone at the door.

Karen.

For a moment he lay there. He was too tired for this, too beaten up to endure any further torture. He didn't need to answer the door. He wasn't going to answer the door.

The knocking became louder, more fervent.

The curtains thunder-clapped in a sudden blast of cold wind.

He got out of bed.

He hadn't really known what to expect, but it certainly wasn't what he got. When he opened the door, Karen literally fell into his arms, throwing herself around his neck, and crying uncontrollably into his shoulder. He pushed the door closed with his foot, and held her, smoothing her hair. He didn't speak, he couldn't find the words to say.

For a while, they just stood that way, holding each other, uncertain why they needed the contact, but certain the contact was a good thing.

She trembled against his body and, as once before, he felt a sudden rush of blood that suggested he derived a certain degree of pleasure from her obvious pain. He kissed her forehead and hoped, beyond hope, this time Jamie had gone too far.

'What's wrong?' he whispered.

Karen pulled away slightly, not far enough to extricate herself from his embrace, but far enough to be able to look up at him with terrified eyes. 'Ethan,' she said, and that was all before fresh tears melded their bodies back together. This was not the time for words, this was a time for comfort of a far more physical nature.

He carefully led her through to the lounge, and sat her on the couch. He sat beside her, never once letting her go, vowing never to let her go ever again. Whatever had happened, whatever they may have said or done, they were together now, thrown together by hurt and despair, but together. Here, now, he could convince himself it was forever.

Time drifted away in the soft ticking of the clock.

She stopped crying, was finally able to speak without the words dragging another sob from her chest.

'I'm sorry,' she said.

'What for?'

'For everything. For how I made you feel.'

'It's okay.'

'For what I said.'

'It's okay.'

'For leaving you at the river.'

'It's okay, really.'

'No, it's not. I used you horribly. There's no way you can defend those actions. I used you to get what I wanted.' She almost laughed, but the sound was desolate and cold in the quiet lounge. 'The problem was, what I thought I wanted wasn't what I wanted at all.'

'What did you want?'

'I wanted the dream.'

'And the dream isn't obtainable any more?'

'I thought Jamie and I had hurt each other so badly it couldn't get any worse. I thought we'd come to the point where things had to change. I didn't want you, Ethan, not to start with. You were just another man like all the others.'

'Others?'

'Jamie's possessive, he always has been, and I've always played on that, using people to hurt him, to get a reaction.'

'You don't need to tell me anything,' Ethan said. Each of

219

Karen's words cut like a razorblade, more painful than any physical assault he had been subjected to in the last week. She didn't need to tell him anything. He didn't want to hear.

'It's a game we've always played. I would cheat on him, he would hit me. We'd forgive each other.' She burrowed further into Ethan's chest, digging ever closer to his pounding heart. 'But it was always just a game. I never cared about the men I slept with and he knew that, and he never hated me for it. When he hit me, it was more like . . . routine. He did it to show he did care what I was doing. His intention wasn't to injure me, just like my intention wasn't to injure him.'

'Karen, listen to me. You don't have to tell me any of this. It's okay. I understand.'

'No you don't. You don't understand, and that's the hardest part. You changed everything. You turned the game upside down.'

'How?'

'You made me love you. I didn't want to admit it, I tried to convince myself you were just like the rest. I've spent so long trying to get Jamie to love me the way I love him, I couldn't let myself believe I could just . . . stop. I wouldn't let myself believe all my hard work could be thrown away because of the way you smile.'

'You like the way I smile?'

Karen squeezed Ethan tighter, and for a fleeting moment he was worried she might rupture his spleen. 'You don't even know what you do,' she said. 'You walk around looking like you were pulled out the pages of a fashion magazine, you smile and the world tap-dances. You probably think I'm silly, but I've never known anyone like you. You're brave, impossibly gentlemanly, strong, handsome, funny, intelligent . . . You say you love me without even using the words. You're everything I wanted Jamie to be.'

'You're going to be good for my ego, I can tell.'

'Don't do that. Don't make this into a joke.'

'I'm not.'

'You are, and it's just making it harder. Don't you understand? I never wanted to love you. I wanted to sleep with you to make my boyfriend jealous, and then I wanted to forget about you. I'm evil. I wanted to hurt you.'

'No you didn't, you wanted to be loved.'

Karen pulled back, punching Ethan in the arm. 'Don't do that. Don't try and protect me. Don't say this is all okay. I saw what I did to you, I saw your face at the river yesterday. Don't just say that doesn't matter. Don't say I'm not a bad person.' She hit him again, harder, her knuckles squeezed white, and her eyes staring. 'Don't.'

'Karen, it's okay.'

She moved to strike him again, on the cheek this time, but he snatched her wrist and held her clawing fingers away.

'Stop it, Karen. Let this go. I don't hate you for what you did. The only person you're hurting is yourself.'

Fat tears rolled down her cheeks. 'I need you to hate me,' she sobbed. 'You have to hate me. I'm bad.'

He drew her back into his arms, wrapping his hands around her back. 'You have to tell me what happened,' he said.

'Jamie came back, that's what happened. He came back like he always does, and I managed to convince myself he didn't know the truth. I thought we were still playing the game, but Jamie wasn't having fun any more.'

'Why not?'

'I told you at the river, if you knew the truth about me, you wouldn't feel the same way. I believed that. I believed that after everything I'd done, Jamie was all I had. He was the only person who wouldn't hate me.'

'I could never hate you.'

'Of course you could. If I had allowed myself to be with you, if I hadn't told you this.' She shook her head. 'You would have hated me sooner or later. I had convinced myself Jamie was the one, and I'd done everything in my power to make sure I got him. I just wanted to be loved. I just wanted him to love me.' A wet sob reverberated against Ethan's chest. 'Why couldn't he have been like you? Why couldn't he have loved me the way I am?'

How could Ethan answer? What could he say? He didn't know why he loved this girl, why he still loved her after this terrible confession. He didn't know why Jamie didn't, how Jamie couldn't. This girl was the last of a dying breed, a girl who only wanted to be loved. A girl who believed in true love, fighting for the lost cause. A girl who had, for better or worse, made a choice, and who was prepared to do everything in her power to make sure she was proved right in making that choice. The choice was wrong, but at least she had the conviction to stand by it.

'I'm sorry,' Ethan said, feeling more useless than he had ever felt in his life.

'After all this, you say sorry to me. You are either very nice or very stupid. I'm not sure I care which.'

'Nice people are just people who are too scared to go after what they want. My father used to tell me that.'

'And what do you want?'

'You already know.'

'Even now?'

'Even now.'

'You shouldn't say things like that.'

'Why not?'

'Because I might hold you to them, and I haven't told you everything yet.'

'I've already told you, it doesn't matter. You don't have to tell me anything. It doesn't change the way I feel about you.'

'You don't know that.'

'I know how I feel. I've always known that.'

Karen took his hand. Their fingers entwined in a way that was more sexual than Ethan could have imagined.

'When I was young, about twelve years old, I discovered boys liked me. I wasn't popular, I was lonely most of the time, but the boys were always there. Normally they would just stand around in packs, giggling, pushing each other. Sometimes one of them would come over and sit by me. I never really knew what it meant at the time.' Her grip on Ethan's hand tightened. 'I found out eventually. I learned that being with them, even though I knew they didn't care . . . that was better than being on my own. By the time I went to university I knew what I was doing. I'd learned what I needed to do to stop being lonely. I hopped from man to man without even thinking about it.'

'What are you saying, Karen?'

'I'm saying this has always been with me. I've always wanted to be adored. I just . . . I just don't know how to do it the right way. I thought being with Jamie . . . I thought that would help me put the past behind me. He seemed to understand why I'd slept with so many people. He understood my pain, and I thought he could make it go away.'

'Karen, you have to tell me what this is all about.'

'When Jamie phoned me, it was the same as always. He said he wanted to talk. That was what he always used to say. Talk never figured too highly though. He would hit me and call me a slag, then he would say he did it because he cared, and then we would have sex. Angry sex. It was always the kind of sex that hurt. But that was part of it.'

'Jesus, Karen. How could you go on like this?'

'Because I loved him. Because I thought . . . because I didn't think I deserved any better. Because I hate myself as much as I hate him now.'

'You could have walked away.'

'Not many people walk away from car crashes, Ethan. It had got to the stage where we needed each other. I needed him to validate my existence, he needed me to prove he was a man. We were always on a collision course.'

'I don't understand.'

'I think you understand better than you think. When someone believes they are worthless they create their own prison. You're fiancée walked out on you, and you've been alone ever since. Do you think that's because you love her, or because you're afraid to try and live without her? Maybe you'll realise you're happier without her, and then all that time mourning her will be shown up for the waste it really was.'

Ethan was silent.

'I was afraid. I didn't want to be alone. I couldn't even conceive of the night when I wouldn't have to cry myself to sleep. I was existing on the pain.' She laughed at herself. 'It was like a drug I couldn't stop taking, and I know how crazy that sounds.'

'You wanted him to hurt you?'

'Because I thought it meant he cared. But I was wrong. He never cared. This time I pushed him too far. It was too much.'

'What happened?'

'I should have gone with you, once you'd told me how you felt. I should have taken the chance. I should have known you wouldn't hurt me that way, but I was scared. If we didn't work out, I didn't want to hurt you. I didn't want to be hurt.'

'I would never have hurt you.'

'People seem to get hurt whenever I'm around. I can't change that, and I couldn't let it happen to you. So I went back to him. I should have known something was wrong when he turned up with his friends. He didn't even want to talk about it.'

'Did he hit you?'

'No. He said he understood. He said he always understood.' She began to shake more fiercely in Ethan's arms. 'He said we could try again, and this time we would make it work. But the look in his eyes . . .'

Although the sun was rising, spreading yellow fingers of light across a purple landscape, the lounge appeared to grow darker. Karen had brought something black into Ethan's flat, and though he could not see it, he knew he was afraid of it.

'Karen?'

'The look in his eyes told me this wasn't finished. I'd never seen him look that way. He looked in pain, like what I'd done had cut him for the first time. He looked like somebody who wanted revenge.'

'I don't understand. What was different?'

'It was the journal. I wrote in the journal I thought of you when I was sleeping with him. It was the first time he had ever felt threatened. All the other times, I had been using men to make him notice me, it had been strengthening his position in my life. You were the first person to ever make me think less of him. You were the only person to take his strength away. You were the only person I ever fell in love with.'

'And that was why he set the thugs on me?'

'He knew punching me wouldn't be enough. He had to do something to make me take notice of him again. What happened the other night wasn't a warning to you, it was a warning to me. He was telling me that if I didn't disassociate myself from you, he was going to make sure you turned up dead somewhere.' She moved away, curling up into a ball on the other side of the couch. Sunlight leaked through the gaps in the kitchen curtains, doing little to alleviate the chill in Ethan's spine. 'That wasn't all, though. He wanted to make me suffer for what I'd done. He wanted to make sure I never had any choice but to stay with him.'

Ethan reached for Karen's arm but she withdrew further. 'What happened, Karen?'

'He did something so vile that nobody else would ever want to look at me, let alone spend the rest of their life with me.'

'Karen?'

'You have to understand, I wanted it to happen. They got me drunk, put something, some drug, in the alcohol, to make me crazy.'

The knots in Ethan's chest tightened like wire springs. 'What did they do?'

Karen buried her face in her hands. 'It wasn't rape. Not at the time. I wanted it to happen. He made sure I agreed to it. That's what he wanted. If it was rape, someone else would understand, they would forgive me.' She began crying again. 'But he made me agree to it. He made me want to be the dirty, uncontrollable thing I was.'

'What did they do?' Ethan repeated, stonily.

'They took turns. Him and his friends. He said that if I was . . . If I was thinking of you then it didn't matter how many people did it to me, it was all the same.'

Ethan drew a deep shuddering breath. Fire raged in his chest, threatening to consume reason in its hungry coruscation. 'How many people?'

'Does it matter?'

'How many?'

'Six.'

Ethan was already on his feet. 'Are they still upstairs?'

Karen nodded.

'This isn't your fault, Karen.'

She smiled, a frightened, icy smile. 'Yes it is. I should have been with you last night.'

He took the steps two at a time, and didn't worry about knocking. He put his shoulder into the door and broke it off the hinges with a triumphant scream that drowned out the pain exploding through his injured body.

They were all in the lounge - the things that could perhaps have been mistaken for men - draped across the couch or lying on the floor.

Ethan located Jamie and dragged him to his feet, slamming him against the wall. 'Son-of-a-bitch,' he screamed. 'How could you do it? How could you?' His hands drew Jamie's shirt collar into scrunched balls, pulling the material tight against the jockey's throat. 'How could you?'

Jamie tried to break free, but Ethan dragged him forwards and then thrust him back against the wall more forcefully, smashing the breath from his body. Around the room, disorientated and confused animals were staggering to their feet, wiping bleary eyes, and trying to organise the world coherently.

'What is this?' Jamie gasped.

'This is me doing something I should have done a long time ago.'

Ethan dragged Jamie away from the wall, spinning, and sending the smaller man spiralling over the back of the couch.

Two of the hungover animals made to approach Ethan, but Ethan's withering glare was enough to convince them to stay back.

Jamie, coughing and spluttering, heaved himself to his feet. He shook his head, blinked, and was almost cognisant before Ethan's fist pounded into his left ear. Jamie jolted across the room, caught the edge of a coffee table, and tumbled backwards. Ethan was on him in a second, pulling him up, and pushing him back against the door.

'Okay,' Ethan hissed. 'Tell me. How could you do that to her? She loved you.'

Jamie grinned bloodily, shook his head. 'I have no idea what you're talking about.'

Ethan pressed his arm up under Jamie's chin, crushing his larynx. 'You know damn well what I'm talking about.'

'You're crazy.'

Ethan's lips drew back with bestial rage. He pressed harder against Jamie's throat. He didn't want to hurt this man. He wanted to kill him. He wanted to break him, destroy him totally, and ensure there was nothing left of him, not even a memory. 'Why did you do it?' he snarled.

Jamie choked, his face reddening, his fingers grasping spastically at Ethan's arm. 'I don't understand. What have I done?'

Ethan released Jamie's neck, and spun him into the nearest couch. As if acting on some unspoken command, the other five animals in the room advanced as one. Ethan drew his fingers into sharp fists. 'Who's first?' he asked.

'No,' Jamie coughed. 'No, guys. Leave him.' He stood, rubbing his throat. 'Developed some guts over the last few days, haven't you, Ethan?'

Ethan took a step back, making sure all six of the animals in the room were in his line of sight. They were all big guys except for Jamie. One of them looked as though he had recently been kicked in the face by a horse. 'I've met you before,' Ethan said. 'I thought I'd killed you.'

The animal was silent.

Jamie shrugged. 'Ethan, why don't you tell me what's on your mind before I get angry and decide to let my friends beat on you for a while?'

'That's right,' Ethan laughed. 'Leave your friends to fight your battles for you. That's what you always do, isn't it? Oh, you're a real big man. You're a top jockey, well respected, money to burn, but it's all nothing without these goons. First sign of trouble, first threat to your perfect life, and who has to clean up the mess? You've never fought one of your own battles, have you?'

'I've never had to.'

'You weren't even man enough to keep your girlfriend under control without the assistance of these . . .' Ethan gestured at the man-mountains surrounding him. 'These people.'

'I'm afraid I don't know what you're talking about.'

'You know.'

'Enlighten me.'

'You and your friends here did something to Karen last night that was beyond evil. I'm going to make sure you suffer for it.'

Jamie looked down at his fingernails, a sly look transforming his face. 'We had a little bit of a party last night, that's true. But evil? Consenting adults having some fun?'

'But you weren't all having fun, were you?'

'Nothing happened that wasn't wanted to happen.'

'You spiked her drink.'

'Prove it.'

'You all raped her.'

'Prove it.'

'You raped her.'

'So you say.'

'You raped her.'

Ethan lunged forwards, but two of the animals had already grabbed his arms. He struggled to pull free but his strength was draining fast, and they were bigger and stronger than he was. He was helpless, unable to do anything. He roared uselessly in his fury. 'You raped her, you bastard. You raped her.'

As Jamie moved, his shadow slithered after him, popping in and out of shape as it glided over tables and chairs. He took a penknife from his pocket with slow deliberation. His shadow did the same.

'Well, well, well,' he mused. The blade of the knife shimmered sickeningly. 'You seem to have got yourself into something of a predicament, Mr Hunter.'

'Go to hell.'

The knife glistened close to Ethan's eye before resting on his cheek. It was cold, like an icicle on his skin.

'You're going to pay for this, Jamie.'

'This is hardly the time for that sort of machismo nonsense, is it, Ethan?'

'I know what you did to Karen, and I know what you did to the

229

horse. I'll make sure you don't get away with that.'

'The horse? Emphatic? I think you should look a little closer to home if you want to know who doped that poor thing.'

Ethan twitched as the knife glided over his skin, pressing into his soft gullet. Not hard enough to break the skin, but hard enough for him to know it was there; a terrible full stop that could punctuate his life with just the slightest of movements. 'So what are you going to do now?' he spat.

'I told you once that if you ever touched me again, I'd kill you.'

Ethan drew a sharp breath.

The knife moved.

Nobody came when he started screaming.

CHAPTER 25

Ethan looked in the bathroom mirror, but what looked back out was no longer him.

The mirror was no longer just a mirror, it was a portal into another world. In that other world, Ethan the apprentice jockey did not exist, because in that other world, Ethan was the disfigured, burned creature from his dreams. In that other world, the world of nightmares, Ethan was an abomination. The true horror was, when Ethan had looked in the mirror for the first time, his world and the nightmare world had collided, and now, who could truly say where one began and the other ended?

Ethan ran his finger over the cold surface of the glass, half-expecting it to ripple. What if he was trapped on the wrong side? What if the cruel, unnatural-looking thing that stared out at him had taken over his life? His breath quickened. What if, when those two worlds had crashed together, all trace of his former self had been erased?

To the left of the mirror, a dirty, damp patch spread across the wall. It was like the wall itself was crying.

The cut of Jamie's blade had slashed in an angry red sweep across Ethan's cheek, and down his jaw line, twisting the right side of his mouth into a lazy and - the doctors said - permanent droop. It was an ugly wound, and designed to be such. It had required seventeen stitches.

The stitches were the only part of his life, until now, that had not yet unravelled.

He poked at the cut. His head was full of animals. Millipedes and beetles and the scurrying creatures that lived just below the surface of civilisation; fat maggots that gorged on the putrid flesh of forgotten corpses.

Perhaps, if he kept poking, if he aggravated the wound enough, tiny spider-legs would start wriggling through the puckered, red flesh of his face.

He couldn't think. It was so hard to think. The world was smothered in a terrible blanket, and all his thoughts were fuzzy, misfired synaptic connections.

He wanted to be able to think again. He needed to be able to think. He had so much left to do. He was standing on the precipice, but he couldn't allow himself to fall, not until he was sure that . . . that what? What did he need to be sure about?

He didn't know. Couldn't think.

Sleep, drugs, alcohol, sex. Nothing could help. Nothing could stop him falling deeper into the marshmallow world on the other side of the mirror.

Jamie had said he had wanted to kill Ethan, and he had. He had killed the last human part of him. He had taken the last part Ethan recognised.

He had taken Ethan's face.

So what was Ethan now? Without a face, was he without an identity? Would anybody know him if they passed him in the street? Would he even know himself? If he was nothing more than

232

flesh and blood, with those things gone, was he even human anymore? Was he recognisable as a man?

He turned on the cold tap and watched water slosh and gurgle into the drain. If he could have physically done it, he would have followed, gone down into the sewers where the other abominations hid.

There was no sound from upstairs.

Karen wasn't there. She wasn't anywhere. She had driven him to the hospital and left him there. He hadn't seen her since.

The water bubbled and rushed. He put his hands in it. His breathing was slow, his face painful. There was no sound from upstairs.

Karen wasn't there.

After Jamie and his friends had dumped Ethan outside his flat, Karen had appeared from nowhere, a faceless angel in a haze of red pain.

His own face had been on fire, burning up from a thousand bee stings. His skin crawled. His head was full of memories. Falling in briar patches. Stinging nettles. Ant bites. All the incomprehensible little hurts from a honey-glazed childhood.

Karen was screaming, but he couldn't make out what she was saying.

He had tried to tell her he was all right, that it wasn't as bad as it looked, but it was. It was worse.

She had hauled him into the car. God knows how she had done it, but she had.

'You can't be here,' Ethan had said, over and over again. 'You can't be here.' He had been talking through a tea towel he was holding over his face. Over what was left of his face. 'You can't be here when they question me.'

She was driving fast. Too fast. Her fingers were white on the steering wheel. The streetlights flashed by like a disco, stuttering illumination over cars and buses and trucks, plotting the vague outlines of inconsequential buildings. The world was without colour or detail.

'How could they do this?' Karen said, her voice twisted with panic.

'It's okay. I won't tell anyone what happened.'

The dial on the speedometer wiggled over ninety. The dark road stretched on.

'It's okay,' Ethan repeated. 'I won't tell anybody. Nobody ever needs to know.'

'Know what?'

'What they did. I'm not going to speak to the police.'

'You have to.'

'I can't. If I talk to the police . . .' His mouth was full of blood and muddled words. Thoughts were painful shards, grinding against each other and shredding his mind. 'They will want to know why, and I can't do that to you.'

'This isn't about me.'

'Of course it's about you. It's always been about you. If I talk to the police they'll find out what happened to you. I can't let that happen. He knew I wouldn't talk, that's why he did it.'

'Don't you dare try and protect me, Ethan. Not after what I've done to you.'

Ethan closed his eyes and listened to the road rushing by. It was hard to talk, to concentrate. The pain was everything. He tried to separate himself from the hurt, but there was too much of it. It was everywhere.

'Ethan?'

'It's okay, I'm still here. I just don't want to talk any more.'

'Ethan, you have to tell the police.'

He tried to string a sentence together, but in the end all he could manage was one word. 'Emphatic.'

'Ethan?'

'Need sleep.'

'Ethan, what about Emphatic?'

'She was murdered. If I talk to the police, that will all come out.' He laughed, a throaty gurgling noise. 'There's something else too. A friend of mine did something the other night, and I helped to cover it up.'

'But you can't let Jamie get away with this.'

'You did.'

'That was different.'

The universe started falling away from him in neat sections, each part of the greater whole folding away until there was nothing left except the single white-hot dot of his conscious pain floating in a black sea. Then even that was gone, and, for a few minutes at least, he slept.

He awoke as Karen screeched into the hospital car park. White coats were moving around excitedly.

'You can't stay here,' he said, as Karen pulled him out of the car.

'I have to.'

'I don't want you involved. I need to deal with this myself.'

'Don't be silly.'

'I don't want you here.'

'You don't mean that.'

She put her arm around his trembling shoulders, but he threw her off, staggered away. 'Leave me alone,' he screamed. 'Get away from me.'

'Ethan?'

'Go.'

He turned and half-ran, half-fell, through the doors into the emergency ward of the hospital.

Karen watched the double-doors swinging, got in her car. Drove away.

She had gone.

She had disappeared the same time Ethan's face had.

She had gone.

Ethan watched as the blood started seeping out of his knuckles, turning the water a translucent pink. There were shards of glass over the porcelain sink.

When he looked up, his reflection was gone, replaced instead with a bare, flat piece of wall.

He couldn't remember smashing the mirror, but the mirror was broken. His knuckles were stinging. He started laughing.

Karen wasn't there.

His face wasn't there.

He wasn't there.

*

'Jason?'

'Ethan, is that you?'

Ethan spoke with the phone wedged under his left ear, wrapping new bandages around his hands. 'Yes, it's me.'

'I thought you . . .'

'You killed him, didn't you?'

'Sorry?'

Ethan's voice was flat and hard, each word driven with the resolution of a sledgehammer. 'You weren't fighting to keep your money, were you?'

'I'm sorry, Ethan, I had -'

'They took your money, didn't they? They beat you up and took every penny. You wanted some payback. There was no self-defence, no brave battle against insurmountable odds. There was just you beating on some kid with a baseball bat because you thought he was responsible.'

'Hooper set me up.'

'So you killed him.'

'I never meant to. I just wanted back what was mine.'

'Looking in the wrong place, weren't you?'

236

'He was involved.'

'And now he's dead. Guess you're even.'

'Are you judging me?'

'Yes.'

'Screw you. Nobody made you lie to the police. You did that of your own accord.'

'You really are a callous bastard, aren't you?'

'So why ring me?'

Ethan glanced over his shoulder towards the front door. 'I need a favour.'

'A favour?'

'You owe me for that shit you pulled with the police. You made me lie for you, and you didn't even have the decency to tell me what I was lying for.'

'Would you have done it if you'd known the truth?'

'No.'

'Then you know why I had to do it.'

'I don't care why you did it, but you owe me, and I'm calling in the favour.'

'Okay, shoot. What do you need?'

'I need a gun.'

'A what?'

'A gun.'

'I'm not sure I can -'

'Get me a gun, Jason, or you may find yourself one alibi short the next time the police come sniffing around here.'

'You wouldn't, you'd be incriminating yourself in a murder investigation.'

'I don't have that much else to lose, Jason. Don't test me.'

There was a long sigh on the other end of the phone. 'So that's how this is playing out then?'

'We aren't friends, Jason. This doesn't change anything. I did something for you, now you do something for me. We're quits, we never have to speak to each other again.'

'What do you want the gun for?'

'Why does anybody want a gun?'

'Are you serious?'

'I need it today.'

'Today? Are you crazy? These things take time.'

'Today, Jason.'

Ethan slammed the phone down. His lounge was terribly quiet. The curtains hung on either side of the window like thick, iron bars, cutting black squares out of the daylight.

He poured himself some whiskey, filling his glass to the rim.

Thirty minutes later, Jason rang back.

## CHAPTER 26

Ethan sat alone in his lounge and stared at the telephone. There was an untouched glass of whiskey on the table beside it, over two-thirds full. He had already drunk two similar sized measures, which had gone some way to shrinking the hollowness he felt inside. Once he finished this third drink, he would be drunk. Once he finished the fourth, he might be able to walk out of his front door without caring what people said about his face.

He picked at the stitches in his cheek. The whiskey glinted in the cut-glass crystal tumbler. The flat was silent and contemplative.

He still hadn't paid this month's rent.

A trickle of blood ran down his face. He stopped picking.

It was just coming up to five o'clock in the afternoon. The air was fresh, the sky clear. It was an afternoon that brought to mind a hundred other afternoons, each identical to the last.

But this was no ordinary day. After today, nothing could ever be ordinary again.

239

He looked at his hands. There was blood on the ends of his fingers. His face itched.

Earlier, he had tried to phone O'Hara. He had wanted to ask why he had been speaking to Karen that first day at the stables. He already suspected he knew what the answer would be. 'Others', Karen had said. She had wanted Ethan to be just like all the 'others'. The other men she used to make Jamie jealous. The men she wrapped around her little finger.

Others. Just like Ethan. Just like O'Hara.

Ethan hadn't been the only person she used. She had turned up at the stables with a mind to use everyone and everything in it to further her own ends.

Perhaps O'Hara had turned her down. Perhaps he hadn't. Perhaps he had slept with her that same day.

Perhaps, right under Jamie's nose, while he was speaking to Lesterton, Karen took O'Hara into the stables and they rutted like animals.

Ethan snatched his whiskey, swallowed back half of it. His hands shook.

Ethan had intended to ask O'Hara straight out what had happened. O'Hara would have no reason to lie.

O'Hara had not answered the telephone.

Ethan drained the contents of his glass. The bottle was standing on the counter by the sink. Almost empty, but there was enough for what Ethan needed to do. He refilled his glass. He didn't bother with ice.

The phone waited on the coffee table.

He picked up the receiver and pressed it to his ear. He did not dial. His lips brushed against the mouthpiece when he spoke.

'Mum?'

'Ethan. How are you?'

'Not too good.'

'Are you ill?'

'Maybe. Things are a little strange right now. I needed someone to talk to.'

'I've been meaning to call you for such a long time, but we've just been so busy.'

'Business is good?'

'We've got nine horses scanned in fowl at the moment and we're just run off our feet. Your father says he's never had to work so hard in his whole life, and I think he's probably right. And it's so hot at the moment. We just haven't had the time to stop and think, let alone give you a call.'

'It's okay, I've been a little preoccupied myself.'

'We haven't seen you in the paper much over the last week, you are still getting rides, aren't you?'

Ethan wrapped the telephone cord around his finger. Swallowed. His cheeks were wet with tears.

'Of course you're still getting rides,' his mother said. 'What a silly question. Mr Lesterton knows when he's got a good prospect. We're so glad it all worked out for you, staying behind and every-thing. We were so worried when that girl ran out on you like that, we thought you'd go to pieces. We should have known you'd pull through. We were sure you'd want to come out to the stud after that. We would have loved it if you had, we really would, but you're doing so well for yourself at the moment.'

'Am I?'

'If you ever change your mind, there's a place here for you. You know that.'

'Mum.' Ethan's voice was cracked and frail, he barely recog-nised it as his own.

'Yes, Ethan?'

'How are you?'

'Well, I'm fine. Really. Tired at the moment, but being tired isn't a bad thing.'

'I'm tired.'

241

'Why's that? Aren't you sleeping?'

His fingers tightened around the telephone handset. 'I'm tired, mum. I need help, and there isn't anybody here who can help me.'

'If you aren't sleeping, you should speak to Mr Lesterton. He'll want to know.'

Ethan looked out of the window. There was nothing there. 'I've got nothing left,' he said.

'Ethan?'

'Is dad there?'

'Yes. He's out in the sheds at the moment, talking to a couple of the stable hands.'

'How's his back?'

'Much better now. We still catch him carrying hay bales from time to time, but generally he leaves most of the heavy lifting to the staff. You know what he's like.'

Ethan wiped his eyes. 'Yeah, I know. Tell him . . . Tell him to be careful.'

Silence. Silence spanning the globe. His mother was thinking. 'Ethan, what's wrong?'

'There's . . . I'm . . . I'm thinking maybe I should come out and visit soon.'

'Oh, that would be lovely. It's been such a long time since we saw you. It will be nice to catch up. I know you're dad would be pleased. He's so proud of you.'

'Really?'

'Of course he is.'

'He's never forgiven me for not going out there with you.'

'You say that, but you don't see his face when you're in the paper or on the television. He knows you made the right decision, and he couldn't be any more proud of you without popping. He talks about you all the time.'

'He never . . .'

'No, but he's your father, he wouldn't, would he?'

Ethan's tears splashed heavily on the coffee table. 'I miss him,' he whispered.

'Are you sure you're okay?'

'Not really. I've . . . I've done something, and I'm not sure I can live with myself.'

'What have you done?'

'I let myself get worn away. I thought I was winning. I thought I was on top, but it's all gone. I'm gone. I can't get back the things I've lost.' He choked back his sobs. 'I'm going to do something else. Something worse still.'

'What?

'Something I can't avoid. I'm afraid that after it's done, there won't be any part of me I recognise. You won't recognise me. But I have to do this.'

'What are you talking about, Ethan?'

'I . . . I love you, mum.'

'Ethan?'

'Tell dad I love him too. I really do want to come out to the stud, I just don't think I can.'

'What could be so terrible?'

'Me. Only me.' He drew a slow breath. 'Mum, I only ever wanted to make you proud and, if something happens today . . . If something goes bad . . . I want you to know that I never meant to hurt you, and I'm sorry.'

'We'll always be proud of you.'

'I hope so.'

Out of the corner of his eye, Ethan caught sight of movement. He turned. Karen was standing in the doorway, watching him. She was dressed entirely in black: black trousers, black blouse, black, orthodox shoes. She wasn't wearing any makeup, her hair was combed but not styled. Her expression was vague.

'What are you doing?' she asked.

He moved the receiver away from his ear, looked at the phone like it was some alien artefact he had never seen before. Cleared his throat. 'I don't know any more.'

'Who's on the phone?'

'Nobody.'

'You're talking to nobody?' She walked over and took the receiver out of Ethan's hand, putting it to her own ear. Dial tone. Nobody there.

'I was going to ring someone,' Ethan said.

'Who?'

'My mother.'

'Why didn't you?'

'I couldn't figure out what to say.'

'Would it have mattered?'

'I don't know.' He wiped his eyes. 'I'm not sure she would have heard me, whatever I said.'

'If she had, would she have understood?'

'I doubt it. That's why I never dialled.'

Karen put down the phone, took a seat beside him on the couch. 'Next time, make the call. She might surprise you.'

Ethan sighed. The lounge seemed to sigh with him. Moments of unsettling silence rolled by.

'I'm sorry,' she said.

'Why?'

'Because I am, and I need you to know.'

'It's not your fault.'

She touched his hand, and he shrunk away. 'Do you even remotely believe that?' she asked.

He looked back out of the window. There was still nothing there.

## CHAPTER 27

Ethan half-limped, half-walked, through the hallway of Lesterton's house. No signs of life. No hushed voices, no footsteps, no lights. Nothing.

It had just turned seven o'clock, and the blue ink stain of night was seeping through the milky clouds of the day, bleeding the world of colour. The stable hands had all gone home. The horses were boxed up for the night.

Everything was peaceful.

Lesterton's door had been standing open, inviting in any passing travellers like beckoning fingers.

Ethan hadn't knocked, hadn't searched for a light switch. The house may have appeared lifeless, but he had been jumped one too many times in the last week to let anybody know he was around until he was sure they weren't going to stick a knife in his back.

He put his head into the dark lounge. Nobody. Television off. Curtains flapping at an open window, casting spectral shadows like devil fingers on the grey walls.

There was the smell of rain in the cool, evening air.

Ethan pulled the door closed, and headed towards the study. Nobody there either.

Upstairs.

Nobody in the main bedroom. The bed was made with perfect hospital corners, but the wardrobe stood open like a yawning mouth full of wire coat-hanger teeth.

Nobody in the bathroom, just a sink full of discarded medication bottles.

Nobody anywhere.

Finally, he pushed open the glass doors of the conservatory leading onto the wooden decking that overlooked the valley. O'Hara was sat on a bench, head bowed, elbows resting on his knees, and his hands clasped together. He looked almost as though he was praying, but O'Hara had no God.

When he heard Ethan's footsteps approaching, he looked up. His eyes, impossible to read, stared out from a marble face. 'Lesterton's not here,' he said.

'I know,' Ethan said, pulling up a chair. 'Where did he go?'

'Away.'

'How far?'

'Far enough.' O'Hara's hands wrung together agitatedly. He kept his gaze fixed on the decking between his feet.

'Why?'

'You know why.'

Ethan touched the puckered flesh of the stitched cut running across his face. 'It was you, wasn't it?'

'You know that.'

'I do now. I didn't. Not when I came here yesterday and spoke to Lesterton. I had my suspicions, but I couldn't let myself believe you two could be responsible, not after all this time together. I'd managed to convince myself it was Jamie, despite the evidence. I came here to lure him out.'

'Whatever you said yesterday, it shook the Governor up. He rang me, said you knew everything, and you were going to blow the whole thing out of the water.'

'I didn't have a clue.'

O'Hara snorted a cruel and self-deprecating laugh through his nose. 'You were bluffing.'

'I couldn't think of anything else to do.'

'I never knew you were a gambling man.'

'I wasn't.'

'What changed?'

'Everybody else. Where has Lesterton gone?'

'This isn't the first time, Ethan. Lesterton has been neck deep in it for years. Doping, bribing, cheating. You name it, he did it. All this . . . this with Emphatic. It would have brought out everything, all the other crimes.'

'I don't believe you.'

'And that was why he let you play detective, because you wouldn't believe it. You would believe everything other than the truth. He played you from the start. We all did.'

'Why?'

'It's always easier to lie to someone who would rather hear lies than the truth.'

'What do you mean?'

'Most of your races here have been fixed. You aren't nearly as good a jockey as you think you are.'

'That's a lie.'

'The truth always sounds like a lie to a man that's never heard it before.'

'Don't say that.'

'Why? You wanted to be a detective, don't tell me you can't stomach it any more.'

'I'm a good jockey. You can't take that away from me. I've had everything taken away from me, but you can't have that.' He swallowed hard. His insides twisted and spasmed uncontrollably. 'I'm a good jockey.'

'Good, maybe. But you aren't great.'

'This can't be right. Where did Lesterton go? I need to speak to him about this.'

'You're too late. He didn't tell me where he went.'

'So he's running?'

'He's finished. You finished him. He's taken whatever money he could get and he's gone, left the country.'

'Then he's got away with it?'

O'Hara looked out across the valley, then up at the dark expanse of the house. Horses snuffed and snorted, evening bugs zig-zagged in the air. 'I wouldn't say that.'

'And what about you? Why haven't you gone?'

'My money's all tied up. Stocks and shares, property, cars, women. I haven't got the kind of cash to run. I've got to stand and fight.'

'That's what you're doing? Fighting?'

'Something like that.'

'So, was it worth it?'

'In hindsight, no. But it could have been. By God, it could have been.'

Ethan sat back in his chair, resting his hands in his lap. 'Why do all this?' he asked. 'What was the plan?'

'Didn't you even figure that much out?'

'My bluffing's better than I thought.'

O'Hara laughed quietly, shook his head. 'Emphatic was favourite, by a mile. She could have walked the race backwards, everybody knew it, and she was eating up a huge percentage of the book. No other horse was getting a look.'

'I know.'

'Jamie Redthorn knew it and he didn't like it. He wanted to win that race. He'd got himself into a bit of trouble racing up north for a rough set up, the kind of men that don't take kindly to losing. Jamie was prepared to give us a substantial sum of money for making sure Emphatic didn't win. It was the kind of offer Lesterton couldn't refuse.'

'That doesn't make sense. If the horse was supposed to lose, why not race her and then pull up on the course? Why stick her full of Ephedrine?'

'It's not that easy to race badly and be convincing about it, especially not in a race like that, which could only ever be seen as a one horse affair. Cheating would have showed up like neon.' He paused, rubbed his palms together. 'Besides, that bloody Dalton had been sniffing around again, looking to take a couple of rides. We didn't want him snooping around asking awkward questions, trying to steal Emphatic out from under me.'

'But why try to give the horse a boost?'

'Jamie supplied the goods. Said it would do for the horse so badly she wouldn't even make it to the stalls. This rough sort he's been riding for, they've got some enemies, and they were trying to knock a couple of birds off the roof with one stone. We were supposed to get Emphatic to the course and scream blue murder, claim she had been got at, doped so bad she couldn't run. Jamie's friends were going to make sure there was enough evidence found on their enemies to justify a prison sentence. It would have worked too, but somebody screwed up with the needles. We got the wrong stuff, Ephedrine instead of Etorphine. We pumped Emphatic up rather than knocking her out.'

'Jesus.' Ethan rose, began pacing angrily. 'You're all criminals, the bloody lot of you. How could you let yourself get involved in this, O'Hara?'

'It was a lot of money.'

'I hope it was.'

O'Hara stared at the back of his hands. 'At least, it would have been a lot of money, but Jamie's a twisting little bastard.'

249

'He reneged on the deal?'

'There never was a deal as far as he was concerned. In the morning, when it was all going down, he came back to the stables with a camera. He got pictures of everything we did. Pictures of Sally administering the injection' He shook his head in disbelief. 'We should have known.'

'He's been blackmailing Lesterton, hasn't he?'

'He's here now, waiting for another payment. He'll be waiting a long time.'

'He's here?'

O'Hara nodded towards the wooded valley. 'Down at the sauna room. He doesn't know Lesterton isn't here.'

Ethan tried to smile, but felt the muscles and nerves around the right side of his mouth refusing to participate. 'Think I'll go and have a chat with him,' he said.

'So what happens now?'

'I guess that's up to you. The only people who know about this are right here, right now. You want to keep fighting?'

'I don't think so.'

'Then wait for me. When I come back, I'm going to phone the police and we're going to have this conversation again.'

O'Hara nodded. Ethan headed towards the sauna room.

*

Jamie was waiting just inside the entrance to the gymnasium, a large whitewashed foyer with stone tiles on the floor, and chrome pegs on the wall. He was sat on a bench that ran along the left wall. He did not stand when Ethan walked in, neither did he seem overly surprised.

'You?' he sneered.

'You were expecting someone else?'

'Not really.' He ran a finger along his face, tracing a similar

250

path to Ethan's scar. 'That's nice, it suits you. But why so glum? You should smile more.'

'You are a sick bastard.'

'I'll take that as a compliment. Where's Lesterton?'

'I know what you've been doing.'

Jamie stood. 'Really? What have I been doing?'

'O'Hara told me everything.'

'About what?'

'He told me about your little arrangement, about Emphatic. He told me about the mix up with the needles. He told me about the blackmailing. Everything.'

'You sound delusional. Are you on medication for the pain?'

'Are you just going to stand there and deny it?'

Jamie's grin widened into a jagged dagger blade. Ethan had always thought Jamie was handsome, but there was nothing handsome about this man. How could he have been so wrong? 'Now I come to think about it, I probably will just deny it. Is that going to cause you a problem?'

'Not at all.' Ethan reached into his jacket pocket, and pulled free the handgun Jason had provided him with earlier that day. An old service revolver. It felt heavy in his trembling hand as he pointed it at Jamie's chest. It was a good weight.

Jamie's smile faltered, but did not wane completely. 'Are you serious?'

'I think so, yes. Is that going to cause you a problem?'

Jamie wiped a hand across his mouth, shifted his body awkwardly. Ethan took a half step closer. His shadow wrapped up around the wall behind him in a gruesome, clawing shape, like the hunched visage of Nosferatu.

'I should have come to expect this of you,' Jamie said.

'Really?'

'Yes, you're clearly deranged. Karen told me that last night. She said you went crazy down by the river. She said,' he stifled a spiteful laugh, 'you said you loved her. Surely not the actions of a man entirely in control of his senses.'

'Did she tell you I meant it?'

'She did.'

'Did she tell you she felt the same way about me?'

'Is that what she told you? I'm afraid that may not be the case. She loves me, Ethan. She always has. I'm a part of her, she needs me.'

'Not any more. Not after what you did to her.'

'This again?' Jamie threw his hands up in despair. 'How many times do we have to go around this? I don't know what you think I am, but I'm not a monster. I didn't do anything to Karen, I didn't do anything to your horse.'

Ethan took the gun in both hands to stop the weapon rattling in his grasp. His eyes blurred with angry tears, the world shimmered. 'Don't think I won't shoot you,' he hissed. 'Don't think I won't do it, because I'm not joking here.'

'I didn't think you were. That is why you came here, after all, isn't it?'

'I came here to make you confess.'

'But I have nothing to confess to.'

'You're a bloody liar.' Ethan's entire body was shaking uncontrollably, his arms shivering with the thrill of anger and pain and fear. He took a step closer. 'You're a damned liar. You've been behind all of this.'

Jamie shook his head apologetically. 'Do you want to know the saddest thing, Ethan?'

'Tell me.'

'Tonight, I'm going to go back to Karen's flat, and she'll be waiting for me there. She'll throw her arms around me and say she loves me and then she'll let me do it to her any way I want. You'll have to sit downstairs and listen.'

'Not this time.'

'Nothing will have changed.'

'Everything's changed, you made sure of that.'

'So you keep saying. But you don't appear to be able to prove anything. Worse still, you don't seem to be man enough to do anything about it yourself.'

Ethan tried to blink his vision clear, tried to stop himself from collapsing in a useless pile of flesh, tried to stop the anger roaring in his gut from setting fire to his brain and burning away the last of his reason. Tried.

'You bastard.'

'Are you going to shoot me or not?'

Ethan's finger flexed on the trigger. The oiled barrel gleamed in the overbearing halogen lights. Somehow the gun seemed heavier, too heavy. 'Just admit it,' he whispered.

'Sorry?'

'I just need to hear you say it.'

'Say what?'

'Just tell me you did it. I can't stand being lied to any more. I need to know the truth. Tell me you did it.'

'I can't.'

'Tell me,' Ethan screamed, taking another step forwards.

Suddenly Jamie was moving. He was fast, much faster than Ethan's battered reactions could cope with.

Too damned fast.

Ethan felt his arm snapping back, saw the gun fly out of his hand, heard it dance metallically across the stone floor. He turned to see where the weapon had landed, felt the hard, flat crunch of Jamie's fist pounding into his right cheek. Stitches split. There were no spiders, but blood filled his mouth. The ground came blazing towards him.

His palms slapped against the slabs, and, running on instinct, he scuttled on hands and knees towards where he thought the gun had fallen.

Movement. Behind him. He braced himself.

Something slammed against his back, driving the air from his wheezing lungs.

He could hear Jamie's breathing by his ear, moist and sinister, could hear the growling menace in his voice, 'You had enough warnings.'

Ethan jerked his head back, cracking it hard against Jamie's nose, quietly revelling in his adversary's yelp of pain. Then, there it was: the gun. Glinting just a few feet out of reach.

He lunged forwards with a scream, fingers clutching the air uselessly.

Too far away; needed to be closer.

He struggled to gain those last few inches, pulling his own weight, and the weight of Jamie who remained latched on his back.

Then it happened.

For a moment he was only aware of something long and thin puncturing his right side, just below the ribs. It took several seconds for him to realise Jamie still had the knife. The same knife with which he had taken Ethan's face.

It didn't hurt, which was something of surprise. There was a moment of terrible coldness as the slick metal ran up inside his body, then a warm gush of blood. Sticky, hot blood, running into his trousers, creeping through his shirt, taking his strength as though his muscles were withering away.

'No,' he gasped, vision swimming out of focus as the blade slid deeper, right up to the handle. 'No.'

With whatever he had left, Ethan reared up, shaking Jamie off his back, and threw himself towards the gun. His sweating, trembling hands found the handle, gripped. He rolled on his back, aware of the blood pumping rhythmically from the tiny but deep wound in his lower abdomen.

Not long now.

The darkness - the fog of forever - was already rolling in. But he could still see Jamie's shadow lurching over him, still had enough wits to aim, pull the trigger.

The universe exploded in a yellow teardrop; white shapes jittered across the walls. The shadow fell away. There was the clink of a knife and an empty gun cartridge hitting stone tiles, then the wet thud of a body collapsing.

Ethan let his head rock back, closed his eyes. God, he was tired. So tired.

Needed to sleep.

If he slept, just for a few minutes, he would be okay. He would be able to walk back up to the house and phone the police. The police would be able to clear up this mess.

It would be okay.

He would . . . He gasped for breath . . . The air was like a wet sponge in his throat . . . He would be okay . . . The air was . . . A few minutes . . .

A few minutes here on the floor . . . Just a chance to get his strength back.

Just . . . Time to sleep.

Just . . .

There was a faint groan.

His eyes flicked open.

Somebody, other than himself, wasn't dead.

Somehow, and God knows how, he sat up. Blinked. The world came back, fuzzy, disjointed, but clear enough for him to see what had happened.

Jamie was sat in the corner, one hand pressed to his right shoulder. Blood was running between his fingers and down his arm. He looked over at Ethan. 'I can't believe you shot me,' he said.

'Doesn't look too bad.'

'I think I might live.'

Ethan looked at the gun in his white hand. There was a

numbness spreading outwards from the knife wound, like thick ice fingers freezing through the sinews of his body. 'I wouldn't be so sure of that,' he said. 'We aren't finished yet.'

He pulled himself painfully across the floor until he was kneeling in front of Jamie. He held the gun loosely down by his side.

'You're going to shoot me again?' Jamie said.

'Did I get your attention?'

'How far are you going to take this?'

Ethan pressed the revolver to Jamie's forehead. 'How far are you going to make me take it?'

'Stop this, Ethan. You don't want to kill me.'

'You think?'

'If you want Karen, take her. I don't want her any more. You win. Okay?'

'This isn't about winning and losing. This isn't even about Karen.'

'Then what is it about?'

'This is about knowing.'

'Knowing what?'

'You have a choice. You can die as the man you are, or the man you could have been. Which is it to be?'

Tears shone in the corner of Jamie's terrified eyes. 'Ethan, please?'

'Too late for begging, Jamie.'

'What do you want from me?'

'I want you to be honest. Just once. I want you to take responsibility for your actions.'

'You don't want to kill me, Ethan.'

'Oh, I do. I really do. I want to kill you more than I've ever wanted to do anything in my life.'

'You kill me and you go to prison. Do you want that?'

'Chances are I won't live to see prison.'

'But are you prepared to take the chance? Do you really want

256

to lose your freedom?'

'That's nothing to what I've lost in the last week.'

'Be rational.'

'Admit it.'

'Ethan.'

'Just admit it,' Ethan screamed, pressing the gun harder against Jamie's head. 'I need to hear you say it. Admit it.'

'Okay, okay. I did it. I organised to have Emphatic doped, I blackmailed your Governor afterwards.'

'And the rest?'

Jamie looked up at Ethan in horror. 'Please don't make me say it.'

'Say it.'

'I can't.'

'You don't have a choice.' Ethan's finger twitched on the trigger. 'I've already shot you once.'

'I . . .' Jamie closed his eyes, drew a slow, shuddering breath. There were tears coursing down his cheeks when he spoke again. 'I raped my fiancée.'

Ethan sighed, lowered the gun. 'I know,' he said. 'I know.'

## CHAPTER 28

Ethan couldn't remember crawling out of the sauna rooms, but he must have done because he was about halfway back up the valley towards Lesterton's house when he woke up.

He was face down in the damp grass. There was the copper-salt taste of blood and sweat in his mouth. It was dark. Surely now he had to be dead.

He had to be.

He had fallen through the mirror. This is what it was like on the other side, just beneath the icy surface of the ocean's ripples. This was what it was like to be dead.

He coughed, nearly choked. This was death. This was all there was once the lights went out. Only the cold and the night and the rain, frozen on the tongue of winter winds. This was death, his death. This was all he had waiting for him.

He raised his head slightly, blinked.

No Heaven, no Hell, no Purgatory, no Judgement. Just simple, blissful, nothingness.

Who could tell him now whether his life had been worthy? Who could say whether he had paid the price for allowing Jason to get away with murder? Where was his God? Where was his Devil?

He blinked again. His vision cleared, then quickly furred over. He felt like he was about to implode, that he was going to shrink down into a microscopic dot, and be lost in the rolling waves of death's endless rivers. He liked that idea. He didn't want to be him anymore, or the abomination that had once been him. He wanted to be part of something bigger, better. He wanted to be a small piece in an infinite puzzle. He wanted to be a pebble, a grain of sand. Smaller still.

He wanted to be so tiny and so insignificant that even he didn't remember who he was. He wanted to erase himself from history, throw a curtain over everything he had seen and done. He wanted to be so small he had never touched the world, that his image had made no imprint on a photograph negative, that no camera film had ever captured his presence, that no person had ever noticed him in a crowd, or heard him speak.

He wanted to go back, and back, and back, until his life had never been.

'Ethan?'

On this vast and featureless plain, he could almost believe it was possible. He could almost believe he could undo all the wrongs he had committed, and all the wrongs that had been committed against him. He could almost believe he could be happy, floating timelessly on this blank canvas.

'Ethan?'

He closed his eyes, and everything rushed past him. Thoughts, feelings, emotions, memories; a soaring kaleidoscope of life with him at the centre, holding all things together. When he opened his eyes again, he was no longer alone.

'Melissa,' he said, without moving his lips.

Melissa looked at him. 'What are you doing?' she asked.

Her lips didn't move either. She didn't even have any lips. She had no means to physically produce those words, they simply came straight out of her head and into his. He did not hear what she said, he felt it being imprinted on his brain.

Of course, this was a hallucination. On the brink of death, his mind was busying itself with some routine housework, attempting to tidy up the scraps of life that remained unresolved.

'Melissa.'

He reached out to her, but she backed away. For a second her image flickered and distorted, like an old reel of cinema film. He felt her speak again.

'What are you doing?'

'I'm leaving,' he said.

'You said you'd always be here.'

'I don't even know where here is any more.'

'Here is where it's always been.'

Ethan opened his hand. A small engagement ring was nestled in his palm. It couldn't really have been there though, he had taken it to a pawn shop months ago. 'This is the place you took with you when you left,' he said.

'I couldn't stay with you,' she said. Her voice, not a real voice at all but the suggestion of a voice that existed only in his mind, was full of the sadness of autumn.

'Why?'

'I did write you a letter.'

'I never got it.'

'I never sent it.'

'What did it say?'

'Do you think it really matters? After everything that has happened?'

'I think I deserve a reason.'

'Life is change. Most changes occur without reason or

explanation. We can't alter that, we just follow the path. Knowing doesn't help.'

The ring suddenly seemed impossibly heavy in Ethan's hand. He placed it carefully on the ground. 'You can take it back, if you like,' he said.

Melissa shook her head. It was a strangely mechanical motion. 'No, I can't.'

'I'm giving it to you.'

'But it isn't yours to give any more.'

'I want you to have it.'

'You lost it.'

Ethan glanced down. The ring, that tiny little startled mouth, had disappeared. 'I just put it down,' he said.

'You said you were leaving. Maybe it's time you did.'

'I'd like to think some part of me will stay here.'

'Only the dead part. You know it's impossible to stay here and live.'

Ethan blinked the tears from his eyes. 'I know,' he said. 'I have to move on sooner or later.'

'We all do.'

'I can't be lonely forever.'

'So what are you going to be instead?'

'Something else.'

Melissa faded away.

'Ethan?'

Slowly, carefully, he looked to his right. It was dark, but not dark enough to conceal the silhouette of somebody sitting next to him with their arms wrapped around their knees.

His breath caught painfully. 'Are you . . ?' He stopped.

The silhouette turned towards him. He couldn't see a face. Perhaps there was no face to see.

Ethan's throat was almost too dry to speak, but, eventually, he managed to thread a semi-coherent sentence together.

'Am I still not dead?'

'Not far away. You've lost a lot of blood. Probably enough to kill you.'

The voice was familiar. Sad and alone.

The voice was O'Hara's.

'I think I screwed up,' Ethan said, rolling over on his back and staring into the silver-studded blackness of a night without end.

'What makes you say that?'

'I thought I was dead.'

'You're not.'

'But I am dying. And the only person who might be able to save me would rather I just finished dying.'

'Is that what you think?'

'I'd like you to prove me wrong.'

'Maybe I will.'

Ethan reached down to where he guessed his knife-wound was. His fingers came away warm and wet. No pain though. What did it mean when it stopped hurting?

He clamped his hand over the wound. 'This is a real mess,' he said.

'Did you kill him?'

'No.'

'It's not so bad then.'

'I wanted to.'

'Over a horse?'

'A woman.'

'It's always a woman with you.'

'I know.'

'Has anybody ever told you, you're a little on the possessive side?'

'Once or twice.'

'Was she worth it?'

'Yes.'

'Will she thank you for it?'

'Unlikely.'

'Then what was the point?'

Ethan laughed, and the sound transformed in his throat into a cancerous death rattle. It was beginning to get frighteningly cold. 'The point was, she's free.'

'Did she want to be?'

'I hope so, because she's on her own now.'

'Does that mean it's over?'

'Perhaps.'

'Did you find out what you needed to know?'

'I don't know.' Soft feathers of rain fluttered across Ethan's face. 'I found out something.'

'Sometimes it's best not to know everything. Sometimes things happen that we just aren't supposed to find out about. It's what keeps us sane.'

'Well, I know, for better or worse.'

'And what do you do with that now?'

'Wait, I suppose.'

'Maybe you were wrong.'

'You don't know Jamie like I do.'

'He's a bad guy, I know that much. Begs the question, if he's still alive, why aren't you already dead?'

'I shot him.'

'Bad?'

'In the shoulder. It's not lethal.'

'Do you still have the gun?'

Ethan felt around in the grass. His stupid, dead fingers ran over metal. He handed the gun to O'Hara. 'It doesn't look too good, does it?'

'It's not all bad. Guns can get lost. Jamie isn't likely to want to press charges. You might not die.'

'Feeling positive, O'Hara?'

'I'm in a good position right now.'

'That's what makes me nervous.'

'I could walk away and there's more then enough mess here to make sure my absence isn't noticed for a few days.'

'Is that what you plan to do?'

'I'm feeling strong, in control. I haven't felt that way for a while now.'

Ethan coughed into his hand. He couldn't feel his legs any more. He couldn't feel anything any more.

'Are you going to walk away?' he asked.

O'Hara was silent.

'O'Hara?'

The darkness came spilling back in all too quickly; the clammy touch of eternity.

'O'Hara?'

No answer.

Ethan watched the stars blinking out one by one, until he was the only star burning in the quiet sea of the universe.

## CHAPTER 29

Karen put her suitcase in the back of her car, and closed the boot with a clunk of such terrible finality that tears immediately sprang to her eyes. She had been crying a lot in the last two weeks, more than she had ever cried before. Perhaps they were new tears; perhaps they were just the ones she had never been allowed to shed before.

It was a long time since she had last been on her own. For years, Jamie had been a terrible and important part of life, a defining feature of her existence. Without him, how did she even begin to discover who she was?

Hunching her shoulders from the fine spray of rain that was marking out angular patterns on the wind, she looked up at the gloomy edifice of the flats. All the windows were dark and lifeless. As far as she was aware, there were no new tenants moving in.

Without any residents to keep up the pretence of liveable accommodation, the place would quickly run to ruin. The owners had tried their best to make the flats look new, but you could only paint over the cracks for so long. The building would be torn down before the end of the year for certain. Maybe that was no bad thing.

Grey clouds trawled across the sky, thinning out towards the horizon. She crossed her arms over her chest defensively.

Deep breaths.

Time to go.

Get in the car, turn the key in the ignition, carry on driving along the road she had come in on. Carry on the journey, and forget she had ever stopped. Forget all about this flat, the man she had thought she loved, the other man she knew she did love. Forget the hurt, the suffering, the lies, the deceit, the violence, and the screaming.

Forget who she thought she was.

Just get in the car, and drive.

There was nothing here for her anymore. Nothing. Not even the man limping, with the aid of a crutch, down the road towards her. The man who had saved her, who had lost everything because of her.

'You're leaving then?' Ethan said.

Karen shook her hair back. 'It seemed like the best thing to do.'

'You're probably right.'

'I need to . . . try again. I can't do that around here, there's too much . . .' She waved the rest of the sentence away. She didn't sound convinced.

Ethan stopped, leaned heavily on his crutch. His breathing was thin and laboured. He made no gesture of kindness. His mouth was as straight as a knife.

He was within reach of her hand. It seemed further.

'I know,' he said. He paused, searching for a way to sum up in words that which, even now, he could barely comprehend. 'There are things I feel for you . . . emotions that are too much.'

'I never meant for it to be this way.'

'Neither did I, but the way I feel . . . It's dangerous to feel that strongly. We couldn't be together, not after this. It would be just as destructive as if you stayed with Jamie. Every time you looked at me, you'd remember what he did. You'd remember that it was because of me, and the way you felt about me. Sooner or later you'd hate me for that.'

'Maybe. Maybe not.'

'And look at my face. He took my face, damaged me badly enough to make sure I couldn't race again, turned me into someone I don't even recognise. He did that because of you. I can't stop myself from hating you for that.'

'You said you loved me.'

'And I do. I love you, I hate you, I need you, but I can't bring myself to stay here for you. Just being near you, it tears me up inside. It hurts to be with you and I've had too much hurt in my life to go inviting more.'

'Then he succeeded, didn't he? He made sure we wouldn't work.'

'Even if none of this had happened, I'm not sure we could have worked. You're another Melissa, another obsession. I loved her so much it was like I was part of her, and I could never get over that, not completely.'

'That was her.'

'But I couldn't bear to love you that way, and I would have. I would have sacrificed everything for you. I would have wrapped you in the world, and carved myself up until there wasn't anything left. Then one day the hurt would have got too much. You would have gone, and I wouldn't even have known who I was anymore. I don't have the strength for that.'

'So you're giving up on relationships?'

'No, but I need to back off from this. I can't be part of another relationship that tries to strip me to the bone. I need something different, something other than passion.'

'And what's life without passion?'

He touched his cheek thoughtfully. 'Painless.'

His mobile phone started ringing. He took it out of his pocket, and looked at the screen.

Jason.

He switched off the phone.

'Who was that?' Karen asked.

'Somebody I used to know.'

The wind whistled around the eaves of the flats. It was as if the building itself mourned the loss of its inhabitants. Perhaps it could see its own impending destruction.

'So what are your plans then?' Karen asked.

'I'm going away.'

'I saw you packing yesterday. I knocked this morning but thought you must have sneaked away in the night.'

'I did.'

'So why did you come back?'

'Melissa walked away from me without an explanation. Not a day has gone by when I haven't questioned that, when I haven't wanted five minutes with her to find out the truth. Being left isn't hard, not knowing why is the difficult part.'

'So here you are.'

'I couldn't do to you what she did to me. I couldn't do that to anybody.'

'I'm touched.'

'I had to talk to you first.'

'We haven't spoken since before the night you were stabbed. And as I recall you didn't have too much to say then, either. What's so different now?'

'Like I said, I'm going away, and I needed to let you know before I went that this wasn't your fault. What happened to you . . . that wasn't your fault.'

268

Karen shook her head, and glanced up. Thin ribbons of bright blue sky were clawing through the strata of the clouds. 'What happened?'

'When?'

'The night you met Jamie. The night he stabbed you.'

'It doesn't matter.'

'Who phoned the ambulance for you?'

'I don't know.'

'Where did Jamie go?'

'I don't know.'

'It's been a while. Nobody has seen him.'

'Do you care?'

'They said there was a lot of blood, consistent with a gunshot wound. Was there a gun?'

'The police never found one.'

'Did you shoot him?'

'He walked away, Karen. This was one car crash we all walked away from.' He looked at his shaking hands. 'Even those of us that died.'

Karen stared out at the white line of the horizon. 'So where to now?'

'I'm going to Africa.'

'Your parents' stud?'

'There's always been a place there for me, and I'm never going to be able to ride again. Not like this.'

'Going to Africa. Isn't that giving up? Isn't the lost cause worth fighting for any more?'

'I've done enough fighting. Gone through enough rough patches.' He straightened up as best he could. 'I think I'd like to stick to the flats for a while.'

'Then I guess we won't see each other again.'

'I think neither of us will lose too much sleep about that.'

'We'll see.'

'There was just one thing I needed to ask before you went.'
'Go ahead.'
'Did you ever sleep with O'Hara?'
'Is that what you think I did?'
'You were seen talking to him at the stables.'
'And you think that means I slept with him?'
'I don't know.'
'You're right, you don't.'
Karen moved around to the driver-side of the car, and got in.
'Karen?'
She looked out of the window. 'What?'
'I'm sorry.'
'What for?'
'For not being strong enough.'
'I could have been strong enough for both of us.'
'I know.' Ethan's eyes glazed with tears. 'I just don't think it would have been worth your while.'

Karen turned the key in the ignition. 'You'll never know,' she said.

He watched exhaust fumes billow, and tyres crunch on gravel. He did not wave as Karen pulled out onto the main road, and neither did she, but he did watch her until she was just a smudged dot on the horizon.

The rain spiralled and twisted, dancing with the wind. A white dove perched on the apex of the roof, craning its neck to watch Ethan.

Ethan switched his mobile phone back on, and dialled. The call was answered on the second ring.

'Anne, it's Ethan.'
'Hi, Ethan. How are you feeling today?'
'I'm okay, how's the job hunting going?'
'Not good.'
'I'm sorry. Is there any word on O'Hara's trial?'

'Not yet. He's got enough money to make sure he has the best lawyers behind him, though. I wouldn't be surprised if he gets away with it.'

'We'll see.'

'I guess we will.'

'Are we still on for tonight?'

'Of course.'

Ethan smiled his new lop-sided smile that remained unable to twist any life into his maimed right cheek. The smile Anne said was surprisingly sexy. 'Good.' He paused, looked up at the dove on the roof.

The dove stared, unblinking, with black eyes full of secrets.

'Is there something else, Ethan?'

'Yes.'

'What?'

'Have you ever been to Africa?'